L

of the
Heart

Sandy Sheehy

2021 White Bird Publications, LLC

Copyright © 2021 by Sandy Sheehy

Published in the United States
by White Bird Publications, LLC, Austin, Texas
www.whitebirdpublications.com

Paperback ISBN 978-1-63363-523-4
eBook ISBN 978-1-63363-524-1
Library of Congress Control Number: 2021937096

PRINTED IN THE UNITED STATES OF AMERICA

Dedication

To my mother, Jean Dunkle Granville,
who taught me to read and to love books.

Acknowledgments

Often called "New Mexico's Williamsburg," El Rancho de las Golondrinas inspired me to write a novel set in the late 18th Century near Santa Fe. The layout of fictional Rancho de las Palomas and the numerous tasks performed by the people who contribute to its day-to-day functioning are based on what I learned from this sublimely evocative living history museum. I am grateful to the staff and volunteers who bring the Spanish Colonial Southwest to life.

Albuquerque's Pueblo Cultural Center was another valuable source of information and inspiration. Fictional Pueblo San Miguel represents a conflation of richly diverse and complex Pueblo traditions. Any errors in interpretation are my own.

I developed the first draft of *Deserts of the Heart* in Heidi Carlson's facilitated writing workshop offered by the University of New Mexico. For their encouragement and insights, I am grateful to her and to my fellow workshop members Krista Burlae, Horatio Chavez, Julie Fulcher, Gale Hannigan, Dallas Hunter, Ruth Mueller, Elizabeth Newton, Sonda Andersson Pappan, Dale Pino, and Rowan Wymark. Rosina Lippi (aka Sara Donati) and Ruth Boutin Kuncel provided valuable advice on narrative and psychology.

My thanks go to Charlotte Raymond for her longstanding belief in me as a writer and to Evelyn Kusch of White Bird Publications for her faith in this book and for the personal attention that she and her editorial staff have devoted to it.

I am beyond grateful to my husband, Charles McClelland, for his love, support, and patience and for teaching me that history is a limitless source of rich story material.

Deserts of the Heart

*White Bird
Publications*

In the deserts of the heart,
Let the healing fountains start.
—W. H. Auden, "In Memory of W. B. Yeats" (1940)

CHAPTER ONE

Sofia leaned around the side of the covered wagon, grasping the bowed frame to steady herself against the sway and the occasional jolts delivered by rocks and ruts. A gust blew her broad-brimmed straw hat back on her head, but the faded violet ribbon held tight.

"Come back down here, Valeria!" Sofia shouted. "You'll ruin your complexion sitting up there in this sun."

A glimpse of her sister's face as the younger girl bent around to reply showed that this prediction was fast becoming fact. Valeria's once-fair cheeks bore splashes of terra cotta, and the skin on her upturned nose was beginning to peel.

"But I prefer it up here!" Valeria called back down from her perch next to the teamster. "I like to see where we're going."

Clutching the wagon frame tighter and bracing her feet, Sofia stood.

"We have some things to discuss, and I don't want to

yell them." *Like I'm yelling now,* she thought. *I'm beginning to sound like a governess. Maybe I'm practicing for my new position.*

Taking a deep breath, she closed her eyes and reminded herself that she loved her sister deeply and that the willfulness Valeria exhibited all too often was only the reverse of her warm and vivacious nature—like brocade, rough and dull on one side but smooth and shimmering on the other. If during the past year Valeria had acted more like a nine-year-old than a girl of fourteen, on the brink of womanhood, her irritating behavior was at least partly a reaction to all they had been through. Sofia took another full breath and let it out slowly, reminding herself that, at twenty-one, she was an adult and should cultivate empathy rather than surrendering to impatience.

She watched as Valeria swung nimbly onto the side rail of the wagon in a blur of honey-blond curls and billowing white muslin—well, off-white. When the right front wheel bounced over a rut, she swayed as gracefully as a spider monkey swinging from branch to branch in the forest near Veracruz.

The image startled Sofia. When they left the lush coast of the Gulf of Mexico more than six months earlier, she resolved not to feel homesick, yet the thought of all those shades of green, of the blend of orchids, plumeria, and loam scenting the air, prompted an unexpected spring of tears. *It's just irritation from the dust.* She wiped her eyes on her sleeve and looked across the arid hills and mesas, all the way to the blue-gray mountains that jutted up like broken teeth.

"Why should I have to sit back here?" Valeria plopped onto the wooden seat. "This is *so* boring. It's so bumpy I can't draw, let alone paint. And what would I sketch, anyway? All you can see is the ten wagons lurching along behind us, with their stupid oxen plodding through the dirt. You can hardly see them, anyway, thanks to the dust."

"You should be glad we're in the first wagon," Sofia said. "Any further back, we'd be eating the dust, not just seeing it, like the poor fellow with his sheep back there."

Glancing to the rear of the caravan, she noticed that the man riding along beside the sheep had pulled his straw hat down to his eyebrows and his neckerchief up to cover his mouth and nose. The fabric was so soiled that she couldn't tell whether it had begun the day white or brown. He did, however, seem to sit his horse comfortably, not with the elegant posture of a military man, but with the relaxed confidence of a rancher. With its cream and chestnut markings, the paint mare looked like an extension of his slender hips and long thighs.

He and his little flock—five ewes and a ram sporting twin spirals of heavy horns—had joined the wagon train just north of Socorro. Sofia and Valeria had speculated about his story: Maybe he was taking the sheep to market in Santa Fe. Maybe they were his sister's dowry, on their way to the groom's family. Maybe they were a tribute for one of the Pueblo chiefs.

After all, the fellow did look at least half Indian, with his straight black hair and broad nose. Valeria had dismissed him as nicely built but not handsome, in fact, bordering on ugly. But, Sofia had countered, there was something about the way he carried himself that indicated character. More like arrogance, Valeria had retorted.

Now Valeria sighed dramatically. "I don't know why we had to come to this wilderness in the first place. Why couldn't we have found positions back home in Veracruz, or at least in Mexico City?"

Sofia felt a twinge of grief thinking of *la vomita*, the disease the English-speaking people of the West Indies called "yellow fever." It had raged through Veracruz, killing her parents and her fiancé and upending her life and Valeria's.

"Because we had no strong connections there. There were plenty of educated young women orphaned by the epidemic and not enough families needing governesses. People with money sent their children up to the convents and monasteries in Mexico City or to live with relatives in the interior to escape the epidemic. Don Alejandro was kind enough to write to his cousin in Santa Fe. Since he was one of Father's closest friends and has known us since you were five, he was able to vouch for us."

"Santa Fe is nothing more than a dingy outpost," Valeria retorted. "'Provincial capital of *El Norte*' ha! More like an overgrown Indian trading post. You saw Albuquerque. We were barely able to find a bed and a bath at that pathetic excuse for an inn. They're so proud of their new church, San Felipe de Neri, but did you notice the saints' statues? They looked like a seven-year-old carved them."

Despite her resolution to banish irritation and replace it with empathy, Sofia clenched her hands into fists. When was Valeria going to start acting like a young woman, rather than a spoiled brat? Surely, they had been through enough together in the past year—the death of their parents, who had spent their last days delirious with fever, spitting up what looked like coffee grounds, their skins turning a nasty yellow with blue-black blotches. Mateo, her fiancé and soulmate, dying the same way, his medical knowledge no help for his or anyone else's suffering. Then four months in a grief-stricken daze, waiting for the reply to Don Alejandro's letter to his cousin asking whether he might have a place in his household for two accomplished young women from a distinguished family.

Sofia mourned Mateo, with his unruly brown hair and sea-green eyes, his quick intelligence, his keen curiosity about nature, and his conviction that science could banish ignorance and superstition. During those flower-scented evenings of intense conversation, she felt her intellect and imagination soar to meet his. Almost as keenly she mourned her lost vision of the life they would have shared.

They had planned the wedding for the second Sunday in June, when the flowering shrubs and trees around the cathedral would be at their peak. She imagined that they would live four or five blocks from the center of Veracruz, within walking distance of the university, in a comfortable house, not grand but with a pretty garden.

Mateo would devote his days to teaching and practicing medicine. She would spend hers playing the piano, perhaps taking on three or four students—invariably enthusiastic and promising. Maybe she would try her hand at composition, at first simple sonatas, eventually chamber pieces for three or four instruments. At least once a month, she and Mateo would host lively gatherings of the city's best-read and most talented young intellectuals and artists.

There would be children, of course, but Sofia pictured them less clearly. A girl and a boy, perhaps a third if the first two turned out to be the same sex. But no more than three. They would be bright, sunny, and affectionate. And, of course, they would be well-behaved. Although the children would have a nanny, Sofia had vowed to take a few hours a day with them herself, reading to them, encouraging their creative talents, and making her expectations gently but firmly clear.

Sofia felt confident of her ability to guide and discipline infants and toddlers. Of her four closest friends, she would have been the last to marry. Three of them had had babies during the year before the epidemic and had seemed content and relaxed about motherhood. All four had moved to relatives' *haciendas* in the interior when the first cases of *la vomita* had appeared in Veracruz, leaving their husbands to carry on with their families' businesses and professional practices in the city.

However, Sofia had been completely unprepared to take on responsibility for Valeria, especially when she herself felt like she was moving through a dense mist that numbed her senses and made her mind sluggish. Even when Sofia had been at her best, Valeria had been able to defeat her in any test of charm or determination.

5

As if to demonstrate, Valeria broke through Sofia's dark reverie.

"Besides, we won't even *be* in Santa Fe," Valeria said. "We'll be on some filthy ranch three hours away. I've read about those. Remember the diary that Franciscan priest kept? He wrote that each of those *haciendas* has a watchtower manned day and night, to warn of Indian attacks. And the Apaches steal Pueblo children who get caught out tending the fields and make them slaves."

"The last Apache raid near Santa Fe was decades ago," Sophia said. "In two years, it will be 1800, a whole new century. Don Emilio's letter to Don Alejandro assured him that the Indians around Rancho de las Palomas are civilized. They live in villages, grow crops, and work at the *hacienda*. He said we would be completely safe."

The staccato clopping of horse hooves interrupted Sofia's lecture. She looked up at the rider, a young corporal with the platoon of thirty soldiers accompanying their caravan. Sweeping off his black leather hat, he bowed deeply.

Sofia noticed the medallions embroidered above the hem of his thigh-length deerskin vest, intricate work in crimson and gold thread, the design matching the crest on the shield that hung from his horse's halter. A fine bay gelding and fine embroidery, too fine for an ordinary corporal. He had to be from a prominent family.

This wasn't the first time he'd ridden by since he and five of his fellow cavalrymen from the Albuquerque garrison had joined their platoon of protectors. Although he always had some excuse or other, Sofia strongly suspected that his true mission was chatting up Valeria, who was peering coyly from under her tousle of curls.

"Good day to you, *señoritas*," the corporal said as his horse pranced side to side. "I bring you greetings from Sergeant Carlos Gomez and his *esposa*, Maria Josefa. She would like to know if there is anything she can do to help prepare you for your arrival at Rancho de las Palomas. As you know, we have only three more nights on the trail. *La señora* thought there might be some, ahh, lady things with which she could assist you."

Sofia opened her mouth to reply to the offer made in almost too-elegant Spanish. Although not Castilian, his accent reflected the cultivated precision of Mexico City rather than the rougher speech of the North. But Valeria rushed ahead.

"Oh, yes!" Valeria said. "We've been saving our good clothes for our arrival. After all this time, they must be dusty even packed up in our trunks. And they're certainly wrinkled. If one of the *parajes* where we stop has facilities where we can bathe and wash our hair…"

"Valeria!" Sofia snapped. "Maria Josefa has the whole caravan to cook for morning and night. She's not our personal maid. I'm sure some of the soldiers have tunics with ripped seams or missing buttons and no idea how to mend them. They'll need Maria Josefa's help making a good impression when they reach Santa Fe. You and I can do our own laundry and sewing."

The corporal smiled, the ends of his waxed moustache lifting. Making a show of looking right and left, as if to check for eavesdroppers, he leaned over and said, "Personally, I think that *la señora* would welcome your company. You know, you are the only other women in the caravan. Maybe you can help her sew those buttons back on the soldiers' tunics. I've noticed that a lot of them are missing. And maybe, as you share this chore, I will do my best to lighten your labor with a serenade on my guitar. I hope you will forgive my being out of practice."

Then, with another bow, he set the wide-brimmed leather hat back on his head, tilting it ever-so-slightly to the right, and rode off, spurs jingling like silver bells.

Valeria clasped her hands to her ruffle-trimmed bodice, threw back her head, and sighed.

"Did you ever see a more handsome man?" she asked. "And one with more refined manners! And a better horseman!"

"I admit he sits his horse well," Sofia said. "Growing up here, what else would there be to do but learn to ride? Shear sheep? As for his looks, I've seen plenty better, and so have you. And his manners? He sounded like a provincial bumpkin playacting the son of a grandee."

"You know that's not true. You're just jealous because he clearly preferred me to you. That shouldn't surprise you. I will always be fair, and you will always be as dark as a Moor. And you will always be more than six years older than me."

"And will you always be a self-centered shrew?"

CHAPTER TWO

For the next two hours, the sisters rode in silence. A dust devil cutting across the flat to the right provided the only relief to the monotony. When the road swung toward a grove of cottonwoods along the river, Sofia felt her shoulders relax. This *paraje* was more basic than some along their route, where they'd overnighted in villages, but it had three sturdy-looking corrals for the animals and, along the riverbank, a stretch of grass green with spring, beckoning with its soft, fresh scent.

Sofia watched as four young soldiers helped Maria Josefa unload the supplies for their dinner. The menu promised to be all too predictable: stew made from dried and salted remains of the elderly ox that had died three weeks earlier in their crossing of the Jornada del Muerto, a ninety-mile shortcut across the bend of the Rio Grande. The route had saved thirty miles but was totally dry, so the caravan had taken it as a three-day forced march, traveling around the clock, carrying just enough water for the humans. The head teamster had told her that losing just one animal to the ordeal was amazing good fortune. He unyoked two other oxen whose knees were beginning to buckle, switched a few of the teams around, and hitched two of the pack mules to the lightest wagon. The ailing oxen looked like they were recovering. In fact, they almost trotted toward the river.

"Poor old ox." Sofia overheard Maria Josefa say to one of her helpers as she hoisted a haunch out of the tub of salt water and laid out onions, chili peppers, and a braid of garlic along the trestle table. "At least, thanks to him, you soldiers don't have to ride up into the mountains to hunt deer and boar for our dinner."

Sofia noticed that Valeria seemed to be in a better mood now that she was out of the wagon. "We're here to help with the cooking and mending," she called, almost skipping up to the sergeant's wife and bending slightly to kiss her on both cheeks. Maria Josefa was a sturdy woman. Her waist-length glossy black plait and high cheekbones confirmed the Indian half of her ancestry. However, her eyes were a startling shade of blue-green, almost the same color as the three strands of turquoise that hung from her neck.

Smiling, Maria Josefa replied, "Thank you, Valerita! You are most kind." Gesturing toward the boards strewn with vegetables, she said, "I have my cooking routine down, thanks to a couple of the young men who help me with the chopping. But the mending! If you two could give me a hand with that, with your young eyes and nimble fingers, the boys will be grateful. If you sit there, on that bench, I'll have someone bring a lantern."

In the fading light, Sofia noticed the tall man with the sheep had taken his flock over to a spot along the river near a clump of rushes and perched on a flat rock whittling. "Who is that?" Sofia asked Maria Josefa. "And why isn't he sitting around the fire, with the soldiers and the teamsters?"

"His name is Roberto, but everyone calls him Beto," Maria Josefa said. "He manages the ranch operations at Las Palomas—the planting and harvesting of crops, the blacksmithing and tanning, the carpentry and construction, the breeding of the livestock. He bought those sheep from a breeder near Socorro, and of course moving them with a guarded caravan like ours is safer than herding them cross-country alone. My Carlos tells me that the army is enlisting more soldiers and therefore needs more wool for their uniforms and blankets. The biggest customer for Rancho de las Palomas is the Santa Fe garrison, but that has been for meat and hides. These sheep you see here are famous for the abundance and quality of their fleece, so my understanding is that these animals will help Don Emilio take advantage of this new market."

With the hint of a lascivious smile, she added, "Isn't that ram a fine fellow? And, look, one of the ewes is clearly quite pregnant already."

Maria Josefa's smile vanished as quickly as it had come. "As to why Beto is sitting alone," she said, "sometimes it is hard to take your place if you do not know what your place is." She turned toward the table, ending the conversation.

Sofia settled herself next to a tall stack of dark blue woolen tunics, some with small rips along the seams, others with missing buttons. Valeria sat on the other side of the pile of mending. A lantern rested on a rock behind them. Maria Josefa's ample wicker sewing basket held dozens of brass buttons, plus needles, thread, thimbles, and two pairs of scissors.

Valeria said, "I wonder about the boys who wear these. Will they have sweethearts greeting them in Santa Fe, or will it just be mothers and sisters?"

"Half of them are from Mexico City or El Paso del Norte," Sofia said, "so they'll only be met by their fellow soldiers from the presidio. Maybe the commander's wife will make them a nice dinner of something besides old ox. Anyway, you shouldn't be thinking about those soldiers. You won't be marriageable age until your birthday in July, and these fellows are years away from being free to settle down."

The sisters sewed quietly for the next thirty minutes.

Sofia was surprised at the progress they were making. One tunic after another received a brisk brush with a horsehair whisk and its final inspection, before taking its place on the growing stack of mended garments.

"Let's practice our French verbs," Sofia said. "What's the simple past tense of '*être*'?"

"'*Fus*,' '*fus*,' '*fut*.'"

Then, dropping the tunic she was mending in her lap, Valeria grasped her head in both hands and asked, "Why do we have to learn French? No one in New Spain speaks it. We won't be teaching the children at Las Palomas to speak French. We'll have enough to do teaching them to speak decent Spanish without sounding like their mouths are full of uncooked beans."

"We need to learn French because the greatest thinkers of our century wrote in French—Diderot, Voltaire, Rousseau," Sofia said. "Learn their language, and you can unlock their ideas."

"The ideas that got all those people beheaded during the Terror in Paris? The ideas that got our family exiled from Barcelona?"

Sofia didn't bother to correct her, as she hadn't the last few times the subject had come up. Although no soldiers had come in the middle of the night to force the family to flee at gunpoint, not even a bewigged official functionary at a decent hour brandishing a serious-looking document declaring them *personae non grata*, Sofia understood why her parents chose to depart Spain promptly.

When they left the thriving Mediterranean port, with its orange-scented gardens and vibrant social life, Valeria had not yet turned five. She had no memory of the lively salon their parents had hosted, where the most intelligent, best-read people in the city—women, as well as men—had gathered to discuss ideas late into the night. Sofia's parents had allowed her to listen for the first few hours, provided she sat quietly in the back of the drawing room and left without a fuss when Imelda took her hand to lead her to bed. With both the ideas and the *cavazos*, the notoriously strong Spanish brandy, flowing freely, the debates about the rights of all human beings or the wisdom of separating the civic and ecclesiastical spheres had become so heated that she could make out both sides of the arguments from her bedroom a floor above.

Stacks of books and broadsides by Thomas Paine and Benjamin Franklin always seemed ready to topple from the side table next to her father's favorite armchair. When Sofia asked him what they were about, he chuckled and said, "Oh, some wise sayings: A penny saved is a penny earned. A stitch in time saves nine. That sort of thing."

But she had gotten the impression that some of the ideas in those books went beyond accepted homilies. She noticed that her father had been in an atypically gloomy mood after losing a civil case in which he represented a local vintner in a land dispute against the Catholic Church. At breakfast a few weeks after that, Sofia's father announced: "We are going to be moving to America. Your mother and I have decided that it will be just the thing—a new life in New Spain as we look toward a new century."

Their mother smiled, but little lines framed her mouth. "We will be moving to Veracruz, a beautiful city on the Gulf of Mexico. Orchids grow everywhere, and parrots fly around wild. And your father will have plenty of work as a lawyer for shipping companies."

The next three weeks passed in a blur as Sofia watched her mother march through their four-story townhouse with paper and pencil, directing their five servants and a team of young longshoremen to pack this, leave that, making one list of everything that would go with them, another of what would stay to be sold by the agent who was also selling the house. The workmen unscrewed the four lion-footed legs on the rectangular piano, then swathed the instrument carefully in old blankets and covered the whole bulky bundle with a canvas tarp, but the heavy sofas and armchairs stayed—except for the one that Sofia's father favored. His law books went into wooden crates, with the French and English political and philosophical treatises secreted at the bottom. When Sofia expressed shock that the long, elegant rosewood dining table and its sixteen chairs were marked to stay, her mother assured her that they would buy a beautiful mahogany dining set in Veracruz.

All their cold-weather clothes would remain behind. There would be no winter in Veracruz. Sofia and Valeria had to select five toys each. The rest would go to the nuns to give to the orphans in their care. Sofia sobbed as she said good-bye to her three closest friends at the convent school and cried even harder as she bid farewell to Imelda. Sofia's mother had wanted Imelda to come with them, but the young maid and nanny who slept in the same room as the two sisters all their lives hadn't wanted to leave her family in Barcelona.

As they climbed into the hired carriage on their day of departure, Sofia took a last look at the stone façade of the house where she and Valeria were born. Rows of floral tiles framed the wrought-iron balconies. Gauze drapes billowed from their open bedroom window, as if waving good-bye.

First, there had been the ship to Seville, where Sofia's father insisted that they spend several days, to make sure that they wouldn't miss the departure of the Plate Fleet, the heavily guarded convoy that set sail from Spain to Veracruz only once a year. For the trans-Atlantic crossing, the family had two staterooms, small but comfortably appointed, with little brass railings around the nightstands and dressers to keep objects from sliding off when the ship heeled over. They ate their meals at the captain's table with the ten other first-class passengers, none of them children. Although she had been forbidden to do so, one calm morning Sofia scampered down the ladder to take a look into the hold and was hit with the musty scent of wine and the sharp smell of brandy, the casks stacked tightly in racks.

The ninety-day passage was unusually trouble-free—no hurricanes, no Barbary pirates, no British or French buccaneers. Sofia suspected that pirates would find raiding the returning ships, laden with gold, jewels, and silks and spices shipped from Manila and hauled overland to Veracruz, more profitable than attacking the outbound vessels, which likely held nothing more valuable than barrels of amontillado, bolts of bobbin lace, and mantle clocks with their faces flanked by porcelain ladies and gentlemen.

After stopping for supplies in the Canary Islands, they headed due west across the Atlantic. When the water turned from deep blue to turquoise, the Tierra Firme Fleet split off from the convoy and headed southwest to Cartagena just off the coast of South America, while their ship and the rest of the New Spain Fleet bore straight on, then bent slightly north to Veracruz.

Sofia and Valeria spent their first three weeks in Veracruz in the Dominican convent just inside the city walls, while their mother and father stayed at an inn just above the port. Their mother explained that the girls would continue taking lessons from the nuns but would be living with her and their father once they found a suitable house. "Your father and I don't want you to become too fond of the cloistered life," she said with an impish smile. "You must learn what the good sisters have to teach you, but you needn't believe everything they say."

One of the nuns, Sister Hortencia, was an accomplished pianist. Recognizing Sofia's talent, she was encouraging but demanding and even taught her how to tune a piano herself using a tuning fork, a set of rubber wedges to dampen the keys not being tuned, and a tuning hammer. This wasn't really a hammer at all, but a small, specialized wrench for tightening the pegs that held the strings.

"Here in Veracruz, pianos need to be tuned every time

the humidity changes," Sister Hortencia explained. "Otherwise, they will sound flat—which will neither contribute to the glorification of God nor to the pleasure of dinner guests."

Valeria showed a precocious knack for sketching, and the nuns soon put her to work drawing designs for the embroidery on ecclesiastical robes. They learned to sing all the responses to the Latin Mass *a capella*, and Sofia spent six hours a week studying Latin, not just the liturgy, gospels and epistles, but the meditations of Saint Teresa, the philosophical works of Marcus Aurelius and the military memoirs of Julius Cesar, as well. The girls also sewed clothes and hemmed blankets for the orphans.

Sofia's first reaction to the new house was shock. Her parents had picked them up just after morning prayers and loaded them into a wagon—not a carriage—with her father driving. They headed out the city's southern gate along a narrow road paved with oyster shells. The air smelled faintly nauseating, like a blend of jasmine and rotting guavas. After about a mile, her father pointed to the left with one of those grand, sweeping gestures he employed when rehearsing his presentations for the High Court.

"There it is!"

Almost obscured by palms and tropical hardwoods was a two-story white frame house with a steeply pitched green roof and black shutters secured at the top but tilting out at the bottom. To Sofia, it looked like a simple farmhouse—wood, not brick or stone—and the verandah wrapping it on three sides was bigger than the first floor.

"It's so small!" Valeria exclaimed.

"Your father and I thought it was just the right size," their mother said firmly. "We have no need for fifteen rooms here. Eight will be plenty, especially since the servants won't be living in. They have their own cottage in the back. Besides, we will have the jungle as our home. Imagine going to sleep to the calls of the frogs in that lily pond over there and waking up to the songs of the tropical birds."

The jangle of a soldier's spurs roused Sofia from her memories of Barcelona and Veracruz and brought her attention back to the wagon train. Handing each sister a bowl of stew and a large flour tortilla, the sandy-haired soldier bowed slightly. From the other side of the campfire, Sofia heard the tentative pluck of a guitar key—the corporal tuning up for his serenade. Soon he launched into a faintly recognizable Andalusian folk tune, something sad about a beautiful gypsy woman from Ronda abandoned by her lover on the Puente Nuevo spanning the gorge. With a flourish of strumming, the corporal brought the story to its inevitable close, the fiery gypsy hurling herself from the bridge. The corporal played better than he sang.

As Valeria applauded enthusiastically, he bowed over his guitar, then shifted to another tune, this one entirely instrumental. Valeria let out a long sigh.

Maria Josefa settled onto the bench next to Sofia, a bowl of stew in her left hand. "It is nice to have some music," she said. "But you must be careful about flirting with the soldiers, especially that one, Valerita. The North is old-fashioned compared to what I hear about the capital and the coast. Here a young lady your age does not talk to a man unless at least one member of her family is present, preferably her father or her brother, but maybe her mother. Sadly, you have none of those, so you must avoid not only conversation but also those pretty gestures with your eyes and your hair."

"But what harm can flirting do?" Valeria asked.

"It can harm your reputation, which is the most precious possession you have, apart from your virtue itself," the older woman said. "It can even make you unmarriageable."

Valeria drew back, a look of shocked disbelief flashing across her face.

"Maybe this is not as it should be, but it is the way it is here, at least among the Spanish, the *criollos*. The *norteña* women who have money and position, they have nothing to do all day but sit around and gossip. Even the servants and laundresses and cooks, they chatter together like hens when they gather to work at the riverbank or around the well in the plaza. And what do they talk about? Whose son or daughter might be a good match for who else's son or daughter. For the rich ladies, the details will involve the girls' beauty and perhaps artistic accomplishments and of course her dowry, the boys' manners and maybe horsemanship. But always—always—the boys' prospects and the girls' reputations will be number one.

"For you, Sofia, the rules will not be quite so strict. You are what, twenty, twenty-one?"

"Twenty-one last month."

"And you told me that you were engaged, formally, but your fiancé died sadly a month before your wedding date."

Feeling a lump rise in her throat, Sofia nodded.

"So you can allow yourself to be seen conversing with an eligible man on the plaza in Santa Fe or even taking his arm, for example, to cross the street. But you must not allow him any further liberties. You might consider modeling your behavior on that of a respectable widow."

That shouldn't be hard. I've thought of myself that way since Mateo's death.

Maria Josefa raised the metal bowl toward her mouth and took a spoonful of stew.

"How was it for you and the sergeant?" Valeria asked. "How did you meet? How did he court you?"

Maria Josefa laughed fondly. "It was a little different, because my mother was Tiwa, and my father was a blacksmith whose great-great-great-great grandfather had come up from Zacatecas with Oñate in 1598. My father's family had only their land and their skills, but they were proud. My mother was a little shy around the *criollos*, so my father's oldest sister took on the job of finding me a husband. One day as the working women were chatting at the town well, my aunt learned from the carpenter's wife that they had a nephew who was a corporal in the army and was being assigned to the garrison in Santa Fe. He was a kind man, brave, and the younger soldiers respected him. The family expected him to be promoted to sergeant in a few years. Of course, because of his humble background, he could never become an officer."

"So your aunt and the carpenter's wife arranged the marriage?" Sofia asked.

"Oh, no!" Maria Josefa laughed. "They just arranged for us to meet, after Mass, and Carlos and I took it from there—under *very* close supervision. His family liked that I was a hard worker, and they didn't mind that I was *mestizo*; there was already a little Indian blood in their veins. Carlos liked that I had a sense of humor; also, he told me he thought I had beautiful eyes. But none of that would have mattered if I hadn't had a spotless reputation."

As the tempo of the guitar slowed to a sultry *bolero*, Maria Josefa added, "You must be especially careful about that one, Corporal Fernando Valdez y Guzmán, Valerita. Don't give him any encouragement at all. The stories about him are hard to believe.

"In fact, even though men are allowed much, much more freedom than women, and a certain way with the ladies can even be considered a good thing, this one has left broken hearts and ruined reputations all across the North. I have it on good authority that one daughter of an excellent family had to enter the convent because she succumbed to his sweet words and the hopes raised by his position as the son of one of the largest sheep ranchers in the region.

"He's engaged to be married next month to a girl whose father is the wealthiest merchant in Santa Fe, which just goes to show that for men, fine prospects can cancel out a wicked reputation. Poor thing. I hope she'll enjoy having a lot of time to herself."

Valeria looked as if her fondest fantasy had turned into the dust at her feet. "And we don't even have dowries, at least not to speak of."

"I know," Maria Josefa said, reaching over to pat the

19

girl's knee. "My Carlos has the duty—and the pleasure—of guarding your dowries, such as they are. He carefully hid the sack of silver and gold coins and the velvet bag, with your poor mother's pearls and her ruby earrings, in our most battered trunk under my most worn chemises. I have seen the two bags, and I know that they're rather small."

"And there is the piano," Sofia said.

"Of course. The piano and your ability to play it. And you girls have something else—in fact, two somethings, in your case, Valerita, because you are blond. I don't think there are more than half a dozen *rubias* of marriageable age in Santa Fe. And both of you are *peninsularas*, born in Spain. Even the *criollos* whose blood is pure Spanish—and this is a lot rarer than they would have you believe—would consider it a social coup to have a *peninsulara* as the mother of their grandchildren.

"But," Maria Josefa said, standing and collecting their bowls, "that holds only if that well-born young lady has a spotless reputation."

CHAPTER THREE

Swollen by snow melt, the river made a soothing sound as the sisters settled in their wagon. The thought of sleeping under the stars, as the soldiers did, was tempting, but their teamster warned them that snakes and lizards liked to crawl under warm blankets on cool spring nights. Better to be up off the ground.

As Sofia drifted off, Valeria asked, "Do you ever wonder why we had such a mild case of *la vomita*, hardly worse than a few days of the flu, and why Mother and Papa and Mateo seemed to have the same thing and be getting better and then took such a horrible turn for the worse and were dead within a week? I only threw up once, and that was just my breakfast, not that nasty black stuff like coffee grounds. You puked a little more." A touch of smugness colored Valeria's expression. "What? Four times?"

"Three."

"And our servants Guillermo and Lucy didn't get sick at all, even though the same damp night air that filled our house filled their little cottage."

Sofia raised herself up on her left elbow and turned toward her sister, buried under the mound of quilts. "Most people in Veracruz got symptoms like we did and then got better," she said. "And the ones like Don Alejandro, who'd lived through the last epidemic, didn't seem to get sick at all. The doctors say that the *miasmas* that cause *la vomita* come from Africa on the Gulf Stream. Guillermo and Lucy are *mulattos*, so maybe they inherited a resistance to the disease from their African ancestors."

Valeria shifted under the blankets, making the floorboards of the wagon creak as she turned toward Sofia. The moonlight washed across her face, revealing four parallel frown lines between her eyes.

"But the thing that keeps bothering me is why Mother and Papa died, and we didn't."

"And Mateo," Sofia said, feeling her chest constrict with the hard hand of sadness and loneliness she had tried to push away for almost a year now. She hadn't even been able to indulge in pleasant memories—the long walks in the gardenia-scented evenings, the sometimes-heated debates on the verandah about whether, when Mexico became a republic, as it surely must, even those who didn't own property should be allowed to vote and hold office. She and Mateo had heartily agreed on the abolition of slavery in every form and on the separation of Church and State, but Mateo thought that only those who owned land or businesses would be able to cast informed ballots. And yet, Mateo had always been respectful of her, so respectful that her parents had allowed them to spend time alone, unchaperoned. In open-minded Veracruz, educated people assumed that engaged couples would need some time to themselves.

Sofia understood how rare their bond had been. She and Mateo loved each other with their minds, as well as their hearts. She had been confident that once they were married, they would develop an affectionate physical relationship. If that never warmed into passion, that would be fine. She had seen too many passionate couples destroy each other with jealousy or suddenly become cold, sometimes just a few months after the wedding, probably because once their lovemaking became routine, they discovered they had nothing in common besides a boring bed and now, family entanglements. She had been confident that this wouldn't happen with her and Mateo because they shared an unquenchable passion for ideas.

Concluding that she would never find another transcendent love like the one she had with Mateo, Sofia resolved that she would never marry, but she kept this decision to herself, reasoning that Valeria would become obsessed with the outdated idea that older sisters had to marry before younger ones could. That was a bygone custom that had never been followed fully. Sofia knew several leading families with spinsters. In fact, she was almost eager to turn twenty-five so that she could assume that title.

"Did you hear me?" Valeria asked. "The nuns said that it was God's will, that God had some role He wanted our parents to take on in Heaven or else something He still wanted us to do on Earth."

"And what would Papa have said to that?"

Valeria sighed. "I suppose he would have said that *if* there were a God, He would be too busy running the universe to concern Himself with the pain and troubles of individual humans."

Sofia nodded. "And Mother?"

"She told us, didn't she, that our only sacred obligations were to be kind to others, to stand up for what we believe to be true, and to develop our minds and our talents."

"And she said that disease and death were things that everyone suffered, if not at one time of life, then at another. Now, let's go to sleep."

As Sofia settled onto her stomach, the iron grip on her chest began to loosen gradually. But well into the night, what she had come to think of as The Nightmare swept into her sleep, as it had at least once a week since her parents died. Although the circumstances in the dream were never the same, the troubling theme never varied. Valeria would be in peril, almost always the result of an impetuous action on her part, and Sofia would be unable to save her. In one version, Valeria, laughing giddily, tried to cross a stream on a log, only to slip and fall into the roaring current, as Sofia watched helplessly. In another, Valeria skipped along the rim of a cliff, where she lost her footing. Sofia grabbed her hand as she tumbled from the edge but lacked the strength to pull her to safety. In a third, Valeria approached a huge black bear, cooing and singing. When she reached out her hand, the beast grabbed it in his jaws. In the present dream, Valeria rode off with a band of young soldiers, chatting and flirting. When Sofia heard her scream in distress, she tried to run to her rescue, but the cries kept getting farther and farther away.

And then someone caught up with her from behind and was shaking her shoulders.

"Wake up, Sofia! Wake up!" Valeria whispered sharply. "You're having another nightmare."

Emerging from the fog of the dream to find her sister safe, Sofia wrapped her in her arms and sobbed.

"Go ahead and cry," Valeria said. "Mother always told us that tears wash away sorrow."

The next day, Sofia studied the passing landscape. Beside her, Valeria dug out her sketch pad and a soft lead pencil and began to draw. The road was less bumpy here than it had been to the south.

To their right were rolling tan hills with blue mountains jutting beyond them. Sofia watched as a red-tailed hawk soared on an updraft, never once flapping its wings. Dashing Corporal Fernando Valdez y Guzmán made his horse prance and tipped his hat as he passed their wagon, but only at a distance. Perhaps Maria Josefa had warned him off.

When they paused at noon, Maria Josefa lay out a modest spread of cold tortillas, jerked ox meat, dried apples, and figs for their midday meal. Sergeant Gomez rode up to her and bent over as if to say something. The sturdy woman leaned back, laughed, and slapped him playfully on the thigh with her long braid. *After thirty years of marriage and five children, they could still flirt with each other.* A ripple of envy slithered through Sofia. Beckoning Valeria to join her, she strode over to help with the food.

"Everyone is in a good mood today," Maria Josefa said. "Only two more nights until Rancho de las Palomas. My Carlos has already sent three soldiers ahead to alert them that we'll be there May 14th. And, you know, the day after we arrive, May 15th, will be the Feast of San Isidro, the patron saint of farmers. Las Palomas always puts on the biggest fiesta that day. First, there'll be a festive little parade, led by the statue of San Isidro carried on a litter overflowing with flowers. Then the priest from Santa Fe will bless the fields, the irrigation ditches, the animals.

"Then after a *very* quick Mass, the young men will show off their horsemanship with races and fancy roping. The older men will bet on which *caballero* will win which contest, and their wives will pretend they don't see them gambling. Around sunset, the musicians will tune up for the first *jota*, several casks of *cavazos* we're carrying in the fourth wagon will be tapped, and the dancing will begin.

"When we arrive around the saint's day, as we are doing this year, Don Emilio always invites the soldiers to make camp just outside the *hacienda* for two nights, instead of the usual one, so that they can join in the fun."

After the short break, the wagons continued on their journey. The oxen picked up their pace as the caravan passed patches of green pasture and cottonwood trees along the river. By the time the sun stood a hand's-width above the horizon, cultivated fields began to appear. Young plants, all in neat rows, poked their heads above the brown dirt. Narrow irrigation ditches defined the fields. Men in white breechcloths and women in long calico dresses, their hems rolled up and tied, tilled the dirt. Beyond rose a cluster of flat-roofed adobe houses, some no more than huts, others three stories high, with the upper floors set back and ladders leaned against the walls. Smoke curled out of the tops of the little structures shaped like beehives that stood next to each building.

"San Miguel Pueblo!" the driver called back. "I think you *señoritas* will like this *paraje*."

As the caravan slowed, children streamed out from the village, yelling "*Bienvenidos!*" Maria Josefa hopped down from her wagon, a burlap bag in her hand. As if they knew the routine, the Pueblo children formed a line, with the youngest at the front. Once they were all quiet, she peeked into the bag, registered a look of mock surprise, and handed each child a wrapped caramel.

The children scampered off, and a middle-aged man, wearing a white tunic over leather britches, strolled toward them, his gait and bearing dignified. *The chief,* Sofia thought. The head teamster jumped down to greet him, while one of the young drovers lifted a wooden box from the bed of the wagon.

Opening the box for inspection, the driver said, "Macaw feathers, from the jungles far to the south."

Lifting up a bright scarlet feather in one hand and a vivid green one in the other, the chief smiled, "These are most precious. I hope you will accept our humble gift of a few baskets and some seed corn—and also our hospitality. You are welcome to graze your animals along the river. My men will keep guard over them tonight."

Within the next half hour, the women of the *pueblo* set up three long tables with red and blue cloths laid over the boards, small stones anchoring them along their length, and beeswax candles placed on saucers down the middle. The chief and a handful of men, two of them with wrinkled faces and gray hair, gathered at one table, gesturing the sergeant and corporals and the head teamster to join them. Three of the younger Pueblo men led the lower-ranking soldiers and the drovers to the second table.

Sofia was surprised to see Beto heading toward that table, covering the distance quickly with long, confident strides. *Surely, his status as foreman of a large ranch would entitle him to sit with the chief.* Equally remarkable, he wore an expression she had never seen on his face—almost a smile. He and several other young men clapped each other on the shoulder.

"Why is Beto sitting at the second table?" Sofia asked Maria Josefa. "And why is he so, well, animated?"

Maria Josefa shrugged. "I suspect they're his cousins."

A woman wearing an intricately embroidered *huipil* cinched with a leather belt, threaded through turquoise-studded silver medallions, walked up to Maria Josefa and said, "I hope that you and the *señoritas* will join me."

The woman arranged her broad hips on a stool at the head of the third table and gestured for the three to sit at her right. Across from them, three younger women settled themselves, folding their hands decorously in their laps.

"My daughters." The daughters smiled and nodded shyly but didn't make eye contact. "My husband, the chief, greeted your *jefe.* He and my sons will be entertaining the men. Here at the women's table, we will have just as good a time."

Sofia noticed that except for the chief's daughters, the younger the women were, the farther down the table they sat. No one in this village looked especially rich, but it was clear they followed a defined protocol that signified status.

On the grassy riverbank, a flock of children chased each other, yelling and laughing, accompanied by half a dozen yelping yellow dogs and shepherded by five or six older girls.

Suddenly, the enticing scent of fresh-baked bread filled the air as platters appeared down the length of the table, along with tureens of stew that smelled delicious, perhaps because it was mutton, rather than ox. The chief's wife tore off a hunk of bread, then passed the platter to Maria Josefa. Sofia watched as the women along the table picked up fired clay bowls and began ladling stew into them using scoops fashioned from gourds. Some ate with wooden spoons, others daintily with their fingers.

"Help yourselves," the chief's wife said.

The stew tasted as good as it smelled. Noticing that the other women at the table were using the soft bread to mop up the remaining sauce, Sofia and Valeria copied them. Except for the occasional slurp or belch, the table was quiet until their hostess patted her ample belly and declared, "I hope you did not find our humble food too rough for your taste."

"This is the best we've eaten in months," Sofia said. "You and your people are very kind. And very good cooks."

Valeria leaned around her sister's shoulder, staring rather too obviously at their hostess's midsection. "Ah," the woman said good-naturedly. "You are wondering about my belt. Perhaps you have not seen one like it on a Pueblo woman? It was a gift from the Navajo, to celebrate the declaration of peace between our peoples. Their legends and ours agree that we taught them to plant corn and raise sheep. Thanks to us, they became settled and civilized."

"The silverwork is beautiful," Valeria said, adding: "I don't see anyone wearing macaw feathers, and yet your husband mentioned that they were precious."

Sofia noticed Maria Josefa give Valeria a sharp look, as if warning her that she was entering sensitive territory.

"That's all right," the chief's wife said to Maria Josefa, then turned to Valeria. "Our people do not wear the feathers. They are for special ceremonies, men-only, very secret. Even I do not know what goes on in these, except that they honor San Miguel." She cast a sly smile to Maria Josefa, who covered her mouth as if stifling a laugh.

"Of course, we women have our own secret rituals. All I can tell you about them is that they honor the saint you call the Virgin Mary. Only we do not place emphasis on her virginity. In our language we have no words for 'virginity' or 'virgin.' We have a word for a girl before she has her first period and her womanhood ceremony. And we have a word for a woman who has not yet had her first child, but we have no word for a woman who has never experienced the sexual embrace of a man. Except that if she were more than a few years into womanhood, we might call her 'ugly' or 'ill-tempered' or 'feebleminded' or whatever quality prevented men from wanting her.

"We do, however, revere fertility and motherhood. In fact, among our people, the wedding is not official until the bride is pregnant. The very best thing is if she shows just a little bit on her wedding day. This, we think, makes for the most beautiful bride."

On hearing this account of the customs of this *pueblo*, Sofia initially felt shock. They were so different from the strict *criollo* mores that Maria Josefa had described. But as she reflected a moment, they began to make sense. Why honor a woman for something she has refrained from doing rather than for something she has done, especially when that something adds value to her family and her community?

The chief's wife was looking at her with a slight smile, as if assessing her reaction.

"Recent years have been relatively prosperous and peaceful for us," she said soberly. "But this has not always been the case. Our elders recall the days when our corn and squash and beans failed, days when Apaches raided our village regularly and stole our children to use or to sell as slaves, days when many of our young men died fighting invaders, including you Spanish. For these reasons, we place great honor on motherhood, which helps replace the people we have lost. We prefer to think of Mary as the Mother of Jesus, or the Mother of All Peoples. Or," she smiled fleetingly, "as the Corn Goddess."

A roar issued out from the chief's head table, answered by cheers from the younger men's, then gusts of laughter. *Either all the men speak Spanish, or whatever is causing the hilarity transcends language.* Sofia noticed that earthenware jugs were being passed around.

"They have broken out the fermented corn," the chief's wife said. "Our people cannot drink your liquid fire, which poisons our brains and our bodies, but for special occasions, this light drink, which I think is similar to what you call *cerveza*, helps the mood. Of course, this is for the men. The women brew it in big pots, but we don't drink it.

"Except when we do."

CHAPTER FOUR

"Why so gloomy, *chica*?" Maria Josefa asked Valeria, who was wiping her eyes with the end of her fichu, the gauzy cotton scarf tucked into her bodice as part of the "city clothes" the sisters had decided to wear to make a good first impression at Rancho de las Palomas. Standing in the shade of the wagon next to her sister, Sofia fastened the hooks on the front of her own wine-red *robe á l'anglaise*, the overdress that nipped in at the waist and then flared open to reveal a petticoat decorated along the hem with cutwork.

The sisters had debated between themselves and sought Maria Josefa's advice about what to wear for this important occasion. Each had only two *robes*, which were all the fashion both in Europe and in the cities of the Caribbean, Central Mexico, and North America. Sofia wore a wine-colored cotton lawn with a pattern of birds and vines, leaving her deep blue embroidered satin in their trunk beside her sister's rich yellow silk. For their arrival at the ranch, Valeria had chosen her pink lawn printed with darker pink roses.

"The cottons will be best," Maria Josefa advised the previous evening as they unpacked the trunk. All of the women at the ranch would be dressed much more simply, she explained, even Don Emilio's wife, Doña Inmaculada, probably in muslin skirts and *rebozos* of hand-loomed wool. Since the sisters were joining the household as governesses and teachers, it would not be bad to have the family's first impression be that of cultivated young ladies from the city. But neither would it do to create envy among Don Emilio's daughters.

Maria Josefa gave Valeria a hug around the shoulders. "Now that we are about to arrive at your new home, Valerita, maybe you are missing Veracruz," she said soothingly.

"No!" Valeria sniffed. "I am thinking how much I will miss *you*. Sofia and I lost our mother just over a year ago. You have been like a second mother to us, with your warmth and your good advice. And now you won't be with us."

Maria Josefa looked startled. "Oh, *chica*, I am just a simple country woman." She gave Valeria another hug. "But your words touch my heart."

Sofia was surprised as well. She'd had no idea that her younger sister valued advice—from anyone.

"Although I may not be with you every day, we will still see each other," Maria Josefa said. "By horse, Santa Fe will be just a few hours' ride away, and you two will be invited to balls and baptisms and other functions. Perhaps you can come by our little house for a *cafecita* before or afterwards or to spend the night after a party. Besides, my youngest daughter, Camila, works at Las Palomas. She is between the two of you in age. I am proud to say that she is their most skillful spinner and dyer. I come by to visit her every few weeks, to trade family news and to make sure none of the young men of the *rancho* get the wrong ideas about her."

Maria Josefa paused pensively, tapping her forefinger against her lips. "In fact," she said, "when we arrive this afternoon, I will pass a note to Camila suggesting that she ask Doña Inmaculada to give her the honor of showing you around, to explain the life and manners of the *hacienda*. Of course, *la patrona* herself will describe your official role and, in addition, her expectations. You should listen to her respectfully, but you shouldn't trust her. Although she prays a lot, you mustn't mistake her for a saint. She is a pious woman, but not a kind woman."

As Maria Josefa headed off toward her own wagon, Sofia heard the hard thump of boot heels behind her. The morning sunlight cast a long shadow at her feet—a tall man carrying something in his arms. He stopped within three feet of her back, close enough that she was uncomfortably aware of his scent, a mixture of fresh sweat and wild sage. Turning, she recognized Beto. He was holding a newborn lamb.

"This little girl was born last night," he said. "She will be riding the rest of the way in your wagon."

"No!" Sofia shook her head. "This is our bedding, our belongings. That animal will defecate and urinate and…"

"Defecate and urinate, will she?" Beto asked. His eyes had always been so red from dust that she hadn't been able to discern their color. Now, at this close range, she still could tell only that they were light—and that she couldn't make out their expression.

"A newborn lamb might even vomit, and who knows what else," he continued in a mocking tone. "But she is a valuable new addition to the flock. She can't possibly keep up with the caravan. If she were to fall behind, her mother would stay with her, and both the lamb and the ewe would be easy prey for coyotes and wolves. This little one has to ride."

"But why in our wagon?" Sofia asked. "Why not in one of the others?"

"They're all fully loaded, either with crates and casks or with cooking pots and farm tools. On this rough road, loads shift, and a little one like this could easily be crushed. Yours is the only wagon with nice, soft bedding and nothing hard stacked where it could fall over."

Without another word, he turned and arranged Sofia's best pillows to make a nest for the tiny lamb.

What gall! Not even a thank you.

"You were right, Valeria," she said angrily as she watched Beto's swaggering back. "He *is* arrogant. In fact, he may be the most arrogant—not to mention presumptuous—person I have ever encountered in my life."

Bleating softly, the lamb curled up among the pillows. From the rear of the caravan came the answering bleat of the ewe.

Throughout the morning, the caravan rolled past bluffs striped in ochre and grayish-white. To their left rose small, conical hills studded with stubby, dark-green juniper and gray-green chamisa. Beyond them a long mesa sloped gradually northward. The dirt along the road took on a rich red hue.

Sofia noticed that Valeria had taken to twisting one of her curls around her right index finger, a nervous habit she hadn't displayed since the months immediately following their parents' deaths.

"Are you feeling anxious?" Sofia asked her.

"Of course I am. You are, too," Valeria said accusingly. "You keep picking at the hem of your petticoat, as if there were a loose thread or something. Only there's isn't."

Raising her hand to her face, Sofia sighed. "I thought I was concealing my feelings better."

"You're always concealing your feelings—or trying to! Naturally, we're both nervous. We are more than a thousand miles from home, in the middle of the desert, with no family and almost no money. And we're about to throw ourselves into a situation where we'll be at the mercy of people we don't know—people who don't know us, either. We don't even have any idea how we're expected to behave."

"We will simply behave like well-brought-up young ladies, which we are. And we will keep our own counsel and observe, rather than prattle. And no flirting."

When the caravan stopped for an exceptionally brief midday meal, Beto strode up abruptly, lifted the lamb from its cozy bed, and brought it to the ewe to nurse. Once it had released the teat, he settled the lamb back into the sisters' wagon without so much as a word to either of them. Climbing back onto the seat, Sofia noticed a musky whiff of urine. Apparently oblivious to the smell, Valeria clambered into the wagon bed and began stroking the lamb, clucking to it softly, even allowing it to suck her finger.

"Sweet little lamb," Valeria cooed. The lamb's tail thumped in response.

As the sun began to dip toward a tall range of mountains, lighting remaining patches of spring snow with a rosy-gold glow, a compound of whitewashed buildings appeared just over a rise. Although it was not as extensive as some of the *pueblos* where they had stopped along their journey, Sofia found the complex imposing.

Anchoring the far corner was a four-story stone tower, its roof shaded by an irregular square of some kind. *Perhaps a leather smith had fashioned it by sewing cowhides together and lashing them to poles.* She could just make out the silhouette of a boy scanning the horizon with a spyglass. The figure pivoted and turned their way.

From her perspective on the wagon, Sofia could just see over the wall connecting the other buildings. They were one or two stories tall, except for what seemed to be a small church crowned with a bell set under an arch topped with a cross.

Sofia watched as the little figure hurried down a ladder and ran toward the church. In a moment, the bell began ringing—five times, six. Sofia felt her pulse quicken; her heart seemed lodged at the base of her throat. Never had she been anywhere more foreign. Even the *pueblos* along their route north had been comfortably familiar by comparison.

People started moving toward the wide wooden gate

leading into the compound. Four men pushed it outwards. Judging from the effort they expended, it looked heavy. The teamster turned their wagon toward the opening. The fourth wagon followed. Except for Sergeant Gomez, the soldiers headed toward a grove of tall cottonwoods along the riverbank with the remaining nine wagons lumbering behind them.

Leading his paint mare by the bridle, Beto strode up to the sisters' wagon and lifted out the lamb. As he leaned into the wagon bed, Sofia once again caught his scent of wild sage and sweat. This time, he turned to them and touched the brim of his dust-covered hat. Then, cradling the lamb in the crook of his right arm, Beto led his little flock around the far side of the compound, where Sofia could see the slate roof of some sort of stable slanting inward from the adobe wall. The mother ewe trotted close behind his heels, bleating soulfully.

Hearing the brisk thud of hoof beats, Sofia turned as Maria Josefa and the sergeant trotted up beside their wagon. With a sweep of his broad-brimmed hat, Sergeant Gomez bowed gallantly and said, "My wife and I hope you will excuse us. We must ride ahead to the garrison, so that I can report to the *comandante* that the caravan is about to complete a safe and remarkably uneventful journey. Customarily, he and his lady would host a banquet for the soldiers at which he would bestow commendations for individual bravery. But this time, I will suggest that he might find it appropriate to commend the entire platoon. Thanks to their discipline and military deportment, there was no combat and thus no opportunity for any particular soldier to display valor. Several times our lookouts spotted Mescaleros and Jicarillas gathered on ridges, but they never dared attack."

"We always felt safe," Sofia said. "We clearly owe our lives to you and your men."

Maria Josefa leaned across her horse's neck and added, "And to reward them, we are heading home to our *casita*, so that they can relax and enjoy the San Isidro fiesta without stern old Sergeant Carlos making them behave."

Looking anything but stern, the sergeant smiled shyly. Then, his expression turned serious as he reached into his right saddlebag and pulled out a tan burlap sack that jingled slightly and a smaller red velvet bag and handed them to Sofia.

"Here are your dowries," he said gravely. "As soon as you get inside those gates, have Don Emilio open the *hacienda*'s lockbox for you and put them inside yourself, along with any important papers, such as your baptismal certificates. Do this *before* he introduces you to everybody."

"One of the soldiers has taken a note to our daughter Camila," Maria Josefa said. "Once the formal introductions have been made, she will show you to your quarters and give you some tips about life at Las Palomas."

The *hacienda*'s stable yard would have been more than ample for the two large wagons, each with its team of two oxen, had it not been for all the people milling around. Feeling overwhelmed by the throng, Sofia counted four dozen men, women, boys, and girls, plus assorted dogs. The dogs were either black or yellow, short haired, with long tails and pointed snouts. Several were conspicuously pregnant or nursing.

Just as Maria Josefa predicted, most of the women were identically dressed, in full white or tan skirts and loose, unadorned over-blouses with rectangular *rebozos* draped around their shoulders, some in vibrant shades of blue or rose, but most brown or gray. A few of the older women dressed more somberly in tones of near black or dark brown. The men's dress showed more variation, although loose-fitting calf-length cotton pants topped by even looser tunics prevailed. Some of the men wore woolen blankets with simple geometric patterns and a slit for their heads—*serapes*. With the exception of one or two, they all seemed to sport battered straw hats.

"I wonder who that is," Valeria whispered, pointing to the young man directing the unloading of the other wagon.

"Don't point! It's rude."

Sofia had to admit, however, that the object of her sister's attention merited a discreet stare. Not only was he dressed differently from the other men, his white shirt with its billowy sleeves tucked into black trousers with suspenders, his polished black boots rising almost to his knees, he was also uncommonly handsome. His head was covered in short auburn curls that extended in front of his ears and halfway down his agreeably square jawline. Under full brows, his eyes were an almost disturbingly clear gray. His nose was of medium length and narrow, and his complexion was almost as fair as Valeria's. The only feature of the young man's face that Sofia didn't find appealing was his mouth. His full lips were pleasing enough, but the fine lines at the corners suggested that they could easily form themselves into a cruel sneer.

Before Sofia could suggest to Valeria that they might want to disembark, a man who looked about fifty strode up and made a half bow, his right hand to his chest. Sofia noticed that his hair was the same coppery brown as the younger man's, but with glints of silver, and his eyes were the same clear gray. He also had the same square jaw, admirably free of the softening that too often accompanied middle age.

"Please allow me to introduce myself," he said with a formal and somewhat old-fashioned accent. "I am Emilio Chavez y Vega, and it is my pleasure to welcome you to Rancho de las Palomas."

Then he added, "My wife and children are eager to meet you, as are the other members of *la hacienda*."

"Could we beg your assistance for a few moments first?" Sofia asked. "We have a few things we hope you can keep safe for us in your strongbox. I am sure that everyone at the ranch is honest, but these are all we have in the world..."

"Of course, of course," Don Emilio said, offering a hand to each sister as they prepared to step down from the wagon. "If you will follow me to my library..."

Valeria clutched the burlap and velvet bags in her left

hand, while Sofia slid a slender leather document case from under her skirt—their baptismal certificates, the death certificates of their parents, and the notarized bill of sale for the house in Veracruz.

As Don Emilio ushered the sisters along a corridor toward the south side of the compound, his voice took on a solicitous tone. "Please accept my condolences on the deaths of your parents," he said. "My cousin Alejandro tells me that they were people of exceptional accomplishment, as well as hospitality and wit. He praised your mother's generosity— and, of course, her beauty."

"Don Alejandro was one of our parents' dearest friends," Sofia said. "In fact, he was like a caring uncle to Valeria and me. We will always be grateful to him for arranging positions for us in your household."

"And he is in good health?"

"When we left Veracruz, he was in excellent health," Sofia said, "and his import-export business seemed to be prospering."

Don Emilio led the young women up two sets of stairs, their risers adorned with glazed tiles, each bearing the silhouette of a blue dove on a white background. More doves, along with red and yellow flowers and green vines, decorated the wooden door he opened with a long brass key. Inside was a spacious corner room suffused with dappled sunlight. Two tall windows stood along each outside wall. Shelves filled with books ran up to the beamed ceiling. Some with worn leather spines looked quite old. Others, with clearly fresh bindings, bore titles Sofia recognized as having been popular in Veracruz. Tall folios of botanical and architectural drawings seemed to catch Valeria's eye.

Noticing their interest, Don Emilio said proudly, "I try to keep up with what is written in Europe and in the cities to the south. As you would expect, I am always about a year behind. I am eager to open the carton of books your caravan has brought me from the capital. But first, to the business at hand."

Taking a set of small keys from his worn leather belt, Don Emilio used one to unlock a walnut traveling desk set on curved legs. Reaching inside one of the elaborately carved drawers, he withdrew three keys on a red satin ribbon. These he took to an ironbound wooden chest set in a corner. After a bit of fumbling, he released its trio of locks and opened the lid. Sofia could see that wooden dividers separated the interior into compartments.

After shifting the contents of one on the right to others in the center, he said, "There! I think this will do. I apologize that the stipends we arranged for you are necessarily modest, but they should be sufficient to cover any personal items that the ranch doesn't provide, so you will have no need to access your dowry money—until you marry, of course. If some of what you are entrusting to me for safekeeping is jewelry you might want for some special occasion, I will be happy to retrieve it for you at the time."

Sofia and Valeria handed over the two sacks and the leather document case. Together, they barely occupied half the space that Don Emilio had prepared for them.

"Now we must hurry back down," Don Emilio said as he locked up. "My wife and children are eager to meet you. They must be wondering where we are."

Ushering Sofia and Valeria to the left at the bottom of the stairs, Don Emilio led them to a patio shaded by peach and apple trees in full, fragrant bloom. Seated beneath them on a long, low wooden bench was a middle-aged woman, her erect bearing accentuated by an abundance of thick, wavy black hair affixed to the top of her head with a tall filigreed tortoiseshell comb. Arrayed on either side of her were a lanky adolescent boy and four younger children.

"Allow me to present my family." Don Emilio gestured toward the group. As the woman rose and walked toward them, the children stood in unison, their arms straight at their sides. A sudden image of the marionettes she had seen as a child in Barcelona flashed through Sofia's mind. Although the woman was no taller than Sofia, her hair and her bearing made her seem regal. Her mouth displayed the same fine lines that bracketed the lips of the otherwise handsome young man supervising the unloading of the wagon.

"Inmaculada Gallegos de Chavez," the woman said, her accent revealing her northern origins. "These are my children Juan, Consuela, Diego, Emelia, and Sebastian," she added, going from oldest to youngest. "You will be teaching them and also seeing to their deportment."

She turned abruptly to her brood. "How do we greet our new governesses?"

"*Bienvenidas al Rancho de las Palomas, estimadas señoritas,*" they said in unison.

Smiling faintly, Doña Inmaculada gave Sofia and Valeria appraising looks, her penetrating dark-brown eyes running from head to foot, then returning to Valeria's face and hair. She seemed satisfied.

"You may also have noticed our oldest son, Alfonso, who was directing the delivery of the goods we ordered from Veracruz and the capital," Doña Inmaculada said, a note of affectionate pride warming her voice. "He assists my husband in managing the business affairs of the ranch."

Just then, the bell gave one long peal. "We must hurry to the chapel for evening prayers," Doña Inmaculada said brusquely. "If you will remain with me for a few minutes afterwards, I will explain your duties and my expectations. Then my husband will introduce you to everyone else at supper, and one of the girls we employ will show you to your quarters."

CHAPTER FIVE

Even with the candles lit in the circular wrought-iron chandeliers, the chapel seemed oppressively gloomy. Narrow slits near the barrel-vaulted ceiling let in no more than a hint of twilight. Twelve rows of pews ran across the square room. The aisle down the center led to a raised platform bearing a rustic altar. *More like a refectory table than a proper altar.* Draping it was a simple white cloth with nothing atop it. Because there was no tabernacle, which would have protected the communion host in its monstrance, Sofia concluded that this was indeed a family chapel, rather than a church.

Mounted on the wall behind the altar, the crucifix was almost jarringly ornate, its finely carved gilded arms gleaming in the dim light. The Christ was well-wrought but defeated-looking and quite gory, with his head flopped to his right shoulder and rivulets of painted blood running from his crown of thorns, his hands and feet, and the gash in his side. The two *santos* flanking the platform were of a primitive style similar to those in Albuquerque that Valeria had dismissed as worthy of a schoolchild. One was clearly the Virgin Mary, clad in her familiar blue robe, her feet resting on a crescent moon. Sofia guessed that the other *santo*, a male figure with a broad-brimmed black hat, his right hand clutching a pitchfork, had to be San Isidro, the patron saint of farmers.

The pews were largely full, mostly with women, all wearing *rebozos* in somber colors. Covering their heads with their fichus, Sofia and Valeria settled onto their knees in front of the last pew on the left. Although the floor was bare stone, there were no kneeling rests or cushions, so the two bunched their petticoats under their shins.

Doña Inmaculada began intoning the Padre Nuestro, and everyone joined in that familiar prayer and in the five renditions of the Ave Maria. Then she paused and, in a clear and commanding voice, delivered an appeal to the Virgin to bless the two "young ladies from the Peninsula" and bring them success in teaching virtue and, especially, piety to her children.

"Go with God," she concluded. When the others filed out, she strode back to Sofia and Valeria, gesturing to them to sit, and said, "I will leave the manner of teaching my children to you. From what my husband's cousin wrote to us, you have received excellent instruction at the convent school in Veracruz and," she added with a curt nod to Sofia, "in your case, in Barcelona.

"Undoubtedly, the methods employed by the good sisters will provide a model for you. You will face a challenge in that your pupils will range in age from six to fifteen, but I am confident that you will figure out a way to manage that. If the children misbehave while under your instruction, you should feel free to discipline them verbally, but not to strike or slap them, which would be inappropriate to your somewhat delicate position as members of the household but not fully family. And you must never correct my children outside of lessons. Am I clear?"

"Quite clear, Doña Inmaculada," Sofia said as Valeria nodded.

"By the way," Doña Inmaculada added, a sly note entering her voice, "I am pleased that you speak pure Castilian. Yet you are from Barcelona..."

"Our father was a lawyer, so he spoke Castilian in his profession and at home," Valeria said. "Our mother spoke Catalán as well, but only to the servants."

"Quite appropriate. And one of my expectations of you is that you will train my children to speak and act as if they were *peninsulares*. They must grow up to be accepted in the best society—not just in Santa Fe or even in Mexico City, but anywhere in New Spain and even in Spain itself."

Sofia noted that she expressed this desire in the distinctive and somewhat rough tones of a native *norteña*.

"Now to my most important expectations. First, as I hope I need not say, your own behavior must always be above reproach. You will be models of virtue and comportment, not just to my children but to all the women and girls of the *hacienda*. Despite all the hard work and practical demands of a *rancho* such as this one, our faith is the true focus of our lives. The priest comes from Santa Fe only about once every six weeks, to say Mass, hear confessions, and perform baptisms and weddings for the help. Of course, you two will attend and take the Sacrament. You may say your morning and midday prayers privately, but I expect everyone to be present in the chapel for evening prayers. At least all the women. Many of the men complain that their responsibilities in the fields, at the mill, at the forge, and so on demand they labor right until supper is served."

She added with a wry smile that touched her mouth but not her eyes, "I suspect them of impiety, but what can I do? I only direct the domestic side of things. Men are in charge of the ranch operations."

"And what do you expect of the formal instruction of your children?" Sofia asked.

"Ah," Doña Inmaculada said, as if this were an

afterthought. "The older children can read, but one or two not so well. And I suppose that even the girls should be able to write, although in my day this was not considered proper. They should know their numbers and at least enough Latin to master the responses in the Mass. They should be able to read simple music, enough to sing hymns. They should all learn to draw. Take the boys outside to sketch landscapes. This is a skill they will need if they become military officers. Have the girls focus on flowers and vines, so that they can create embroidered designs for altar cloths and for vestments for the priests. You see how sadly sparse in adornment our own chapel is, and even La Parroquia in Santa Fe lacks appropriate textiles for the liturgical seasons."

Rising, she added, "In teaching reading and so on, I strictly forbid you to use secular texts. None of the writings of heretics like Cervantes, of whom my husband is so fond. The only exception might be for the history of the Spanish Empire, where I might sanction brief passages from ship's logs or the journals kept by missionaries. Otherwise, the Bible, the lives of the saints and the like should be sufficient. The Old Testament contains plenty of stories that will hold the attention of young children."

Agreed, especially if one wanted to teach them about brutal slaughter, deceitful conniving, and outright fratricide. Following behind Doña Inmaculada's rigidly straight back, they walked out of the chapel and toward the savory smell and animated chatter coming from a room across the stable yard. Valeria was wobbling a bit, her breath shallow.

"Here, take my hand," Sofia whispered. "We're doing fine so far."

Gently taking hold of her sister's hand, Sofia gave it a squeeze she hoped was reassuring. Fainting would not make a good impression.

The refectory was more than large enough for the six wooden tables arranged across it, each seating eight or ten, with ample room left between the benches for the young women who were bringing out the food. Sofia and Valeria began to move toward one of the tables nearest the door, where children jostled each other, but Don Emilio gestured for them to join him, Doña Inmaculada and Alfonso at one of the tables in the back. Sofia noticed that Beto was nowhere to be seen.

"This will make it easier to introduce you this evening," Don Emilio explained as Sofia and Valeria settled themselves to his left. "When the next day isn't a fiesta or some other special occasion, the children eat early, and you might want to join them occasionally, to teach them proper table manners."

Rising, Don Emilio intoned a simple grace, thanking God for the safe arrival of the caravan and especially the accomplished *señoritas*, who brought both culture and beauty to this humble *hacienda*, and asking Him to bless the ranch and all who worked it and to grant abundant crops and livestock. Then, motioning the sisters to rise, he said, "I am happy to introduce Sofia and Valeria Alcantara y Pasqual, daughters of one of the most distinguished families in Barcelona. They have come to us by way of Veracruz to teach the children of the *hacienda* their letters and numbers and, I hope, to instill in them a bit of *peninsulare* polish."

He is overstating our backgrounds somewhat. Sofia curtsied slightly. *But better that than introducing us as well-educated but destitute orphans.*

A young woman wearing a *huipil* embroidered with blue and yellow flowers placed a platter stacked with rounds of fluffy bread in front of Doña Inmaculada, who tore off a piece and handed the platter to her right. Then she passed three bowls and three spoons to her left. The bowls were simple glazed terracotta, but the spoons seemed to be silver, their handles plain but nicely balanced.

To her surprise, Sofia felt hungry. Beginning with Doña Inmaculada and then moving first to the left, then to the right, the young woman in the *huipil* came along behind their seats with a steaming tureen of beans, dark red mottled with white dots. Sofia had never tasted this variety, but they had a nutty flavor clearly enlivened by peppers and some sort of salt pork. The meal was simple but filing.

As he signaled for a second bowl, Don Emilio turned toward Sofia. "I understand that you brought with you a novel musical instrument called a pianoforte, rather larger than a harpsicord but played somewhat similarly. And my cousin Alejandro writes that you are quite an accomplished musician."

"You are correct that we brought our mother's piano with us. But as to my skill, it is modest compared to what Don Alejandro has witnessed even at informal *musicales* in Veracruz."

"Be that as it may," Don Emilio said in a gracious tone, "we are privileged to have you and your instrument here at our remote *hacienda*. With your permission, I thought we might set it up in this refectory, so that on occasion you might favor us all with your playing. If any of the children show aptitude for the pianoforte or perhaps for any instruments that might appropriately accompany it, we could hold the odd recital."

Pointing toward a canvas-covered mound in the far corner of the room, he added, "Thinking that your instrument should be protected from the weather, I had the teamsters bring it inside, over there. Once we have all recovered from the excitement and demands of tomorrow's fiesta, you can select an appropriate spot for our men to assemble it, under your supervision, of course."

Touched by his thoughtfulness, Sofia said, "Thank you so much, Don Emilio. You are exactly right that the piano will do much better protected as much as possible from the dust. As you may have noticed, we kept it as tightly wrapped as possible on our journey north."

Don Emilio nodded toward his wife. "And now, I think we are all a bit tired, and we need to be up promptly at sunrise to complete preparations for the fiesta. Remember, five bells, and everyone jumps out of bed. Have a comfortable night."

He stood and nodded once more to Doña Inmaculada, who nodded in turn to a young woman standing in the shadows along the wall. "This is Camila," Doña Inmaculada said, striding off abruptly. "She will show you to your quarters."

As they approached each other, Valeria whispered to Sofia, "She has Maria Josefa's turquoise eyes." And indeed, she did, along with her mother's high cheekbones and glossy black hair, worn in two braids rather than one. Yet if Sofia hadn't known, she might not have guessed that Camila was a quarter Pueblo. Her figure was almost willowy, her complexion light olive, like Sofia's own.

"You must be *señoritas* Valeria and Sofia," the young woman said. "I am Camila. My mother said in her note that she held you both in great affection, as well as esteem. I will be pleased to assist you any way I can, starting with showing you to your room and helping you wash up and prepare for tomorrow. You must be tired from your long journey and from meeting all these new people."

Sofia smiled gratefully, feeling her knees buckle slightly. *It has to be almost ten o'clock.*

"She doesn't like me," Camila whispered with a quick glance over her shoulder at Doña Inmaculada's retreating back.

Valeria looked startled. "Why would that be?" she whispered back. "Maria Josefa told us you are the best spinner and dyer on the ranch."

"It's not my work that displeases her. It's that I am mixed race. She likes full-blooded Indians better than us *mestizos*. She says the circumstances of our birth, or more accurately our conception, are an offense to the will of God."

Camila led them out the side door of the refectory into a large room with a wide hearth at one end and a trestle table down the middle.

"This is the main kitchen," she explained. Then, pulling aside a curtain of yellow and red striped homespun flax, she said, "And this is the auxiliary kitchen, for preparing coffee and *atole*, that sort of thing."

Camila ushered them next into a smaller room with a corner adobe fireplace and two simple wooden cots piled with quilts. Suspended from one of the ceiling beams was a little platform fashioned from sticks about the width of Sofia's thumb, with smaller sticks woven between them, the whole topped with a fluffy layer of lambs' wool.

Camila gave the platform a little push, as if to demonstrate its function. "This is the cradle for Julio, the baby boy of Jimena, the assistant cook. She and I sleep here normally, but tonight she has taken little Julio to see his father, who is one of the soldiers. They have been married for only a year, and he has never seen his son."

Ducking through a lower doorway, Camila pulled aside another striped flax curtain, this one blue and tan, and led them into a somewhat larger room. Set into the opposite wall, a door and two windows opened onto a courtyard with cloistered arcades along the sides and a three-tiered fountain in the center flanked by rose bushes just beginning to bud. The room featured two deep shelves perpendicular to the windows, each with a horsehair mattress covered with muslin sheets and a pile of fresh-smelling blankets and pillows. In the corner immediately to the left was a little fireplace, smaller than the one in the adjoining room but with a flickering brazier that partially dispelled the chill of the high desert night.

"I hope you will find your room comfortable," Camila said, nodding toward the spaces under the windows. "As you can see, the teamsters have brought in your trunks from the wagon. Would you like me to help you unpack or draw you baths?"

"Just a basin of water, so we can wash our faces and hands," Sofia said gratefully, noticing that Valeria seemed to be swaying on her feet. "The room is lovely, so spacious compared to the wagon bed."

"It has only one problem. You can hear almost

everything that goes on in the household. Don Emilio and Doña Inmaculada have their room just across the way. Except for Alfonso, who has his own place right below Don Emilio's library, their children share the rooms along the right side. On a mild night with the shutters open, every conversation sounds like it takes place right outside your door. My room is much quieter, good for Jimena's little one to sleep."

Sofia noticed that Valeria had already fallen onto her bunk, fully clothed, and was snoring softly.

"I'll bring you that basin, so that you can wash, and also a pitcher of drinking water."

"You are so kind," Sofia said. Her fingers felt almost numb as she unhooked her bodice and slipped off her *robe á l'anglaise* and her top two petticoats and unlaced her stays. She barely had the energy to wait for Camila's return with the water and to splash her face and arms. Unpacking her short nightdress could wait for tomorrow. Tonight, she would sleep in her chemise.

CHAPTER SIX

Sometime before dawn, Sofia awoke to the sound of angry voices—a woman's and a man's. They seemed to be part of an anxious dream she was having, but as her mind floated up from the murk of sleep, she recognized that they were real. At first, they seemed frighteningly close, right outside her door. Then she remembered what Camila had told her. The voices must be coming from a room across the courtyard. Don Emilio and Doña Inmaculada were having a furious argument.

"The *señoritas* will be teaching *our* children, not the children of the ranch hands and kitchen help," Doña Inmaculada said loudly. "I will not have my children spending their days with those little *mestizos*, sitting beside them, going through the same exercises with no distinctions made as to class or position. Why do the offspring of the ranch hands and the servants need to read and do numbers, anyway?"

"*All* the children at Rancho de las Palomas need to be

able to read and write and do arithmetic." Don Emilio sounded like keeping his voice below a shout required considerable effort. "This ranch is becoming more prosperous and therefore more complicated to manage. Our ranch hands are hard-working, as are the women who cook and clean and help raise the animals. They take pride in what they do. With this attitude and some education, their children will be able to perform tasks that will benefit us all the more in the future."

Taking an audible breath, he continued in a more reasonable tone. "Wouldn't it be useful if the girl who collects the eggs every morning were able to keep track of which hens are producing how many eggs, and whether a particular hen is laying more or fewer eggs than a month ago? If that girl can write and do numbers, she can maintain a record. Or take another example. As you know, we produce fine saddles and harnesses here. I would like to be able to send one of the older boys to Santa Fe to trade them for tools and supplies and be confident that he can tell whether the merchant is cheating us or not. Alfonso and I can't handle all such transactions personally, as we discovered when he was away for two years studying in Mexico City."

Then, sounding almost like Sofia's father rehearsing a court argument, Don Emilio added, "Besides, we are already feeding and housing these two young women and giving them small stipends. It will cost us no more to have them teach eleven children than five. And it may be more effective for our own children, because now there will be several of similar ages."

Rather than dropping the level of her voice to match her husband's, Doña Inmaculada raised it to a ferocious pitch. "That would be against the will of God! The Lord in His wisdom made the races separate. It is His command that they *remain* separate and that the more primitive races serve the more advanced." Then she added in a tone like a blast of wind preceding a thunderstorm, "As you should know but clearly do not, the races are forbidden to mix."

"Do you think that God speaks directly to you, as he did to Moses and reportedly does to the Pope, woman? Well, He has not communicated this prohibition to *me*. And on this ranch, I am *patrón*!"

Valeria began to stir. "What's happening?" she asked sleepily. "I had a dream that two people were fighting, maybe in the heavens, like Zeus and Hera."

"It wasn't a dream, but it isn't our concern," Sofia said soothingly. "Anyway, we should probably get up. The sky is getting light, and you need to change out of those clothes you slept in."

Just then, the first deep clang of the morning bell peeled forth. At the fifth clang, Camila entered their room, a steaming mug in either hand and two *rebozos* draped over her right arm.

"*Atole*," she said, setting the mugs down next to the washbasin. The tantalizing scent of chocolate laced with cinnamon wafted through the room. "Here, we make it with toasted blue corn, coarsely ground with a *metate*, so it's probably darker and grainier than what you are used to. If it's not to your taste, I can bring coffee."

"It smells delicious," Valeria said. "And those?" She gestured toward the *rebozos*.

"These are for you to wear today, to add color to your white cotton skirts and blouses." Camila lay them across Valeria's bed. "I thought that the rose and gold stripes would be best for you, the emerald and wine for Sofia."

"Did you weave these?" Sofia asked, fingering the surprisingly soft fabric. "They're beautiful."

"No. Weaving is men's work. I only cord and dye and spin the wool. But our master weaver, José, made them especially for you when he heard you would be arriving just before the fiesta. He spent considerable time selecting the colors and textures of the yarn. He can be quite particular. He can also be a bit brusque, but a kind word of thanks would mean a great deal to him.

"And now I hope you will excuse me. I have to help lay

out the food in the refectory. There will be no seated meals today, but there will be special things to eat all day, including the sweet *churros* the children like so well."

Valeria rose. "Just one more favor. Can you tell me how to find wherever the new flock of sheep are kept?"

Looking puzzled, Camila said, "Against the wall just behind the chapel."

Pulling on a petticoat over a clean chemise, Valeria followed Camila. "I just want to check on the lamb."

A quarter of an hour later, Valeria bustled up to Sofia, who was helping lay out platters of *churros*, *tamales,* and flat bread in the refectory, and reported that the lamb was doing well, even walking. "But when I tried to pet the darling little creature, the ewe lowered her head and gave me an evil look," she said.

Smart mother, to be so protective of her little one in this hostile desert.

Although Camila had insisted that the sisters were not expected to do such menial work as bringing out the food, Sofia explained that she enjoyed being useful. Privately, she recognized that without something to occupy her, she would become as anxious as she had been the evening before—and that this was true of Valeria as well.

"Valeria, maybe there's some way you can help prepare for the fiesta."

"Ah," Camila said. "Perhaps you could assist with decorating San Isidro's litter. The girls will have finished cutting the flowers, but arranging them so that they look pretty and don't scatter is demanding and delicate work. I'm sure they could use a hand. They would be right in front of the chapel."

Seemingly pleased with the assignment, Valeria ran off, while Camila and Sofia continued working side by side, arranging the delicacies brought out from the kitchen.

As full morning sunlight began slanting through the

windows, Sofia heard the heavy front gate creak open, then a clatter of hooves and creaking of cartwheels.

"That will be the party from Rancho de las Golondrinas, our neighbor to the north," Camila said. "Don Emilio invites them to our fiestas, and they do the same for us. Not everyone comes, but the young people do, so the boys can show off their skills in the competitions and the girls can have the opportunity to dance—and maybe meet potential husbands. Father Antonio will be with them. He often spends the night at Las Golondrinas on his way here from Santa Fe."

Looking out toward the chapel, Sofia could see Valeria on top of the litter, bent over a tangle of deep pink peach blossoms and vibrant yellow and purple sand verbena, apparently unconcerned that her hair was in total disarray and her bottom was sticking out in a most undignified manner, accentuated by the brightly striped *rebozo* tied loosely around her hips. The two young men standing in the chapel doorway with San Isidro supported between them bore bemused smiles. Sofia scanned the stable yard for Doña Inmaculada and sighed with relief when she didn't see her.

Valeria stood, brushed her hands on her skirt and jumped down, petticoats billowing, after which the smiling fellows, accompanied by the handsome Alfonso and his gawky brother Juan, settled the *santo* onto the litter, securing the saint's feet and steadying his wobbling pitchfork. When Alfonso called the order to lift, the four picked up the litter, set it on their shoulders, and moved to the side as an oxcart bearing a middle-aged man wearing the brown robes of the Franciscan order rolled past.

Dipping a cylindrical brass aspergillum into a silver bucket, Father Antonio sprinkled holy water on the seventy or eighty people now packing the stable yard. As the cart bore toward the sheep pens, chicken coop and horse corrals, San Isidro and his litter fell in behind it, trailed by two men with trumpets, a soldier and a ranch hand, playing enthusiastically, one of them half a note behind the other. The women and girls working in the kitchen and refectory quickly filed out and joined the jubilant parade. Some attempted to sing along with the trumpeters, but Sofia could barely make out what were probably familiar hymns. Once the oxcart and the flower-bedecked *santo* headed out toward the gristmill and the pastures beyond, most of the celebrants fell back and began to drift toward the chapel.

Sofia felt a tap on her shoulder. "Come with me if you want a seat for Mass," Camila said.

Indeed, the chapel was packed to overflowing by the time Father Antonio marched up the center aisle with the communion host and wine, followed by San Isidro on his now somewhat bedraggled litter. Sitting in the third pew on the left, Sofia spotted Valeria at the door, signaled quickly, and moved over so that her sister could squeeze in.

As Maria Josefa predicted, the Mass was remarkably quick, except for the distribution of communion to the assembled throng, which seemed to take half an hour. The air in the chapel was becoming increasingly stuffy. Pleasantly sweet in the open air, the scent of peach blossoms and verbena emanating from San Isidro's litter became increasingly cloying. Once again, Sofia had the uneasy sense of being somewhere entirely foreign.

No sooner had Father Antonio turned to make the sign of the cross as his final blessing than Sofia felt herself being pushed by a wave of humanity out the door of the chapel and across the stable yard to the refectory. The platters of food, all cleverly designed to be eaten with fingers, were emptied and refilled twice before Sofia and Valeria reached them. Sofia grabbed an *empanada*, which turned out to be stuffed with sweet corn and onion, and headed outside. Valeria, immediately behind her, unwrapped a *tamale*.

The increasingly jubilant flow propelled them around the side of the *hacienda* and through the rear gate to a field of bare dirt alongside four substantial corrals. Stakes topped with pennants and linked with cord defined an area about ten yards on a side. Five men, two of them army privates, and a boy of about sixteen stood at the far end of the square, each with a coil of maguey rope looped around his left shoulder. One of the men held a horse loosely by the reins. The palomino stallion was one of the most magnificent animals Sofia had ever seen. His long blond mane, brushed until it glistened in the noonday sun, hung within a few feet of the ground.

Weaving gracefully through the crowd, Camila came up beside them and leaned close to be heard above the cacophony. "That is Patricio Esquivel from Rancho de las Golondrinas, and that is his famous horse Victor."

"Your mother told us that the men would be gambling at these competitions, but I don't see any money or chits changing hands," Valeria said.

"That is because everyone knows who will win the fancy roping. This will be more of a demonstration than a contest—a chance for the ranch hands to show off a bit, for the soldiers to entertain their comrades and maybe impress some girls, and for all of us to see a performance of the most skillful roping in *El Norte*."

The crack of a pistol cut the air. The crowd turned as one toward the end of the field, where Don Emilio stood on a broad raised platform. Some of the men lifted small children onto their shoulders. A hush washed over the group.

The *patrón*'s voice rang out with warmth and vigor. "Welcome, friends, neighbors, and our valiant soldiers of the Santa Fe garrison, to Rancho de las Palomas for the Feast of San Isidro, patron saint of farmers and herdsmen and therefore of us all. I am pleased to announce the first of today's competitions, fancy roping."

Beginning with Don Emilio's ten-year-old son Diego, the contestants entered the blocked-off field one at a time and performed loops, twirls and jumps, some clearly better than others. The soldiers had choreographed a duet, which they clearly had not practiced sufficiently. They barely completed their second *pas de deux* when one of the privates tripped the other and they both fell, accompanied by hoots from their comrades and laughter from the crowd.

Suddenly, the laughter turned to excited chatter as Patricio Esquivel swung onto the palomino's back and eased the coil of rope into his left hand. Sofia watched Victor step majestically into the center of the field, then, seemingly without prodding, turn to all four directions while Esquivel bowed.

Esquivel began slowly, spinning ever-larger loops to the right, to the left, then completely around himself and his horse. Sofia found the display more elegant than the performances of the earlier contestants, but not particularly novel or challenging. But she caught her breath when Esquivel climbed gracefully onto his saddle. With Victor standing perfectly still, Esquivel danced in and out of the spinning rope, never appearing the least uncertain of his balance or his horse. As calmly as he had begun, he settled back into the saddle and began gracefully rewinding the rope while keeping a loop spinning above his head. Once the entire coil was draped around the pummel, horse and rider took a simultaneous bow.

For a moment there was perfect silence. Then the crowd roared as Patricio Esquivel rode to the platform and dismounted to stand beside Don Emilio. The other contestants positioned themselves behind him. Bearing broad smiles, each clapped the champion on the shoulder, except for Diego, who could only reach his elbow. Sofia saw the *patrón* nod to the boy. His expression wavering between delight and awe, Diego presented Esquivel with a silver goblet.

The next three contests struck Sofia as vaguely anticlimactic, although some of the male spectators began digging into their pockets and whispering as another, his forearms bearing the telltale tracery of small scars typical of a blacksmith, made marks on a piece of paper which he slipped, along with the coins, into a brown wool sack. *This is why we'll be teaching the children to write and do arithmetic. Given that four* cuatillos *make a* real, *if Pablo bets ten* cuatillos *on a horse and Ramón puts twenty-five on the same horse, and the other spectators bet a total of seventy* cuatillos *on other horses, how much will Pablo get if his horse wins?*

For the fourth event, Don Emilio walked to the back of the platform, turned around, and faced the adjacent field. It was longer and narrower, with twenty stakes set down the middle, each eight feet from the next. Affixed to the top were bright strips of cloth, five to a post, the ribbons on each post a distinctive color. Holding aloft a sandglass such as cooks used to time eggs, Don Emilio announced: "This will be our most demanding test of precision riding, of skill of both horse and rider in total partnership. Each of the five contestants here," and he bowed to the five young men on his left, standing next to their horses, "will have three minutes to complete the course, weaving between the posts. As he goes past each post, the rider will attempt to pick up a ribbon. The contestant with the most ribbons wins."

Simultaneously, Don Emilio fired the starting gun and flipped over the sand glass. Sofia watched as the first contestant steered his horse through the course. The mare seemed an able enough cattle pony, but her rider almost lost his balance twice as he bent over to reach the streamers, and he missed two. The next rider didn't even complete the slalom before the crack of the pistol indicated the end of the three minutes. The third contestant came in within time but with only fifteen ribbons.

Up fourth was Corporal Fernando Valdez y Guzmán. He had shed his embroidered vest and woolen tunic and his broad-brimmed leather hat. He now sat astride his bay gelding in a simple muslin shirt, the sleeves rolled up to the elbows. Sofia saw Valeria smile and wave. The corporal replied with a grin and a two-fingered salute. The gelding pranced side-to-side and snorted, then quieted as the corporal patted his neck. Responding to the gun, the horse dashed forward, his head stretched out as he rounded each stake so close that Fernando had only to bend slightly at the waist to snag the streamer. He completed the course with all twenty and time to spare. Valeria squealed and jumped, as did at least a dozen other pretty young women in the crowd.

The final contestant put on a good show but was no match for the handsome corporal and his nimble horse. Sofia took a deep breath and asked Camila where they might find something to drink.

"Along the wall just outside the refectory. There's beer and rum, of course, but if you would like something lighter, the cook has prepared a special treat using preserved lemons and molasses brought on the wagon train."

Refreshed by the sweetly tart drink, Sofia rejoined the crowd moving toward the large grassy pasture beyond the corals. Don Emilio appeared to have abandoned the platform for a tall black stallion with a silver-studded saddle and bridle. When she looked behind her, Sofia was surprised to have lost sight of Valeria and Camila. She tried to make her way back to them, but the throng pressed her forward until she found herself standing next to the starting line for the final event, the twenty-furlong race she'd heard about since morning.

She'd overheard locals and guests ask each other about the length of a furlong. The English racing term made the contest sound prestigious, but just how long was it? One of the stable boys proudly told a visitor from Las Golondrinas that a furlong measured an eighth of a mile. The race would run two and a half miles, crossing the long pasture diagonally to the left, rounding end posts at each corner, and returning to the starting line.

Climbing onto the top rung of the corral fence, the stable boy pulled out a spyglass and trained it on the far-left corner of the field. He turned the cylinder with his right hand, then lowered it to his thigh. Ten horses and riders lined up. Three were soldiers, including Corporal Fernando Valdez y Guzmán, still flushed with his victory in the slalom. Halfway down the line, Alfonso and Beto sat astride their horses. As Sofia watched, Alfonso turned to Beto, who spun around in his saddle to face Don Emilio's oldest son face on, square jaw to square jaw. The look that passed between them was one of pure hatred.

The fury in whatever Alfonso was saying cut through the noise of the crowd, but not the words themselves. However, she clearly heard the close of his tirade: "Son of a whore!" For the first time, Sofia was able to make out the color of Beto's eyes—clear gray.

Stunned, Sofia recognized the singular truth that no one at Las Palomas had seemed willing to reveal. Even Maria Josefa had been evasive when Sofia asked about Beto. "Sometimes it is hard to take your place when you don't know what that place is."

But he did seem to know his place, or at least who he was, and now Sofia thought that she did, too.

At the crack of the starting pistol, the horses took off across the long pasture. The blacksmith who had been collecting the wagers tied a cord around his brown wool sack and shook his head. All bets were now in. Fernando's magnificent bay gelding quickly pulled into the lead. Six lengths behind him, Beto's paint mare galloped smoothly. Another three lengths back, the white stallion charged forward as Alfonso's riding crop flashed across its withers. The other seven horses fell progressively behind, although one of the soldiers managed to push his dappled gray ahead of the pack as they passed the point halfway to the first turn.

By then, the horses had become so small that the spectators around Sofia stopped craning their necks and turned to the boy on the top rung of the fence. He had deployed his spyglass and was calling out the positions.

"Rounding the first turn, white stallion in the lead, paint mare next, bay gelding falling back," he shouted to the suddenly silent crowd. "Gray gaining on the turn, coming up on the bay, passing him on the straightaway."

Some of the soldiers nodded happily at the news. Others frowned. *They'd been on the trail for months with nowhere to spend their wages. Some of them must have bet heavily.*

After taking a sip from a cup that a girl with rosy cheeks handed up to him, the boy raised his spyglass toward the far-right corner of the field.

"White and paint neck and neck rounding the second turn. Bay now well back in the pack, led by the gray." He paused for a full swallow from the cup, coughed slightly, then took another sip.

Lifting the spyglass once more, the boy shouted excitedly, "Paint mare now leading by two lengths on the home stretch. White stallion gaining—a length."

He handed down his spyglass and stood. Everyone at the front part of the crowd could now see the two lead horses. As Beto leaned forward in his saddle, the paint speeded her gallop, but Alfonso charged up on his left, furiously spurring and whipping the white stallion. Sofia watched as Alfonso crossed the finish line half a length ahead, blood running from the horse's heaving flanks.

Jumping triumphantly from the saddle, Alfonso bowed briefly to the applauding crowd and tossed the reins to the boy who had wielded the spyglass. Then flushed and grinning, the heir apparent to Rancho de las Palomas exchanged embraces and shoulder-slaps with the exuberant young men who quickly surrounded him.

Sofia watched Beto dismount slowly, pat his horse soothingly on the neck, and lead her toward the stable. She noticed he wasn't wearing spurs. Up on the platform, Doña Inmaculada had joined her husband. Draped in a bright purple *rebozo*, she beamed and waved. Don Emilio's expression was curiously neutral.

"Wasn't that thrilling?" Valeria shouted in Sofia's ear, startling her.

"I suppose so. But did you see Alfonso's poor horse, snorting foam and bleeding from his flanks?" *Surely, given her love of animals, Valeria should find that sight distressing enough to mute her enthusiasm.*

"Camila and I were too far back," Valeria said nonchalantly. "I only saw him win. Poor Corporal Fernando.

62

His horse is pretty, but not much for distance."

Following the smell of roast goat basted with garlic and cumin, Sofia and Valeria trailed Camila toward the stable yard, where a ranch hand hoisted a haunch onto a long trestle table. Although she'd had nothing all day except the *atole* and the *empanada*, Sofia wasn't hungry. In fact, she felt a bit queasy. The press of the crowd combined with the press of her new knowledge made her dizzy.

"Please excuse me," she said to Valeria and Camila. "I think I need to go lie down for a while."

"But you'll miss the dancing!" Valeria said.

"I'm sure you'll enjoy it. Have fun, but don't embarrass yourself."

Gently declining Camila's offer of help, Sofia wove her way through the exuberant throng, dodged two casks of *cavazos* being rolled toward the stable yard, and made her way to her room, where she lay down fully clothed. Out on the wooden platform from which Don Emilio had overseen the day's competitions, she could hear the musicians tuning up for the *jota*. The reed instrument—she thought it was a *dulzaia*—was slightly flat. Despite the clatter of castanets and the stomping of heels, she fell into a profound sleep.

Well after dark, Valeria burst in, waking Sofia with the announcement that the *jota* danced here was completely different from the version danced in Veracruz—much livelier—but that Fernando had taught her the steps, and Alfonso had complimented her for picking them up so quickly and had danced with her until the band stopped playing.

"I think he likes me," she said breathlessly.

"They all do," Sofia replied before slipping back into unconsciousness.

CHAPTER SEVEN

Except for having awakened briefly when Valeria returned
from the dancing, Sofia slept straight through to the morning
bell. She awoke with a muzzy head and the certainty that she
had been dreaming. Nothing of the dream's content
remained, only the uneasy sense that she had been in a
foreign land where everything—the plants, the animals, the
people—were so unfamiliar that she couldn't tell which were
safe and which were dangerous.

Following the smell of coffee, Sofia made her way
through Camila's room to the kitchen, where a pot sat
bubbling on the hearth. The brew was strong and bitter, but
after half a mug Sofia's head began to clear. Camila sat at the
well-worn kitchen table, finishing a tortilla and beans.

"You should eat something," she said. "You went to bed
without supper yesterday. How about some goat? There's a
nice haunch left over."

The thought of the oily meat made the coffee rise in
Sofia's throat. Looking alarmed, Camila said soothingly, "Sit

down. I know what you need—a couple of *churros* and some white sheep's cheese."

One bite of the sweet pastry and Sofia felt her customary strength return. She watched as Valeria bounced into the kitchen, sniffing the air theatrically as she headed for the coffee pot. She had tied her hair back in at least a semblance of order, and she appeared to have washed her face. Sofia wondered how her sister could look so fresh on what couldn't have been more than five hours of sleep.

Camila got up and embraced Valeria. "You look as beautiful as last night, Valerita. All the young men wanted to dance with you, but Alfonso scared them away."

Returning Camila's hug and then disengaging herself gracefully, Valeria reached for a mug and the coffee pot. "I *do* like Fernando." She sighed. "But since he is about to be married, I guess Alfonso will have to do."

Sofia couldn't help joining in the giggling. Her sister was as vivacious as she was pretty.

Suddenly, Sofia remembered the reason they had been invited to this place. "Today is Wednesday. Camila, do you think Doña Inmaculada will be expecting us to begin lessons this morning?"

"No. Traditionally, the day after a fiesta is set aside for rest and for putting the *hacienda* back in order. The men will be taking down the platform and the race courses. The women will be scrubbing the stable yard, sweeping the chapel, putting away the food. And they will expect the children to help. Apart from that, only the work caring for the animals and preparing simple meals will go on. Those are necessary every day, even Sunday."

As if to demonstrate, loud banging began in the direction of the corrals. A male voice lifted above the racket. "Pile those boards over by the main barn!"

Sofia recognized the commanding tone as Beto's.

"Not so loud," one of the men called back. "Some of us have headaches this morning."

A third worker jeered, "I suspect you mistook the

cavazos for water last night."

"Just get to work," Beto said. "The sooner we finish, the sooner you can go nurse your big head."

There isn't so much as a hint of fellow-feeling in his voice. Where is the man who had patted his mare soothingly at the end of the race?

She heard one of the ranch hands grumble, "Who does he think he is, ordering us around like that? He's a *mestizo*, like the rest of us. In fact, he looks a lot more *indio* than I do."

"Someone has to manage this place," another said. "You clearly don't have the brains for it."

The first man sneered. "The reason he gets to do it is that he's the *patrón's* beloved bastard."

"I heard that," Beto said icily. "I understand that Las Golondrinas is hiring. Why don't you take a ride up there this afternoon—better still, right now, and bring your belongings with you."

That exchange erased any lingering doubts Sofia harbored as to the brusque ranch foreman's identity. She felt a sudden flare of irritation, more because of his high-handed tone than because everyone had concealed this truth from her and her sister. She turned her attention to the challenges she and Valeria faced.

"At least we can plan how we can set up the classroom," she said to Camila. "On the long journey here, we talked about what and how we would teach, but since we didn't know what space would be designated for us, or what materials might be available, we couldn't picture the details."

"If you would permit me to make a suggestion, let's take a look at the refectory," Camila offered. "Everyone here eats breakfast in their quarters or in the kitchen, so the refectory will be free until just before noon."

One look at the now-empty dining hall made it clear that the corner farthest from the kitchen would make the most appropriate classroom. Not only would it interfere least with the cook staff, but it was also close to the front door. Morning light spilled through high windows on each wall.

"We will have five pupils," Valeria said, glancing at the table nearest the corner.

Sofia shook her head. "No, I think eleven. My understanding is that we will be teaching all the children on the ranch between the ages of six and sixteen."

Valeria looked startled, but then shrugged. "That will make it easier, I guess—having an older group, who will already know how to read and do arithmetic, and a younger group."

"I would not count on the skills of the older children," Camila said. "Some of them can barely sign their names. Even Doña Inmaculada..." She trailed off as though embarrassed. "Let me just say that she can read her prayer book and gospels, but she relies on Don Emilio to write any letters on her behalf."

"Then how did you learn to read and write?" Valeria asked bluntly.

Camila smiled. "I grew up in Santa Fe. Both my parents were taught by the missionaries who came to their village. Even though they didn't have much money, they paid to send us all to school—my sisters and me to the nuns at the convent, the boys to Father Antonio and the missionary brothers. But here on the ranch, it's too far, especially for the little ones. That is why we are so happy to have you two here."

"We will need some supplies," Sofia said, "a slate and chalk for each pupil, plus a big slate for us."

"For the big one, one of the men can paint a sheet of tin black. For the small slates, maybe the sisters in Santa Fe have some they don't need, and also some chalk."

"We can make a list and ask Doña Inmaculada to send a request, perhaps with an appropriate donation to the convent," Valeria said.

"I wouldn't ask Doña Inmaculada for anything today regarding the lessons—maybe not ever," Camila said. "Her maid warned us all that she is in a bad mood—a *very* bad mood. She smiled and waved when Alfonso won the horse race yesterday. But right afterwards, when Don Emilio tried to take her hand, she slapped him away. Everybody saw it."

Once again, Sofia felt the now-too-familiar sense of not knowing quite where she stood or what was expected of her. If only her piano were set up, she could sit down and lose herself in the music.

Apparently catching her glance toward the far corner of the room, Camila said, "Let me ask Beto if he can spare a few men to set up your piano." With that, she headed out through the front door.

Valeria looked like she hadn't heard a word—not about Doña Inmaculada's ill temper, not about the piano. "A map of the world, with Spain and the colonies indicated somehow…Maybe Don Emilio has some maps I can copy in one of those portfolios in his library."

She tapped her teeth with a fingernail. "The names of the king and the queen and the viceroy. A copy of the Spanish flag and the flag of New Spain."

Rushing out the side door, Valeria called over her shoulder, "I'm going for my art supplies. If you'll get a little flour and water from the kitchen, we can paste some of my drawing sheets together for the maps."

Sofia sat down at a table facing a corner, imagining the first day of lessons. She and Valeria had agreed that they would have formal instruction six days a week from 9:00 to 11:30, beginning with a short prayer asking blessings for Rancho de las Palomas, for King Charles IV and Queen Maria Luisa and Viceroy Don Miguel de la Grúa Talamanca de Carini y Branciforte… Maybe a shortened name for the viceroy, who at any rate was notoriously corrupt. The younger children would sit at the front table, the older ones behind them. Whatever their ages, each of the pupils would get up every half hour or so to recite something or to solve an arithmetic problem on the large board, both to develop their self-confidence and to keep them from becoming restless. Three days a week, they would spend the two hours after *siesta* in the field, learning about the plants, birds, and animals. The girls would sketch these. The boys would do landscapes. *Doña Inmaculada is right about that point. Future army officers need to be able to draw up battle plans with realistic topographic features.*

As Sofia sat drumming her fingers on the table, trying to identify any flaws in the instructional strategy, Valeria bustled in, her largest sketch pad and box of wax drawing sticks in her left hand, a sheaf of pencils, a sharpened quill, and a bottle of India ink in her right.

"Where's the flour paste?"

By the time the cook staff began bringing out the midday meal, Valeria had sketched out the names of the king and queen of Spain and the viceroy of New Spain in large block letters, which she was inking in neatly. Catching a whiff of fresh sweat mingled with wild sage, Sofia looked up to see Beto leaning on the table not a yard from her shoulder. She gasped.

"A few of my men will be coming by after *siesta* to set up your piano," he said. "You'll need to be here to tell them what to do."

With that, he strode toward the serving table, filled a bowl with goat stew, snatched up a spoon and a round of flat bread, and headed out the side door.

No "Would it be convenient if..." Not even a "Good morning." Sofia recognized that the lanky ranch foreman was doing her a favor, but he hadn't even paused long enough for her to say, "Thank you."

After a bowl of stew and a brief *siesta*, Sofia returned to the refectory with her green suede roll of piano-tuning tools. Valeria was already there, smiling sweetly at three sturdy ranch hands as she directed them toward the classroom corner.

"If you could nail this one there." She pointed to the wall to the left of one window and held up the two pasted-together sheets of paper bearing the names of the king, the queen, and the viceroy, the last in smaller print, both reflecting his lower status and the length of his name.

"And these over there," she said, displaying another two pages from her sketchbook, one bearing a likeness of the Spanish flag, the other the flag of New Spain, "I would be so very grateful."

Sofia marveled that her sister had been able to produce such vivid reds and yellows from her box of wax drawing sticks.

Turning to Sofia, Valeria announced, "I'm heading to Don Emilio's study now. When I told him we needed maps, he invited me to come up and copy some that he just received with his new books."

The ranch hands' appreciative stares at Valeria's retreating form stopped just short of disrespectful. The tallest of the three turned to Sofia and said, "Señor Beto has asked us to set up the musical instrument you brought with you from Veracruz, *señorita*. We understand that it is somewhat delicate, so we are prepared to take great care with it if you will direct us as to how to proceed."

Leading the men to the large canvas-covered mound in the opposite corner of the dining hall, Sofia directed them as they unwrapped it gently. A satisfied warmth spread across her chest and down her arms as she saw the front panel with "Broadmoor" gleaming in gold letters, every curlicue on the ornate "B" unblemished. In fact, the whole rectangular body of the instrument had come through the journey apparently unscratched except for a small dent on one of the legs.

The unevenness of the floor tiles necessitated much fussing with slivers of wood, first on one corner, and then on the opposite, then back again. It took an hour before the piano was set up to Sofia's satisfaction. One of the ranch hands fetched a chair from the kitchen, so that she could test the height. For playing purposes, the chair was a bit low, but the addition of a pillow would correct that. Perhaps the ranch's carpenter could make a proper bench to her specifications. It wouldn't need to be fine provided it was the right height and wide enough that she could have a student sit next to her.

Thanking the workmen, Sofia laid out her tuning fork, the hammer for adjusting the strings, and the rubber wedges for dampening those not in play. She struck the tuning fork and secured its handle between two boards of the nearest table. Then, while the vibrations settled into the clear tone of 'A' above middle 'C,' she lifted off the top and front panels of the piano and went to work. Not surprisingly, the instrument was completely out of tune. Every string would need resetting. Feeling the silken ivory of the first key she touched, Sofia fought to quell the surge of sadness that washed over her as she remembered her mother, sitting at this same keyboard, smiling as she played a Bach prelude.

An hour into her task, Sofia felt an uncanny prickle along her arms. Perhaps it was a faint sound or shift of light in the room. Whatever the cause, she turned to see a broad-shouldered man standing in the refectory's side doorway. Not standing—leaning with his arms crossed. Because he was backlit by the sun, she couldn't make out his features, but from his insolent stance, she was certain it was Beto.

Strolling over to the table on which the tuning fork was wedged, he asked, "Did my men set up the piano to your satisfaction?"

"It's fine." Recognizing that her tone had been rudely sharp, she added, "Thank you."

Her next words spilled out before she could couch them politely. "You're Alfonso's brother."

Beto smiled wryly. "His half-brother. Don Emilio is my father, but Doña Inmaculada is not my mother. Thank God. I wouldn't have her for my mother for all the gold in Peru."

Once again, Sofia caught a whiff of fresh sweat mingled with wild sage as his smile turned bitter.

"I see that someone has been gossiping, maybe more than one someone. I thought that everyone here had agreed to keep this matter quiet, at least until you and your sister had settled in and had a chance to appreciate all of us on our own merits."

"No one told me anything. They all kept your confidence well, even Maria Josefa, back on the trail when I asked her who you were. I saw you and Alfonso at the start of the race yesterday, arguing face to face, and I began to draw my own conclusions."

"Of course." Beto dropped his gaze to the pointed toes of his brown boots. "When he called me a son of a whore, loud enough for everyone to hear his insult and feel his contempt."

"The look I saw *you* give *him* was hardly one of brotherly love. This morning, when I heard one of the ranch hands say you were 'the *patrón's* beloved bastard,' I was certain."

"And did you also hear me fire him on the spot? That wasn't because of what he said. It was because he's always been lazy and uncooperative, and the other men have had to pick up the slack. Besides, his surliness has been bad for morale."

Beto unfolded his arms and leaned toward her across the table. "My mother was no whore. Like your friend Camila, she was a gifted spinner and dyer. Her name in her people's language meant 'Light that Shines;' so when she was baptized, she was given the Christian name 'Lucinda.' She was beautiful, kind, cheerful, hardworking. Everyone loved her, but my father especially. And she loved him with a true heart."

"But your father was married…"

"He was married to a woman without a grain of warmth. Her family owned the ranch immediately to the south. They were country people, barely literate, so having a daughter marry a Chavez gave them a social boost. For her part, Inmaculada had that beautiful hair and was known to be tediously pious. Certainly, no one could question her virtue, and in those days that was especially important among the *criollos*. All the older people here at the *hacienda* say that even when my father and Inmaculada were newlyweds, she wouldn't let him give her an *abrazo* or hold her hand, at least not in public. In private—well, at least they managed to conceive Alfonso."

"And then what happened?" Sofia asked, feeling herself soften a bit toward Beto.

"I only know what some of the older men have told me over a *cerveza*. My father has never said a word against Inmaculada, at least not in my presence. But what I heard was that as soon as she suspected she was pregnant, she denied my father her bed. He moved to a room up near his study. And before long, he and my mother became inseparable. They were crazy about each other, with that kind of passion that can destroy everything around it. Some people call it 'falling in love,' but I think of it as going mad."

"How soon did that happen?"

Beto paused, re-crossed his arms, and fixed his gaze on the ceiling.

"Alfonso is six months older than I am. You figure it out. No one here seems to have had any trouble doing the arithmetic, not even the most thoroughly illiterate."

Shocked, not so much by these revelations as by seeing a man who had seemed so strong, even arrogant, suddenly vulnerable as the boy he must have been, Sofia sat across the table from him and asked softly, "What happened to your mother? You speak of her in the past tense..."

"She died when I was four, giving birth to my baby sister, who didn't make it, either. That's why my memories of her are vague, so jumbled up with the stories I've heard that now I can't sort out my recollections from those tales. But I do know that the three of us lived together in a little *casita* down by the gristmill. And I also know, because I have seen the papers, that my father took me to be baptized in Santa Fe and on that same day he acknowledged me legally."

Grinning broadly, he added, "You can imagine how that sat with Inmaculada."

Beto shook his head, then looked at Sofia directly, his disturbing gray eyes meeting hers. "Shouldn't you be getting back to tuning your piano?"

"That can wait. First, I want to know what happened when your mother died."

"To me or to my father? Everyone knew Inmaculada would have nothing to do with me, and my father was reportedly so grief-stricken that he was in no condition to take care of a four-year-old boy. Like many men who lose the mother of their children in childbirth, he also felt overwhelmed with guilt. So I went to live with the stable master. He and his wife had been unable to have children. Frankly, they spoiled me. My father taught me to read and write, but the stable master taught me about horses."

"And Don Emilio and Doña Inmaculada went on to have five more children."

"That took a while," Beto said, focusing again on one of the rough-hewn beams in the ceiling. "You'll notice that there's a ten-year gap between Alfonso and Juan, their next-oldest child. Father Antonio got them back together, if you can call it that. My father trusts him because he was a man of the world before he became a man of God. Antonio came here from Spain as a cavalry officer. He married a woman from a fine old family in Santa Fe. Reportedly, he loved her very much; but before they could have children, she died of influenza. At first, he cursed God. Then, one day while he was walking in the desert, shaking his fist at Heaven, you know how such stories go, he experienced a conversion—not so much to religion as to science. He recognized that disease was a natural process, not a personal attack from God, and that the best way to honor the woman he had loved and lost was to bring knowledge not just to the Indians but also to the ignorant, superstitious *criollos*. Joining the Franciscans allowed him to do that."

Sofia watched Beto's broad shoulders loosen. Turning toward her, he pulled out the bench alongside the table, swung his long legs over and sat down.

"Of course, Doña Inmaculada trusted him because he was an ordained priest and a *peninsulare*. He is her confessor, although what he makes of her 16th Century version of Catholicism I can't imagine."

A brief hint of a smile crossed his full lips.

"So Father Antonio told Emilio and Inmaculada to resume living together as husband and wife, and they just did that?" Sofia asked incredulously.

"Oh, it wasn't *that* simple," Beto said, turning the full focus of his gray eyes on hers. "First, the good father saw to it that my mother and my baby sister received a proper burial, even though some people would have said that she wasn't entitled to it because she was living in sin when she died. Wisely, Father Antonio didn't bury them here, where certain people might have desecrated their graves, but at San Miguel Pueblo, where she was born."

So Maria Josefa had spoken the truth. The young men at the pueblo feast had *been Beto's cousins.*

"Then, according to the old men who have shared the story with me over a *cerveza* or two, Antonio began spending the night here occasionally when he was making his pastoral rounds of the ranches and *pueblos*. He explained to anyone who asked that he enjoyed discussing books with my father. In fact, they may have been the only people in *El Norte* who read scientific treatises, the classics, and so on. My father had that wonderful library."

Sofia noticed that Beto himself seemed more than comfortable with expressing complex ideas and that, like Corporal Fernando and Don Emilio but unlike Doña Inmaculada, he spoke with the precise diction of the capital—at least he did when he wasn't shouting orders to ranch hands. Don Emilio must have taught his son more than basic reading and arithmetic.

"In the course of those late-night discussions, Father Antonio managed to persuade my father that it was his duty to fulfill his marriage vows." Beto shrugged. "Knowing my father, I suspect that Antonio cleverly led him in that direction and let him think it was his idea all along. After that, convincing Doña Inmaculada, probably in the course of confession, that she should accept her sacred marital duties would have been easy.

"And now," he said, "both of us need to get back to work."

Unhooking a knife from his belt, he struck the tuning fork. As its vibrations coalesced toward a single tone, he added, "When you and Valeria start teaching the children, try to drop the Castilian accent. Inmaculada may consider it a mark of cultivation, but everyone else will just think it's pretentious."

Sofia felt stunned. Here she had been moved by his story, feeling warmth and empathy for a vulnerable human being spreading his poignant past before her, only to have him slip back into his armor of dominance.

Well, she wouldn't allow herself to be trapped like that a second time.

Sofia turned back to the piano, tightening the middle 'C' string so abruptly that it almost snapped.

CHAPTER EIGHT

Although the classroom in the refectory corner was clearly makeshift, Sofia decided that it would serve its purpose. Valeria's artwork had transformed the space admirably. By Thursday morning, a neatly lettered alphabet executed in black India ink ran along the wall just below the ceiling. Valeria's renditions of the flags of Spain and New Spain stood out boldly, and the map of the world with Spain and its colonies highlighted in red was remarkably detailed. Sofia had to admit that her sister was a talented artist.

Ranch hands had painted a sheet of scrap metal black and had hung it beneath the window facing the tables. It was a bit wavy, but it would do for a chalkboard.

Valeria rushed in carrying a rough-hewn but sturdy-looking wooden box. She and Sofia were both wearing white skirts and flounced blouses with plain *rebozos* that Camila had provided—Valeria's a muted rose, Sofia's indigo. "The children will be here in half an hour. I thought the little ones could stand on this to recite," Valeria said, setting the box in front of the first table. "There's a pile of old furniture in the barn. Most of it is just pieces, and you have to watch out for the spiders, but I think I saw some sort of lectern or prayer-book stand in there."

"Why don't you go look? I'll see if Camila was able to borrow a Bible from Don Emilio."

Sofia found Camila in the weaving workshop, stirring a vat of chamisa-based yellow dye. "Let me just get this started," she said, "and I'll bring in the Bible. I told Don Emilio that you wanted an old one that you didn't have to worry about, so the cover is a little tattered, but the type is large. He also managed to dig out four slates and some pieces of chalk. Those should help until we see if the sisters in Santa Fe can provide us with more."

Before leaving the workshop, Sofia went over to José, the master weaver. Propelled by pedals at his feet, his loom clattered so loudly that she had to shout to introduce herself and thank him for the beautiful *rebozos* he had made for her and Valeria. "Thanks to your handiwork, she had so many invitations to dance that she ended the evening exhausted," Sofia said.

Pausing his shuttle in mid-flight, José looked up, his expression changing from a frown of concentration to a faint smile. "Your sister's beauty and liveliness were the cause, *señorita*, not my humble weaving. Even if she had worn a grain sack, all the young men would have wanted to dance with her."

As Sofia turned to leave the workshop, she thought bitterly of her own broad mouth, so out of proportion with her deep-set eyes, and the words that Valeria shot at her back on the road north: "I will always be fair, and you will always be as dark as a Moor."

By the time Sofia got back to the refectory, three children were standing at the door—a girl of about thirteen, already all arms and legs, and two boys, one a head taller than the other. She recognized none of them as Inmaculada's, so these had to be the children of ranch hands. All three were looking down at the toes of their worn but polished boots. The older boy shuffled back and forth as if trying to make a little ridge out of the dust.

"Good morning, children," Sofia said. "I'm happy to see that you are here early."

She nodded toward Valeria, who was wiping down a battered lectern. "I am Señorita Sofia, and this is Señorita Valeria. We will be your teachers. Please tell us your names and ages."

"Marta," the girl said, still addressing her toes. "I am thirteen."

The boys introduced themselves as Reynaldo, twelve, and Nicolás, eight.

Smiling sweetly, Valeria walked over to the door and crouched down, taking Marta's and Nicolás's hands in hers. "The first lesson today is to look up and smile," she said. When the children obeyed, albeit tentatively, Valeria gave their hands a gentle squeeze. "You both have such beautiful eyes, and so intelligent."

Valeria is buttering the bread a bit thick, but the strategy appears to be working. The children seemed to relax somewhat and followed Valeria as she led them to the tables, directing the younger boy to the front one, the girl and the other boy to the one behind.

Moments later, two little girls arrived holding hands, with an older boy behind them. Valeria took the same approach with them—Catalina, seven, and Julia, eight. Tomás announced that he was fourteen. He blushed bright scarlet when he looked at Valeria and muttered how he should be working with his father in the carpentry shop, but that Don Emilio had insisted that he come to classes.

"Perhaps the *patrón* has in mind for you some position of responsibility that will require skill in reading, writing, and mathematics," Valeria said.

Sofia was amazed. She never suspected that her headstrong younger sister would be so good with their pupils.

Just as the elaborately carved grandfather clock in the

far corner struck nine, five more children appeared. Sofia recognized them as Doña Inmaculada's. They all looked straight ahead and said "Good morning" in unison. Even Valeria's charms failed to relax them. They recited their names and ages in order—Juan, fifteen; Consuela, twelve; Diego, ten; Emilia, nine; Sebastian, eight. *They don't seem to know what a smile is.* Holding hands, the five siblings filed over to the far end of the front table and began to sit down.

"Not there," Sofia said, attempting to pitch her tone midway between authority and warmth. "Emilia, Sebastian and Diego, please sit in front, Consuela and Juan behind. And I would like all of you pupils to sit together, about an arm's length apart. Señorita Valeria and I don't want to have to look all over the refectory during lessons."

All the children squirmed uncomfortably, but Doña Inmaculada's moved as directed, and the others spread out. Noticing a slight smirk on Consuela's broad face, Sofia guessed the girl had been assigned to report back to her mother. Maybe it would be best to begin this first day with something irreproachable.

"Now, please rise for our morning prayer," Sofia said. "Repeat after me: Dear Lord we pray you to guide our thoughts and efforts…"

The children repeated, with Sebastian and Julia half a step behind.

"…this day and all days."

Once again, they echoed her words.

"Please bless Rancho de las Palomas, Don Emilio and Doña Inmaculada and all who live and work here."

The children stumbled a bit but seemed to be picking up their pace.

"And please bless Spain, New Spain, King Carlos IV, and Queen Maria Luisa…"

Now they were almost in unison. Here came the hard part.

"…and Viceroy Don Miguel de la Grúa Talamanca de Carini y Branciforte."

By "Carini," the response dissolved into an unintelligible mumble, but that was to be expected. Sofia brought them back together with "in Jesus' name, amen."

Now Consuela could tell her mother that they had begun the school day with a prayer, in fact, one that included patriotic sentiments. If they closed with the Lord's Prayer, that should help balance Inmaculada's predictable outrage at her children sitting with those of the *mestizo* ranch hands.

Because the children responded so readily to Valeria's warmth and, yes, her looks, Sofia nodded to her to describe the rules of decorum, reasoning that the children would want to please her. Valeria explained that everyone in the class was to treat everyone else with respect. No interrupting. No making rude faces. No laughing when another pupil made a mistake.

Diego and Sebastian rolled their eyes. "And no rolling your eyes," Sofia said sharply.

Valeria smiled and continued. No one would be struck, but anyone who misbehaved would be sent to the other rear corner of the room to sit for half an hour, and his or her parents would be informed.

Nicolás looked alarmed at this news. Apparently, he would have preferred to receive a swat on the spot than to face consequences at home.

The older children would assist the younger ones with their lessons. Now it was Consuela who looked alarmed. Remembering what Camila had said about the deficits in Inmaculada's own education, Sofia amended Valeria's statement. "Or, rather, those who already have some mastery of the subject will help the others."

Tomás squared his shoulders. Sofia suspected that as apprentice to his carpenter father, he might already have a good grasp of arithmetic.

"Each day we will spend the first hour on reading and writing," Sofia said. "Then we will do our numbers. And finally, we will have a lesson in geography or history."

Looking down the two rows of pupils, she saw them all

nodding or at least looking attentive. *Good.*

"Monday, Wednesday and Friday, following *siesta,* we will go out into the field or to the banks of the *acequia* to learn about the plants and animals and also to learn to draw." Pausing, she scanned the two rows of pupils. Two of the girls nodded eagerly. "Doña Inmaculada wants all of you to be able to read simple music, so that you can sing hymns at Mass and Sunday prayers. But if any of you also would like to learn how to play the piano, or perhaps the recorder or the guitar, I will be here practicing on Tuesday, Thursday, and Saturday afternoons. You may come then, and I will give you some basic lessons. If you are willing to work hard, we may go further."

Smiling conspiratorially, Valeria rose and said in a stage whisper, "There are two other things that I think you will like. First, every week we will have a different theme for our studies. Next week our lessons will focus on ships. We will begin by reading Bible stories—including the one about Jonah being tossed from his boat during a storm at sea and then being eaten by a whale."

Catalina and Julia exchanged horrified looks. Apparently, this Old Testament tale was new to them.

"Don't worry," Valeria said soothingly. "God saved Jonah. The giant fish spat him out." She paused a half a second before continuing. "Then we'll read about Noah's Ark and all the different animals. After that, we'll learn about our great Spanish fleet and the battles fought by our brave sailors." Here the older boys exchanged nods. "And Señorita Sofia and I will tell you about the galleon that brought us from Spain to Veracruz."

"And the pirates?" Diego asked, then looked down at his hands as if suddenly aware that he'd interrupted.

"We never saw any pirates," Valeria said.

"Not even from far away?" Sebastian asked, clearly disappointed.

"Not even from a distance. Maybe it was because they had heard how brave and ferocious our sailors were."

The boys looked somewhat consoled. Sofia made a mental note to include some accounts of Spanish naval victories in the next week's lessons.

Valeria brought her index finger to her lips, and the pupils quieted instantly.

"Now for the second thing I think you will like, every evening, immediately after prayers, Señorita Sofia and I will take our supper over there." She pointed to the children's table she and Sofia recognized the night of their arrival. "If you have any questions about the day's lessons, you can ask them then, but you must demonstrate good table manners— no talking with your mouth full, no elbows on the table, one hand in your lap except when you're cutting your meat. And here comes the reward: on Saturday evenings, we will have a special party, with candles and real silver. We will pretend that we are at a banquet in Mexico City, and we will all behave like proper ladies and gentlemen of the capital."

The older boys leaned back, several of them crossing their arms. The girls looked at each other excitedly.

"Can we dress up?" Emilia asked.

Deciding that it was time to step in, Sofia said, "We wouldn't want to put your mothers to any trouble, but maybe we can arrange for hair ribbons or flowers."

Sofia knew full well that Inmaculada wouldn't be dressing her daughters herself, and she hoped that Valeria would be able to present the Saturday party idea in a way that would earn *la patrona's* approval. One thing of which she was quite certain, Valeria hadn't checked out the plan ahead of time. In fact, Sofia suspected she thought it up on the spur of the moment.

The rest of the morning and the next two days, Sofia and Valeria spent most of the time assessing their pupils' skills. They ranged widely. As Camila had suggested diplomatically, Inmaculada's children were almost illiterate, even the eldest. When asked to read the Twenty-Third Psalm,

Consuela looked straight at the class, leading Sofia to conclude that she was reciting from memory, rather than reading the text. Tomás demonstrated an impressive mastery of arithmetic and even geometry, but he painstakingly sounded out every word in the Gospel of the Loaves and Fishes.

Not surprisingly, none of the younger children could do more than recite the alphabet and do simple addition and subtraction, sometimes making errors even there. Sofia noticed that the ranch hands' children were better than Inmaculada's at arithmetic and Inmaculada's at reading. When it came to writing, none of them could do more than sign his or her name. Except for Diego. In a sure, round hand, he wrote out not only his own name but also those of his parents and siblings. He also read the first paragraph of St. Paul's First Letter to the Corinthians without much expression but flawlessly, not even stumbling over "stewards" and other difficult words. Stopping Diego before he got to the bits about immorality and the temptations presented by women, Sofia remembered Don Emilio's exuberant reaction to his performance in the fancy roping contest. Like Beto before him, Diego must have learned to read and write from his father.

At their first supper together, the children seemed subdued and self-conscious. After the first five uncomfortable minutes over the savory goat stew, Sofia put down her spoon and said gently, "No one expects you to know city manners yet. Just watch what Valeria and I do and try to copy us. The most important thing is to enjoy this delicious food and talk politely with each other."

By ten o'clock Friday morning, Sofia noticed that the children were tiring of listening to each other attempt to read aloud and watching each other try to do sums on the chalkboard.

"Let's learn some geography," she said.

To her amazement, even the older pupils couldn't locate Spain on the map of the world, and only Juan could find

Santa Fe. Some of the children put Mexico City on the Gulf Coast, others surprisingly close to El Paso del Norte. Most had never even heard of the Philippines.

Leaving the setting up of the party table to Valeria, on Saturday afternoon Sofia grabbed a rush basket from the kitchen and headed out to find pieces of wood to build a model of Noah's Ark. After the second day of class, she and Valeria had discussed the gaps in their pupils' education, even in their experience of the world. They would never have seen a boat, maybe not even in picture books. To illustrate the next week's lessons, Valeria had depicted a storm-tormented sea, with white-peaked waves and lightning bolts zigzagging down the threatening sky. On it was an open boat, its single sail tattered. Three figures stood at the rail. In the foreground a man with a white beard, looking very much like a prophet, struggled in the water, while not more than an arm's length away, a ferocious-looking sea monster spread open its tooth-studded maw. It was a truly arresting scene, sure to send chills up the spines of even the older boys; but it offered only a vague concept of how boats functioned.

So Sofia and Valeria had decided to have the children build a model of Noah's Ark using whatever wood Sofia could find.

As she walked across the stable yard, Sofia caught the now-familiar whiff of wild sage mingled with sweat. A tingle ran from her fingers up her arms and across her breasts. Annoyed at this involuntary response, she turned to see Beto sitting sideways on an old saddle and leaning against the shadowed wall, his long legs crossed at the knee. His left hand held an open book. His right hand absentmindedly fondled the ears of a yellow bitch lying beside the saddle, four little pups sucking enthusiastically on her teats. The dog thumped her tail languidly.

Beto put the book down, marking his place with a stalk of dried grass.

"On your way to pick posies?" he asked, raising her irritation a notch.

"No, I'm collecting pieces of wood so the children can build a model of Noah's Ark."

Why did I tell him my business? I should have just ignored him and walked on.

Pulling his hat brim down, apparently to shade his eyes from the late afternoon sun, Beto nodded. "Not a bad idea. None of them will have seen a boat. If you build it right, you might even get it to float on the mill pond."

Sofia hadn't considered that. She set aside her annoyance, for the moment, and took three steps toward the lanky rancher.

"How could we do that?" she asked.

Beto shrugged. "Maybe by coating the inside with wax. But if you build it right, the wood should make it float on its own. The trick will be designing it so that it doesn't tip over. Tomás should be able to figure out how to do that. He can also bring some pieces of scrap lumber from the carpentry shop. Ask him to take charge of the project. Better still, get Valeria to ask him. If she asked him to jump off the watchtower, he'd do it."

There they were again—her sister's beauty and charm. Sofia turned away angrily.

"Aren't you curious what I'm reading?" Beto asked. "I saw you glance at my book."

"So what is it, a study on sheep husbandry?"

"Actually, it's José Cadalso's *Moroccan Letters*," he said, holding it so she could read the silver lettering on the green leather cover. "It's a brilliant piece of writing, much more than just a military officer's memoirs. Cadalso depicts the landscape of the desert and the ways of the people who live there in amazing detail. You know, *El Norte* is not so different from North Africa."

"But isn't Cadalso better known as a playwright and poet? I've never seen any of his plays, but I've read all his poems. I found them eloquent and elegant."

"Romantic rubbish." Beto snorted. "He wrote those plays as vehicles for his mistress, Maria Ignacia Ibáñez. And as you may know, when she died of typhoid fever at the tender age of twenty-five, he attempted to exhume her. God knows why. At any rate, as you probably recall better than I do, the authorities hauled him off to a madhouse in Salamanca. As for his poems, they might be a little better than his plays, but his purpose in all of them was to woo, and then to mourn, her."

Beto shook his head sadly, then said, "I can think of no better case for what I told you the other day -- what people call passion is a form of madness."

Picking up his book and opening it, Beto added: "I recommend that you read this to see what Cadalso could do when he was in his right mind. After I've finished, you can borrow it from my father. He's proud of his library and generous about lending books from it."

"Thank you," Sofia said—on reflection a bit too curtly. Beto's suggestion of putting Tomás in charge of the ark-building project and asking him to use scrap from the carpentry shop had been sound. However, she didn't want to have to walk back past the man whose very scent seemed to prompt such confusing responses in her, so she turned back in her original direction, toward the blacksmith shop and the grove of cottonwoods beyond.

As she passed the stable, Sofia saw Alfonso standing in the door, a deep blue silk scarf tucked into the collar of his ruffled shirtfront, his black boots gleaming like mirrors.

She could hear his raised voice.

"I'll have my horse saddled immediately."

Sofia watched as the stable boy looked up from rubbing some sort of ointment into the white stallion's still-raw flanks.

"But, Señor Alfonso, your horse needs a few days to rest so his wounds can heal."

His hair gray and his face wrinkled, the stable master emerged from one of the far stalls. Sofia realized that this must be the man who raised Beto and taught him about horses.

"What seems to be the problem?" the old man asked.

"I will have my horse saddled now, so that I can get to Santa Fe by eight o'clock!"

"But *señor*, you must not ride this horse for another two days at least," the stable master said. "Otherwise, you might lose this fine animal to infection. Perhaps one of the other horses here... We have a black gelding with a very comfortable gait..."

"Who are you to tell me what I must or must not do?" Alfonso shouted. "I have very important business tonight in Santa Fe. This is the fastest horse in the stable, the only one that can get me there on time."

Nodding sadly at the stable boy, the old man set about arranging an extra blanket on the stallion's back. He set the silver-studded saddle, cinched it, and turned to Alfonso.

"I must insist, *señor*, that you remove those spurs."

As Sofia watched, Alfonso ripped off his spurs with a gesture that could only be fury and stuffed them in his saddle bag.

"One day this ranch will be mine." Swinging into the saddle, he spat at the stable master's feet. "But perhaps even before that, you will be roasting in hell."

As she watched Alfonso canter toward the *hacienda*'s heavy gate, Sofia wondered what important business the heir to Rancho de las Palomas could have in Santa Fe at night.

CHAPTER NINE

Feeling a need to soothe her nerves, Sofia stopped at her room for her piano-tuning kit, then made her way to the refectory. She still had an hour and a half before the kitchen staff would lay out supper. She could use the time to play through "The Well-Tempered Clavier." Sister Hortencia had explained that Bach wrote the piece to help keyboard musicians assess whether their instruments were in perfect tune and identify which notes were even slightly off key.

As she worked her way toward the end of the third sonata, tightening a string here, loosening one there, Sofia heard a commotion from the direction of the blacksmith's.

"Look at this!" Beto shouted. "You may have ruined this fine horse."

Sofia closed the piano and hurried out the side door. She could hear Reynaldo, the blacksmith's son and now her pupil, stammering an apology.

Beto, his face red with fury, held up the right forefoot of a palomino gelding. Reynaldo took several steps backward, waving his hands helplessly at his sides. Grabbing him roughly by the shoulder, Beto forced the boy's head down toward the horse's hoof.

"Do you see what you have done with your carelessness? You have nailed the shoe so that it split the hoof."

Sofia noticed that the handsome horse was shuffling its other three hooves nervously, but as soon as Beto stood and patted him on the neck, the animal settled down. Not so Reynaldo, who looked around wildly.

Using his teeth to rip off his stained tan work glove, Beto grabbed the boy's chin in his powerful right hand. Sofia thought she could see the veins pulsing, even though she was still several yards away.

"Now here is what you are going to do," he said coldly. "You are going to remove all four of this horse's shoes and put him over there, in the fenced paddock. You will make sure that he gets extra feed and plenty of water. Every morning, you will file that hoof, just a little bit and very gently, until it grows out enough to heal."

Reynaldo nodded miserably.

"And you had better pray to Jesus and to San Isidro and to whatever Pueblo gods your family might secretly worship that this hoof doesn't become infected and we don't have to put this horse down."

Wiping his eyes and nose with the back of his right hand, the boy led the horse away with his left. Beto spun on his heel, his hands clenched, the tendons in his neck looking like ropes. Sofia stepped in front of him, uncomfortably aware of the power of his arms and shoulders. How intimidated twelve-year-old Reynaldo must have felt by the sheer physical presence of this man.

Beto's eyes widened as he noticed her.

"You might get better results if you treated people as well as you do horses," she said. Then she marched off toward her room, experiencing a warm swell of self-righteous satisfaction. Beto could not have looked more stunned if she had slapped him.

That evening's party supper went well. In fact, Sofia felt more relaxed than she had since her arrival at Las Palomas. Responding to her request for varied courses, so that the children could practice something besides spooning soup, the cook prepared wild greens, two plump roast chickens, rounds of fluffy bread, and a sweet of stewed apples with honey, which turned out to be exceptionally tasty. Savory smells swirled from the kitchen. Camila, who had volunteered to serve, moved around gracefully, a white linen cloth draped elegantly over her left arm. She addressed the girls as *señorita*, the boys as *señor*.

Sofia noticed some of the adults seated at the other tables give their little group curious looks, but the children seemed oblivious. After Don Emilio offered the blessing, she asked Juan to cut up one chicken, Tomás the other. Not surprisingly, the carpenter's son sliced his bird neatly and cleanly, while Juan hacked his into sections, leaving considerable meat on the carcass. Reynaldo sat at the far end of the table and never raised his eyes.

Although they all seemed a bit subdued, the children behaved admirably. Mouths remained closed while chewing. Elbows stayed off the table. The only opportunity for correction came when Sebastian reached down the table for the butter. Valeria reminded him gently that he should ask Reynaldo to pass it.

As Camila cleared the empty dessert plates, Sofia asked the children to stand. "Thank you for being our guests," she said, looking at each in turn. "And what do you say in return?"

Julia was the first to respond. "Thank you for inviting us," she said sweetly. The other children followed with their polite thanks, though not quite in unison. With a small curtsy, Marta added her own flourish: "We had a lovely evening."

Wishing the children a good night, Valeria turned to

Camila and hugged her. "Thank you so much, Camila," Sofia said. "You set the perfect tone. Where did you learn to do formal table service?"

Camila smiled shyly. "When I lived at home, I would sometimes help with the dinners given by the *comandante* and his wife at the presidio. She is from a fine family in Mexico City, so she knows how things should be done."

Then, gesturing for Sofia to come closer, Camila whispered, "I have some good news for you. Tomorrow my mother is coming to visit. It will only be for the afternoon, but I know that she would love to see you."

"Let's have coffee in our room," Valeria said enthusiastically.

"Perhaps it would be better that we meet in mine. Remember what I told you about being able to hear from your room everything that's said around the courtyard? That applies both ways."

Now that Sofia knew something about the secrets of the *hacienda*, she recognized that a confidential conversation with Maria Josefa could be enlightening.

As the sisters and Camila made their way toward the kitchen and their rooms beyond, Valeria said quizzically, "I didn't see Alfonso this evening. I wonder where he was."

"I think he has business in Santa Fe," Sofia replied. Beto hadn't been at supper, of course. He never took his meals with the family.

A sharp rapping on the wall connecting her room to Camila and Jimena's wakened Sofia from her Sunday *siesta*. Camila stuck her head around the blue and tan striped curtain suspended from the doorway.

"My mother is here. I thought you would want me to wake you so you could visit. She has to go back to Santa Fe in about an hour."

Valeria stirred suddenly, pushed her blond curls back from her face and swung her legs over the side of the bed.

"Maria Josefa!"

"In here, Valerita," came the cheerful reply. "Your coffee is ready."

The sisters rushed into the room, Valeria first.

"I would give you each a big *abrazo*," Maria Josefa said, looking up from her seat on Camila's bed, "but, as you can see, my arms are full."

Rocking Julio gently, she offered her cheeks to be kissed, then motioned for the young women to sit on either side of her.

"Jimena is helping prepare the bread for baking, so I get the pleasure of holding this fine boy. Camila and I have already finished with the family news. My Carlos, by the way, sends you both his warmest regards. I took the liberty of asking Camila to show me your lesson corner. It is as well appointed as any classroom at the convent. Valerita, your artwork is remarkable."

As Julio reached a chubby hand for her strand of turquoise beads, Maria Josefa extended her right index finger, which he grabbed instead.

"It seems like a month since we saw you," Valeria said. "But it hasn't even been a week."

"I know. I wanted to see how you two were settling in, and I knew I wouldn't have another chance to see you until the wedding."

"The wedding?" Sofia asked.

"Of course. On Saturday, June 30, Fernando Valdez y Guzmán, that handsome corporal I warned you about, Valerita..." Here, Maria Josefa reached over and patted Valeria on the knee. "...will marry Isabella Gutiérrez. Remember, I said that I hoped that she wouldn't mind spending a lot of time alone, because he would be out chasing other women? She is not a beauty like you, but she reportedly has an enormous dowry. Her father is Hector Gutiérrez y Lujan, perhaps the richest merchant in Santa Fe, and her mother is a Moralez, with a fortune of her own. The party after the wedding Mass will be at their house, which is the grandest in Santa Fe. It makes the Governor's Palace look tiny."

Sofia took a sip from the mug Camila handed her. The coffee was strong and sweetened just as she liked it. A spicy hint of cinnamon brightened the taste.

"But surely we won't be invited," Sofia said. "We're newcomers, and we have no family connections here."

A sly smile crossed Maria Josefa's lips. "From what I hear around town, Doña Inmaculada has already arranged for you two to be included on the guest list."

Startled, Sofia asked why.

"First, the official reason: Santa Fe does not have that many young women of marriageable age from good families. Even with you two, there will not be enough dance partners for the single officers from the garrison. I'm sure that Doña Ana, the mother of the bride, was happy to add you to the list for this reason."

"And the unofficial reason?" Valeria asked conspiratorially.

"Doña Inmaculada may be less than perfectly literate, shall we say. She may even embrace superstitions that most people abandoned a century ago. But she is not stupid, either about money or about the expectations of *norteño* society. She knows that she can't keep two such eligible *peninsulares* cooped up here on the ranch. Yet, because you are not family members, giving a party to introduce you in Santa Fe could be a bit awkward, as well as expensive. This wedding provides the perfect alternative. Doña Inmaculada can allow everyone who belongs to Santa Fe society to notice you at the wedding Mass and the ball that follows. It will cost her nothing, either financially or socially."

Not for the first time, Sofia felt a surge of admiration for Maria Josefa's astute knowledge of people.

Camila rose from her seat beside the little corner hearth and refilled the coffee mugs, first Valeria's and then Sofia's.

"Isn't there another 'unofficial' reason, Mother?" she asked.

Maria Josefa sighed. "Well, this is only my own speculation. It hasn't even reached the level of proper gossip. Alfonso is of an age when he should be getting married. Every few weeks Doña Inmaculada goes to Santa Fe, to attend Mass, of course, but also to visit one of her cousins, a widow who lives in town. This cousin's maid says that Doña Inmaculada has been asking about the young ladies of the community and—imagine this—the cousin has made some polite excuse about every one of them as to why they would not make a suitable match for Alfonso. His reputation is almost as bad as Fernando's—worse, in a way. Fernando has a bad reputation where women are concerned, but Alfonso is known around town for his gambling, mostly playing a French card game called *bassette*, where the stakes are high, and the odds heavily favor the house. Oh, he can be seen at Madame Le Ferrier's, the most exclusive brothel in town, but they say he spends more time at the card tables than upstairs."

"But he is so handsome," Valeria said. "And he has such fine manners. How could anyone object to his enjoying a game of chance now and then?"

"They could object if he bets high and seldom wins. A bride's dowry becomes her husband's property on her wedding day. Alfonso could lose his wife's in short order. The young ladies may find him attractive, but most of their fathers would never grant permission for him to come courting. And Doña Inmaculada would never risk the humiliation of having her son's suit denied."

Sofia finished her coffee and held up a declining hand when Camila raised the pot to offer more.

"So Doña Inmaculada is beginning to think beyond Santa Fe for a potential daughter-in-law," Sofia said.

"In fact, she has thought as far as Veracruz. That is one reason, perhaps the main reason, that she supported Don Emilio's desire to bring you two here."

Valeria gasped. Sofia watched as a deep blush rose from her sister's neck to her hairline.

"And, of course, the wedding ball will give Alfonso an

opportunity to dance with you, perhaps to charm you, although he cannot pay suit to you officially until you turn fifteen," Maria Josefa said, giving the pretty young blond a warning wag of her finger. "But be careful, *chica*. You may have more to lose than you recognize."

Just then, Jimena came through from the kitchen, wiping her floury hands on her homespun apron. "Julio," she cooed. "Have you been a good boy?"

Handing the beaming young mother the baby, Maria Josefa said, "He has been a cherub. And now, since I have to leave soon, please let me know if you have any other questions, any way I might help you."

"There is one," Sofia said, "one on which you could advise us, with your wisdom of people."

Valeria nodded in agreement as Sofia continued. "It has to do with the children. We knew that the difference in ages would present a challenge, but we had expected the older children to know more, to be able to read and do arithmetic." She glanced down at her lap, as if trying to think how to phrase what followed. "We also expected Doña Inmaculada's children to be more advanced than the ranch hands'."

"Ah!" Maria Josefa smiled knowingly. "And you have found neither to be the case."

"In fact, the best at numbers is the carpenter's son, and the best at reading is Doña Inmaculada's ten-year-old boy," Sofia said.

"And I expect that she didn't want you to teach the workers' children at all," Maria Josefa said. "After all, they're *mestizos*."

"But Don Emilio insisted," Valeria said.

"That is admirable, but now I suspect that you have the problem of keeping the *patrón*'s children from feeling embarrassed in front of the help and the others from deciding they should know their place and be silent."

"Can you suggest a way to avoid this?" Sofia asked.

Maria Josefa frowned briefly, then smiled.

"It's quite simple. First, you must let all the children learn according to their natural abilities. Praise those who succeed. Try to avoid criticizing those who are slower. All children have fragile spirits, even princes. Then think of things that you are quite sure Doña Inmaculada's children would do well, things that all the children would find interesting, and let them take the lead in projects around those."

Valeria jumped up enthusiastically. "When we told them that next week's lessons would focus on ships, the boys all wanted to know about pirates and naval battles. We could have them stage a famous Spanish victory—maybe the Battle of Cartegena de las Indias."

"And I am quite sure that Doña Inmaculada will have taught her daughters embroidery," Maria Josefa said. "You could have the girls design and sew an altar cloth based partly on the flowers and birds they observe and sketch."

"Brilliant," Valeria said, embracing Maria Josefa. "How I wished you lived here on the ranch."

"Valerita, I love you and your sister like daughters, and I love Camila as I love life itself. But I thank God every day that I don't live here. Rancho de las Palomas has more intrigue than the Spanish court."

Adding that she needed to hurry back to Santa Fe, otherwise, her Carlos would be worried, Maria Josefa kissed Julio on the forehead, gave *abrazos* all around, and headed toward the stable, with Camila, Sofia, and Valeria close on her heels.

"One more thing," Maria Josefa said as she swung onto her pinto mare. "I should probably apologize for not telling you more about Beto. I wanted you to be able to judge him for himself, without any preconceptions about his background."

"We were able to do that," Sofia said, her cheeks growing unaccountably hot. "We found him arrogant, presumptuous…"

"And intelligent and well-read, right?"

Sofia nodded curtly.

"He shares the fiery temper of his father and his brother. Beto is totally direct, perhaps to a fault. He is devoted to this ranch and to his father. And no matter how Don Emilio may try to hide it, Beto has always been his favorite."

"Oh," Maria Josefa said, as if as an afterthought, "he likes women, but he has never had anyone special."

"Why should that concern us?" Sofia asked, regretting as she watched the pinto mare trot through the gate, that she'd been so rudely abrupt to her wise friend.

CHAPTER TEN

The next morning, as Sofia set up the lesson corner, she saw a long shadow spill across the table, accompanied by the scent of wild sage. Looking up, she saw Beto standing in the refectory doorway, a small burlap bag in his left hand. With his right, he touched the brim of his weathered straw hat in greeting.

"You sniffed just then," he said, "before you turned around. What did you smell?"

"Wild sage. Sometimes it mingles with your sweat, but not now."

A smile flashed across his face. It was faint at the lips, but it lit his eyes.

"That's because it's still early. I haven't started work, so I haven't sweated. Every morning I put a few sprigs of sage in my wash water. It lasts longer than that fancy cologne Alfonso has the chemist brew for him in Santa Fe. Mine is free, and it's always available."

Untying the string around the top of the burlap bag, Beto

ambled over to the table and began unpacking it. Sofia was struck again by his size. He stood well over six feet. Although she always considered herself taller than average, she barely came up to his shoulder.

"I thought that since the children would be studying Noah's Ark this week, these might help," he said, drawing out first a ewe, then a ram with a rack of curled horns, next a cow and a bull. In all, he placed ten pairs of animals on the table, each about three inches high. All were two-dimensional, carved from flat pieces of wood about half an inch thick; but they were beautifully painted, the eyes, nostrils, and mouths clearly wrought, the manes on the horses seeming to flow down their necks. In addition to the familiar farm animals and a pair of elk, Beto added elephants, giraffes, and zebras to the Biblical menagerie.

"To help the children understand that the world contains many fascinating creatures," he said.

Sofia was stunned. This was the man she dressed down two days earlier, yet here he was, bearing this gift to which he had certainly given thought and care. "You carved all these yourself? And painted them?"

"Yes." He turned abruptly.

"They're wonderful," she said, but he had already reached the doorway, calling over his shoulder: "I'm needed at the *acequia*."

The following afternoon Sofia returned to the refectory, hoping to tune the last two octaves on her piano. She was so intent on tightening one string that she almost broke it when Valeria burst through the refectory door yelling, "That brute! That *brute*!"

Startled, Sofia looked up, alarmed that someone had attacked her sister. Here she had thought they were safe, and now some ruffian had shattered her sense of security. Then she noticed that Valeria was clutching her sketch pad against her left side and brandishing three pencils in her right. Surely she would have dropped them if she had been assaulted.

Sofia grasped her sister by the shoulders and looked directly into her startlingly blue eyes, relieved that they were narrowed in anger, not wide in fear.

"Calm down and tell me what happened," Sofia said soothingly.

Valeria took three deep breaths and set her sketch pad and pencils on the nearest table.

"I was out sketching by the plowed fields. A man and a woman and two little children, too young to be taking lessons from us, were planting beans, or maybe it was squash. They looked happy, and I thought they would make a good picture—you know, one of those idyllic pastoral scenes."

She paused and took another breath.

"Go on," Sofia said.

"Suddenly, there was Beto on his horse. I guess part of his job is to ride around and check on everything. But he jumped down, tore my sketch out of my pad, crumpled it up, and threw it on the ground. And he shouted that he never wanted to find me sketching people on the ranch again. He destroyed my work. He had no right…"

Just then, a shadow fell across the open doorway. Sofia looked up to see Beto lean against the jamb, fold his arms, and angle one long leg over the other.

"Look, I apologize if I was a little rough and rude." He uncrossed his arms and legs and ambled across the room.

"A *little* rough and rude?" Sofia clenched her hands into fists. "Your behavior toward my sister was arrogant, insolent, and inexcusable. It went way beyond bad manners."

"And by our standards, so did your sister's."

"What do you mean?"

"I mean that your fancy *penninsulare* manners aren't the only ones that matter. In fact, they don't matter much at all here, except perhaps to Inmaculada—and maybe to Alfonso."

He glanced up at a ceiling beam, as if he hoped it might tell him how to phrase his thoughts.

"Beneath the surface, manners come down to one person displaying respect for another. Am I right?"

Sofia nodded curtly. Valeria was still staring at Beto with her mouth open.

"Look, everyone on this ranch works, so they all deserve your respect," he went on. "Even the youngest. If they can walk, they have a useful task to perform. All the children you teach have chores to do before and after their lessons. Even Inmaculada's children work. The girls mend clothes and blankets and sometimes embroider little flowers on things. The boys take shifts on the watchtower—except for Diego, the ten-year-old. He's crazy about horses, so he gets to help clean the stables and oil the tack. Inmaculada doesn't especially like this, because it means he works with *mestizos*, but Don Emilio has overruled her. Don Emilio himself works, of course. Alfonso, Inmaculada, and I report to him, and he makes the major decisions."

Having recovered her composure, Valeria looked startled. "What does Inmaculada do?" she asked. "Surely, *she* doesn't work."

"You think hiring, training, supervising, and firing cooks and cleaning women isn't work? You think keeping track of the kitchen inventory and making constant lists of supplies to be purchased isn't work? You think passing along garrison orders for blankets and wool and checking the quality of whatever woven goods leave this place isn't work? Not to mention that *la patrona* takes it on herself to direct the *hacienda*'s religious life. I consider the woman mean-spirited, superstitious, and willfully ignorant, but I don't consider her lazy."

Sofia had never thought of the ranch in this way, nor of how each of the fifty-odd individuals who lived and worked on the ranch contributed to its functioning.

Suggesting that they all sit down, Beto continued, "Don't worry, Valeria. I'm getting around to the sketch I destroyed—and why I lost my temper."

"You owe me an explanation," Valeria said haughtily,

"and an apology."

"Here's the explanation. We'll see about the apology. I'm going to take you on a bit of a journey, but I think you should understand the background."

"All right," Sofia said. At least he wasn't just ordering them around.

"With a few exceptions, every person who lives on this ranch is *mestizo*. Don Emilio and Doña Inmaculada are *criollos*, of pure European extraction, mostly Spanish but a little French on my father's side. The midwife Marina and a couple of the other women are pure Pueblo. But most Pueblo people prefer to remain in their villages, raise their crops and livestock, and acquire things like sugar and tools by trading with us. For a couple of generations now, the relationship has been friendly. The soldiers from the garrisons help keep the Mescalero and Jicarillo Apaches from attacking the *pueblos*, which used to be a huge problem. When they attacked, they stole not just horses, but children and young women, as well. Sometimes, they kept them for themselves, but mostly they sold them to the Spanish, who sent them south as slaves. The girls and women they used as whores, and the boys were worked to death in the silver mines. Because the Pueblo people lived in permanent villages, the Church considered them civilized and forbid enslaving them—directly, that is. If a band of Mescaleros offered children they'd kidnapped for sale, the authorities weren't so particular."

Valeria gasped. "How terrible for their parents."

Beto nodded gravely.

"But back to the rest of us. Every one of us *mestizos* has a war going on in his or her heart. We've all been converted to Catholicism. Sometimes our families have been Catholic for almost two centuries. But we haven't been converted to Spaniards. The old ways, the old beliefs, are still there, even though they may be buried or translated, so to speak, like when a god or goddess is honored as a Catholic saint with similar attributes."

"So that's what the chief's wife at Pueblo San Miguel

meant when she told us subtly that Mary was the Corn Goddess," Sofia said. She still felt irritated at Beto, but her curiosity outweighed her pique.

"Exactly," Beto said, pointing at her approvingly. "Now, not all *mestizos* are part what you Spaniards call Pueblos. Some have Navajo or Apache blood, some even Comanche way back. And even with us part Pueblos, beliefs vary from one *pueblo* to another, just as language can. Another time, I'll recite the Lord's Prayer for you in Tiwa, Tewa, and Keres. You'll see how different those tongues are.

"Now, to get to the point, superstitions differ from group to group, but they can be amazingly persistent. Some people here believe that any likeness of them steals or at least ensnares their souls, or that it can be used in some sort of witchcraft."

Valeria gasped.

"And you can't tell by looking at a *mestizo* whether that person holds that belief—which is why it is very, very rude, even threatening, to draw his or her picture, at least without first requesting permission.

"Did you ask that family in the field?"

"No," Valeria said softly.

"Did you ever sketch people in Veracruz?" Beto asked.

"Of course. I would go down to the road that ran by our house and sketch the country women walking to town carrying huge bundles on their heads, sometimes even tall bunches of bananas. They made fascinating subjects."

"And I bet they were *negro*," Beto said, "or *negro* and *indio*. They wouldn't have dared challenge a blond girl."

Valeria's face fell.

"Did you ever sketch white people, or people who were mostly white, in the city?"

"Sometimes, during our lunch breaks at the convent school."

"And how would you go about that?"

"If I wanted to sketch a man selling fruit in the market, I would tell him that his display of oranges and avocados and lemons was so beautiful and that he looked so handsome when he smiled that I wanted to make a drawing. Most times, I offered to do two sketches and give one to him."

"And I bet that made him happy, to have a pretty girl admire him and his artistic arrangement of fruit. But you always asked first, didn't you?"

Valeria nodded vigorously. "To do otherwise would be rude."

Sofia could see where he was going.

"I suppose you could try the same approach here," Beto said. "If you see a couple of children milking a goat or chasing each other in a field, you could find their mother and tell her that they look so cute that you want to sketch them. If she says no, don't press the matter. If she says yes, make a second sketch for her. I'm sure she would treasure it."

Valeria nodded again, this time with the hint of a smile.

"Thank you for the explanation," Sofia said. "Now, what about the apology?"

Beto's clear gray eyes locked with hers. The effect was disquieting but also faintly exciting.

Turning to Valeria, he said, "I apologize for losing my temper, but I do not apologize for destroying your sketch. That family in the field needed to see that I respected them."

He rose, bowed briefly, and touched the brim of his hat. Then, without another word, Roberto "Beto" Chavez turned and strode out of the refectory, leaving behind a whiff of wild sage.

CHAPTER ELEVEN

Wednesday afternoon, intent on finishing "The Well-Tempered Clavier" and completing her tuning, Sofia heard Beto's voice, loud with urgency, the sharp beat of his heels on the pavers. "Get Marina," he shouted, calling for the ranch's midwife and healer. "Tell her to bring her wound kit and also Elena. She'll need help. And tell her to bring her strongest medicine for pain."

Beto burst through the refectory door, Tomás in his arms. A torn strip of Beto's left shirt sleeve wrapped the boy's leg tightly just below the knee. Tomás's pants had been slit from there to the hem, revealing a foot-long slash along his shin, oozing blood and so deep that Sofia could see the white glint of bone. The flesh around the wound was turning purple, blending to red at the edges.

Placing Tomás on the table where the children usually dined, Beto ripped off the other half of his sleeve and tossed it toward Sofia.

"Get someone to boil this, will you? And whatever other

muslin might be handy in the kitchen. And bring a basin of water and a bar of lye soap."

As Sofia emerged from the kitchen, Marina, bent with age but with bright brown eyes, bustled through the side door, a worn leather satchel in her right hand, a pair of beeswax candles in her left. Behind her hobbled her middle-aged daughter and assistant. Despite her clubfoot, the younger woman moved quickly, simultaneously tucking her mane of loose, steel-gray hair into a crocheted snood.

Marina took one look at the wounded boy, crossed herself, then shouted something to Elena in a language Sofia didn't recognize, although she did understand the last three words, "tincture of opium." Opening the satchel, Elena extracted a small amber glass bottle. She dipped a blue metal cup into the basin of water, deftly added five drops from the bottle, then handed the mixture to Beto, who slid his left arm under Tomás's shoulders and raised him up.

"Here, Tomasito, drink this," he said in a voice at the same time gentle and commanding. "It will make you feel better."

Wincing, the boy complied. He made a face at the bitter taste.

Suddenly, the refectory seemed full of confusion. Tomás's mother, Juanita, appeared in the main doorway, emitting a wail of dismay as she saw her son. Camila rushed in through the side door. Doña Inmaculada strode regally from the pantry, demanding to know the cause of this domestic disruption, which had interrupted her inventory of the *hacienda*'s root vegetables.

"As you can see, Tomás has suffered a serious wound, and Marina and Elena are treating it," Beto said coolly.

Elena set the candles on the table next to the one where Tomás lay, moaning with pain. Juanita hovered anxiously next to his head. Her presence seemed to distress more than comfort him. Responding to a gesture from Beto, Sofia stepped over and led Juanita to a bench where she could observe her son but leave the midwife, who had probably delivered him, free to mend his leg.

Using the lye soap, Elena scrubbed her hands in the basin, then passed it to Marina, who washed her own hands and proceeded to sterilize a long needle in the candle flame, intoning a rhythmic chant that she muttered throughout the procedure. Although Sofia couldn't understand what she was saying, she found it calming.

"What is that old Indian chanting?" Doña Inmaculada demanded.

"The Lord's Prayer, some Hail Marys, special entreaties to San Lucas and to her namesake, Santa Marina, the patron saint of midwives," Beto said.

"I don't recognize a word. I say that she is calling on the Devil and perhaps her pagan gods. I say that she is a witch."

"That is because you have never troubled yourself to learn Tiwa," Beto said. "If Marina had been a witch, she would have used her dark arts twenty years ago to save my mother and my baby sister."

"With wounds such as this, the injured one always loses the leg," Doña Inmaculada said warningly. "I say that we should send for the garrison surgeon right now, to perform an amputation before gangrene sets in. If you oppose me on this and the leg heals, I will accuse Marina of witchcraft."

An expression somewhere between astonishment and fury crossed Beto's face as *la patrona* spun on her heel and stalked out of the refectory. Abruptly, he turned back to Marina.

"We can't wait for the opium to take effect. You have to sew up the wound now, so that we can release the tourniquet."

The midwife nodded and positioned herself on the boy's right, needle and white silk thread in hand, while her daughter moved around to the left and pinched the edges of the gash together.

Tomás cried out, and tears rolled down his face. Sofia watched as Beto gently lifted Tomás's chin, directing the boy's gaze away from his slashed leg and toward his own gray eyes.

"You are a brave fellow," Beto said, "maybe the bravest of us all."

With the first stab of Marina's needle, Tomás yelped. "It was my fault," he sobbed. "I cut my own leg with my machete."

"That was because you slipped just as you raised it," Beto said. "The bank along that part of the *acequia* is treacherous. What happened to you could have happened to anyone."

Untying his red bandana, Beto gently wiped the tears and mucous from the boy's face.

"I understand that you played a valiant role in your class's re-enactment of the Battle of Cartegena de las Indias. From what I heard, those wooden swords you made were so realistic and the fighting was so fierce that two of the younger girls cried."

Tomás gasped with the pain of another stitch, then said proudly, "I had to portray a filthy Brit, since Juan was in charge of the play, but I got to be an admiral." Here, he only winced. "Even though my nickname was 'Old Grog,' I wasn't drunk. I fought bravely beside my men." He gave another wince, this one slighter. "And if it hadn't been for the great valor of the Spanish, and also for the fact that my sailors fell ill to tropical diseases, the British might have won the day."

As Marina fastened the last of twenty-four stitches and snipped off the tourniquet, Elena came in from the kitchen with a bowl of boiled rags, a jar of honey, and a plate smeared with some sort of green paste. Sofia noticed that the blood was only oozing now. Tomás's mother had gripped Sofia's left hand so hard that her nails left little red half-moons in her palm. With her right hand, Sofia gave Juanita's knee a soft pat.

"Where is your husband?" she asked.

"Down at the sawmill, thank God. I don't know how he would have reacted if he'd seen his son's leg laid open like that, with the bone showing..."

"In just a few minutes, there'll be nothing to see but bandages," Sofia said soothingly.

Examining her handiwork, Marina looked at Elena, who nodded briefly and handed her another boiled rag. Even from six feet away, Sofia caught the strong scent of brandy as the midwife wiped the stitched wound and its margins. Reaching into the bowl, Elena removed a cloth that looked suspiciously like the half of Beto's left sleeve and smeared it with honey and the green paste. She wrapped the wound gently then tucked in the ends of the bandage. To Juanita she said, "I will come by every morning to change the dressing. If your son's leg ever feels hot or looks red and swollen around the edges, come get me right away."

The opium finally seemed to be taking effect. As he slipped into unconsciousness, Tomás gazed up at Beto. Sofia heard him ask whether he would have a peg leg, "like a pirate," and Beto's reply that Tomás would find a peg leg dashing, perhaps, but impractical.

"We'll try to save the leg you have," Beto assured him.

Lifting him carefully, Beto carried Tomás out the side door, with his mother close beside him. Camila walked over to Sofia and gave her a hug as she sat down.

"You were wonderful," Camila said. "If you hadn't kept Juanita calm, I don't know how Marina and Elena could have worked."

Sofia smiled but shook her head. "It was Beto and the way he comforted and distracted Tomás that soothed everyone," she said. "I have only seen him be gentle like that with animals."

"Oh, Beto has his gentle side, even though he tends to hide it. Despite his fiery temper, I have never heard of him striking anyone. Of course, he wouldn't need to. He's so big that the glare from those gray eyes would be enough." Camila paused briefly. "He can even have a sense of humor."

"I wonder why he has such a dislike for me," Sofia mused.

Camila covered her mouth with her apron, as if to conceal a laugh.

"He doesn't dislike you, Sofia. In fact, I suspect that he likes you a lot. It's just that you're the first woman with a fine formal education he's encountered. Even though Don Emilio had the advantage of a university education and devoted himself personally to Beto's learning, Beto is self-conscious about own lack of polish and afraid of saying something that would make him appear foolish."

Camila seemed to know so much about the inner workings of life at Las Palomas, even things that had occurred when she was a little girl living in Santa Fe. She must have inherited her mother's sense of, and interest in, the human heart. Perhaps she could explain something that Sofia found puzzling.

"Why did Don Emilio send Alfonso to study in Mexico City but keep Beto here at home?"

"Ah," Camila whispered. "As my mother would say, there is the official answer, and there is the unofficial answer. The official answer is that Don Emilio decided, probably wisely, that he would delegate the day-to-day running of ranch operations to Beto and the business affairs to Alfonso. Therefore, it made sense for Beto to stay at the ranch, to serve as an apprentice to the various skilled workers so he would be able to supervise their areas and to learn about the stock breeding that generates the profits for the ranch.

"While Beto gained this practical knowledge, Don Emilio would use the books in his library to teach him classics, literature, Latin, mathematics, and so forth. As everyone recognizes, Beto is more intelligent than Alfonso, so he was a quick learner on both fronts. And if Alfonso was to be the ranch's public face, shall we say, having him acquire some of the capital's fine manners and refined tastes, along with a familiarity with trade and business practices, would be a benefit."

"And the unofficial answer?" Sofia asked.

"Well, really there are two unofficial answers." Camila

held up her right hand with the thumb and index finger extended. "The first would be obvious to anyone who knows the ways of *El Norte*. Although Don Emilio has always acknowledged Beto as his son, including in legal documents, Beto is nonetheless illegitimate. Also, like me he is *mestizo*. Either one of these reasons would be enough to prevent him from being accepted into the upper levels of our provincial society, no matter how elegant and accomplished he was. So why bother to send him away to receive polish that would be of no benefit to him or to his family?"

Camila folded down her thumb and drew her index finger across her mouth, as if sealing in a secret.

"And the second unofficial reason?" Sofia asked softly.

"Ah, this is only my conjecture. As my mother might say, it has not even reached the level of proper gossip."

"Nonetheless…"

"Don Emilio couldn't bear to send Beto away for two years. Even after he and Doña Inmaculada reconciled, to whatever extent they did, the *patrón* was a lonely man. As Beto developed under his teaching, he provided Don Emilio with companionship. Also, the *patrón* could look at his son and see the face of his beloved."

That certainly makes sense. Even though Don Emilio expresses fatherly affection to all of his children, his smile takes on special warmth when he's with Beto.

In fact, it was only with Beto that Sofia could recall seeing the *patrón* laugh.

"And have you and Beto ever fancied each other?" Sofia asked.

With a sparkling smile and a faint blush, Camila replied, "There's a boy in town, the innkeeper's son. Ever since we were children, Santiago and I have been sweethearts and have known that one day we would marry. No other could possibly interest me."

CHAPTER TWELVE

Once again, Sofia caught Beto's distinctive scent before she noticed him standing in the refectory's main doorway. This time, it was midday, so he didn't cast a shadow. And this time, sweat predominated over wild sage, but she still found the odor oddly pleasant.

Sofia had been at the blackboard, explaining the last arithmetic problem, so she had no idea how long Beto had been there, but it must have been a while. He was leaning casually against the doorframe, his straw hat pushed back, his left leg crossed over his right, his hands in their worn leather work gloves cradling his elbows. The children were filing out of the side door, on their way home for the midday meal. Valeria was rolling up some watercolors of an orange, a pyramid of lemons, and a bunch of bananas. The day's lessons had closed with addition and subtraction—and, for the older children, fractions—involving fruit.

"Those are lovely pictures of tropical fruit," Beto said, nodding to Valeria. "But do you mind if I make a suggestion?"

"Go ahead," Sofia replied. She turned from the makeshift blackboard and lowered the rag with which she'd begun to wipe it clean.

"Your arithmetic problems would be more relevant to the children if they dealt with ranching matters," he suggested, bowing slightly. "The children have never seen an orange—well, Inmaculada's may have been given one on Christmas Eve. And I can tell you if they had one, they certainly wouldn't give it away. They might have seen the occasional lemon, but it would have been preserved in a cask. And a bunch of bananas?"

Rather than being offended, Sofia found herself fixing him with a direct look and arching her eyebrows.

"Go on."

Crouching, Beto removed his gloves, took the rag from her hand, and finished erasing the board. Then he picked up a stub of chalk. "So instead of 'Maria has twelve oranges, and she gives Ignacio half, then gives Consuela a third of those she has left,' how about something like: 'The upper pastures measure 40,000 acres. If it requires 640 acres to support one cow and her calf, how many cows can we put on the upper pastures?'"

He wrote the division problem quickly on the board then drew a circle around the answer, 62 1/2.

"However, I would recommend running only 60," he said. "It's better for the pasture, as well as for the cows, to graze a bit light, especially in this desert."

Beto's grin as he stood was at once so pleased and so playful that Sofia couldn't bring herself to scold him for being presumptuous. After glancing at Valeria, who shrugged, she smiled.

"You're right, on both counts," she said.

"And maybe," Valeria added impishly, "to please Doña Inmaculada, we could concoct a problem something like, 'On an average Sunday, 225 people take communion at La Parroquia. On Easter, the attendance is 28 per cent greater.

How many communion wafers will Father Antonio have to order for Easter?'"

After all three of them finished laughing, Beto said: "The reason I stopped by was not to advise you on your instruction methods, but to ask you to join me at the stable tomorrow after *siesta*. It's Saturday, so if I remember correctly, you should be free after the morning lessons."

"Yes," Sofia replied quizzically.

"I have something down there that I'd like to show you both." Then, he tipped his hat and strode out into the sunlight.

After *siesta* the following afternoon, Sofia and Valeria hurried down to the stable. Both had been too curious about Beto's surprise to take a nap, so they had tried to read, interrupting each other every few minutes with guesses about what he had in store.

When they arrived at the gate, they found Beto standing next to a dappled gray filly, brushing her back and patting her flank, all the while speaking to her gently. Next to the filly stood a dark brown gelding with a black mane and tail. Both horses wore simple rope halters, which were slung loosely over the middle fence rail.

"Good afternoon," Beto said, turning to the sisters and touching the brim of his battered straw hat. The corners of his full lips twisted up into a smile.

"Even before you arrived at the ranch, my father and I agreed that you two would need your own horses, so you could explore the countryside and ride into Santa Fe occasionally for whatever reasons young ladies sometimes feel the need to go to town."

Valeria let out a yip of delight. Sofia felt her mouth drop open and her face flush.

His smile broadening, Beto said, "In the month since you got here, I've watched you, I hope unobtrusively, as I tried to decide which horse would be right for each of you. I raised and trained all the horses in our stable myself."

He beamed proudly.

"It's a bit of a hobby for me, a profitable hobby. Although it can't compare to raising sheep, goats, and cattle, which are the main sources of income for the ranch, the prices our best horses fetch make it worth my efforts."

Untying the gray's halter, he led her over to Valeria.

"Of the five horses that are ready to ride, I think this one is right for you. She's a quarter horse, nimble and spirited, like you. To bring out the best in her, she needs an athlete. Take her halter gently and stroke her checks softly with your other hand."

Sofia felt a stab of jealousy. *Of course, Beto is attending to Valeria first and giving her the better horse. After all, he's a man.*

As Valeria followed his directions, Beto untied the brown gelding and handed the end of the lead rope to Sofia.

"When it comes to gait, this fellow is the best horse I have ever trained. Once you get him into a canter, you'll feel like you're floating. You will never want to ride in a wagon, or even a carriage, again. And see how beautiful he is? His conformation is perfect, and that brown coat and black mane will set of your elegant Spanish coloring."

Beto's smile grew even broader.

"I'm confident that you both have some fine Andalucian blood."

Sofia was stunned. Was this proud breeder really giving her one of the best horses he had ever trained?

"Thank you," she whispered, looking directly into those gray eyes smiling back at hers.

Then, something occurred to her. "Clearly, this animal is beautiful. And if he is otherwise so fine..."

"Ahhh... Why did we geld him? I said I was confident he had Andalucian blood. I don't know for certain, because I'm not sure of his sire. I do know that his dam was one of our finest mares. One day I noticed she was pregnant; but I hadn't bred her, so I had no idea which of several stallions might have done the deed. All I can tell you is that the sire was smart enough to jump the fence or shoulder his way through a carelessly closed gate, have his way with this excellent mare and then return to his own pasture. Since I couldn't confirm which stallion was the culprit, I knew that I'd never be able to sell or hire the offspring out for breeding. And once I could tell how lovely this fellow's gait would become, I decided to keep him."

Turning to a shelf next to the stable door, Beto grabbed a pair of grooming brushes and handed one to each sister.

"How much do you two know about horses?" he asked.

"We began riding when we were four or five, around the park in Barcelona," Valeria answered. "Once we got to Veracruz, we sometimes rode from our house outside town to the convent for school, but mostly Papa took us with him in the wagon on his way to his office."

"These were family horses, I suppose, not your personal mounts. And who took care of them?"

"In Barcelona, the young man who drove our carriage took care of the horses," Sofia said. "In Veracruz, it was Guillermo. He and his wife were our only servants."

"So let us assume that you know little of horses. That's actually good, because you will have little to unlearn."

Beto looked to Sofia, then to Valeria. They both nodded.

"The first thing to understand—and this is very important—is that by instinct a horse fears anything on its back. Cougars, jaguars, almost all predators except packs of wolves attack horses by jumping onto their backs. The horse's natural reaction is to throw that predator off. And this is why you must approach your horse carefully and speak to it softly and pat it on the neck before you put on its bridle and saddle. You must make your horse *welcome* your weight on its back."

He shrugged. "After that, instinct will work in your favor. Horses like to run."

Gazing up at the passing clouds, as though searching for a way to phrase what he had to say next, Beto continued: "Both you and these animals need to recognize that they are *your* horses. The only one who has ever ridden them is me. The stable boy, Diego and I are the only ones who have ever brushed them, saddled them, fed them or checked their hooves for stones. Whenever we do any of this, we speak to the horse soothingly and pat it gently. You must do the same. That way, your horse will become accustomed to your voice and your touch."

Beto paused, and Sofia and Valeria nodded again.

"Beginning today, I want each of you to spend some time each day with your horse, whether or not you plan to ride. The stable boy and Diego will clean out the manure, spread fresh hay in the stalls, make sure your animals have plenty of water. But you should be the ones to brush and comb them and give them the occasional treat. If a nail in your horse's shoe starts to come loose, *you* should be the first to notice it."

Turning on his heel, Beto lifted the lid of a covered barrel and rummaged inside, appearing with two apples. He threw one to Valeria, who caught it deftly, the other to Sofia, who fumbled but then recovered it before it hit the ground.

"The cook rejected these as too bruised and wormy for her to use, even for baking," he explained. "But the horses find them plenty sweet. Now, put the apple flat on your hand under your horse's nose, and speak softly while the animal eats it."

"Do these horses have names?" Valeria asked.

"You mean like a pet dog or cat? We don't tend to name horses here. Some people might say 'the brown one' or 'the dappled gray.' I just call them 'Boy' and 'Girl.' But you can call yours 'Horsie, Horsie' if you like, Valeria, as I heard you do just now."

Valeria blushed, and Sofia giggled.

"Your horse will learn to respond not to whatever name you might give it, but to the sound of your voice," Beto continued. "Try walking your horses around the paddock a few times. Speak to them, pat them on the neck, and don't pull on their halters. You just gave those animals something nice to eat. They will want to follow you to see what's next."

As Beto predicted, the horses followed the sisters docilely. Sofia held the end of the halter rope in her hand but refrained from tugging on it. At the start of the third circuit, Valeria dropped hers, and the dappled gray filly didn't seem to notice.

Throwing them each another apple, Beto said, "That was well done, all four of you. You don't need to give your horses apples every time they do what you want, but it's good to get them to associate you with pleasant things. In fact, you must always treat your horse with kindness. Even if you tried to control your horse by brute force—using a riding crop and spurs and yanking this way and that on the bit—you couldn't. An average riding horse like these outweighs you by eight or nine times."

Beto paused and looked directly at Valeria. "Alfonso is a handsome fellow with gracious manners, at least toward people he considers his equals or betters, but never use him as a model for how to treat a horse."

Valeria frowned slightly but nodded.

"When do we get to ride?" she asked, the frown vanishing.

"Tomorrow morning, right after Inmaculada's obligatory and often interminable Sunday prayer service."

Sofia could see the racks of saddles and tack just inside the stable door.

"I don't see any women's saddles," she said.

"You mean side-saddles? We don't use them here. Even grand ladies ride astride."

"But..." Sofia began to object.

"The reason is simple, Sofia. Given the rough country in *El Norte*, the weight on a horse's back must be balanced equally. This is essential for the safety of the rider and of the horse. Also, you'll need to learn to grip with your knees, both for stability and to steer your horse. That's how the Mescaleros became such a formidable light cavalry. They don't even use saddles and stirrups."

As he ushered the sisters out the stable gate, Beto said, "I bet your parents didn't let you ride side-saddle in the jungle around Veracruz."

"They didn't let us ride in the jungle at all," Valeria replied. "There really were jaguars, you know."

"Yes," Beto said. "I've read about them."

It took Valeria less than an hour the following morning to master riding astride. The biggest challenge seemed to be getting her skirt and petticoats to stay down, but Sofia noticed that her sister eventually developed a strategy of mounting in such a way that she sat on the back of her skirt and then could tuck the front under her thighs. Sofia copied her.

Initially, Sofia tended to shift her weight to the left, a habit left over from riding side-saddle. After trying without result to describe what she should do to correct this, Beto spoke softly to her horse and then jumped nimbly up behind her saddle. Grasping Sofia around the waist, he shifted her to the right, then ran his hands up her back to her shoulders and squared them. Sofia took a sharp breath and felt her heart race. This broad-shouldered horseman had rearranged her full hips as easily as if she had been a child.

Sliding off the horse's back, he said, "Now see if you can hold that posture as you walk him around the paddock."

After Sofia had done so twice to Beto's satisfaction, he opened the gate to the pasture. "Give this fellow just a slight nudge with your knees and feel him take off."

Sofia did as Beto directed. Suddenly, she understood what he had meant when he told her that the brown gelding's canter would feel like floating. A mere shift of the reins on the fine animal's neck brought him around and headed back to the stable.

Beto was standing at the gate with an apple in his hand and a grin on his face.

"Well?" he asked.

"I've never felt anything like it!"

"Maybe you will one day," he said, cocking an eyebrow as he helped her down.

That night as she was falling asleep, Sofia heard three packs of coyotes. Each group yelped its distinct call. Sofia remembered Camila telling her that every pack had its own series of barks and yelps that it exchanged with neighboring packs, maybe to say "Hello," maybe to say "Keep your distance."

This time, one of the packs sounded unusually close to the *hacienda*. From the direction of the henhouse came an agitated clucking. *Of course, the chickens don't like having the coyotes nearby.* Sofia rolled over and fell back to sleep.

Shortly after the five-bell wakeup, Sofia heard a woman's distressed cry. Like the hens' clucking during the night, it seemed to come from the chicken coop. Slipping on her shoes and wrapping her dark blue *rebozo* over her night dress, Sofia ran toward the noise. Now she recognized Beto's shout and a small boy's sobs.

The door to the chicken coop was ajar, and feathers littered the ground. Beto towered over a child too young even to have been in lessons. He had to be no more than four, at most five. Hovering next to him protectively and wringing her hands, the woman explained that her youngest son was responsible for rounding up the chickens every evening and putting them securely in their coop.

The child was weeping, snot and tears running down his face. He hiccupped as he wailed that he thought he had turned the wooden latch properly, but that it was heavy, and the wind was blowing, and maybe he didn't push it all the way.

Crouching down, Beto patted him on the shoulder and said firmly but kindly, "And because the wind was able to blow the door open, the coyotes ate four of our best-laying hens."

The boy howled. Beto patted him again and ruffled his

hair. "Yours is a very important job, a lot of responsibility for one so young. Will you promise me that if you ever have trouble with the latch again, you will get your father or older brother to help you?"

Nodding, the child wiped his nose on his sleeve.

Clearly, Beto took my advice. He treated the boy as gently as he would have treated a horse. Sofia slipped quietly around the corner to the latrine.

Late that afternoon, as she returned from taking the boys to an overlook where they could practice drawing mountainous terrain, Sofia heard angry voices emanating from the direction of the stable.

"This is *my* horse, and you will not tell me what I can and cannot do with him," Alfonso bellowed.

"This horse is yours to ride, not yours to abuse!" Beto shouted back. "Look at him! His flanks are bleeding. There is no excuse for you to spur him like that riding home from Santa Fe."

Rounding the corner, Sofia could see the two half-brothers, standing not more than six feet apart in the corral in front of the stable, their fists clenched at their sides. She wondered if they were about to trade blows. Beto had a slight advantage in height and reach, and daily physical labor had clearly built up his shoulders and arms; but Alfonso radiated the sort of fury that could be decisive in a fight.

Still standing upright, the two men circled each other slowly in the dust. The white stallion pawed nervously beside the stable door. Holding the horse's reins in his left hand, the stable boy brought up his right as if to shield his eyes from the impending violence.

"My horse was well-rested and well-fed," Alfonso said. "He had three days in the best livery stable in Santa Fe."

"Right. A stable where everyone in town could see how mistreated he was. Do you have any idea what that does to the reputation of our horse-breeding business?"

"Business? It's no more than your little hobby. And remember, Rancho de las Palomas will be mine someday, and the minute it is, you'll be out of here."

Alfonso's face glowed bright red. His mouth was contorted in a snarl. He no longer looked handsome in the least.

Beto stepped back, straightened his shoulders, and announced levelly, "Until it is, I run this ranch's operations, including the horses. And let me remind you that our father is only fifty-two and in excellent health. Eventually, of course, he will die, and you will inherit Las Palomas—not for yourself, on behalf of your family."

"I notice you say 'your family,' not 'our family,'" Alfonso said triumphantly. "I'm glad you understand that you have never been a part of my family and never will be. The second biggest mistake our father ever made was acknowledging you."

"What was the biggest?"

"Conceiving you."

Alfonso Chavez y Gallego turned on his heel and strode off, spurs jangling.

Shaken but relieved that Beto and Alfonso hadn't actually come to blows, Sofia ducked quickly along the wall and into the refectory, where her piano, her refuge from all turbulence and uncertainty, sat waiting.

Over the next two weeks Sofia noticed that Alfonso was spending less time in Santa Fe and more around the *hacienda,* although he and Beto avoided each other, never getting close enough to do more than exchange wrathful looks. When Alfonso did ride into town, he tended to leave early in the day and return by nightfall. On the three occasions when he was gone overnight, it was only one night, not two or three as had been his custom. And he seemed to apply his custom-blended orange and spice cologne excessively. Sofia found the scent a bit cloying and not altogether manly, certainly not at all appropriate for a rancher.

If she read in their room after supper, Sofia sometimes heard Valeria's lilting laugh coming from the courtyard, a pleasant baritone accompanying it. Alfonso's furious tones she had heard earlier were transformed to honeyed warmth. Rising from *siesta* one afternoon, she spotted a smooth board, about two by three feet, leaning against the wall next to Valeria's bed.

Curious, she turned it over. Tacked at the four corners was a large sheet of sketching paper bearing an almost-finished charcoal portrait of Alfonso drawn in profile. It was quite good. Valeria had even caught the slightly cruel cast to his lips. *When had he sat for the portrait? Probably some afternoon when I was playing my piano.* Sofia suddenly felt guilty that she wasn't taking better care of her beautiful younger sister who had such poor judgment when it came to handsome men.

Maybe I should be spending more time with Valeria, rather than heading automatically to my piano when I have a free moment. Turning the portrait back to the wall, Sofia walked over to the stable. Valeria would either be there, brushing and cooing to her lively gray filly, or sketching at the mill pond.

Mingled with the earthy smell of horses was the whiff of wild sage, so Sofia wasn't surprised to encounter Beto just outside the stable door, carefully combing burrs from his mare's mane.

Glancing over at Sofia, he said evenly, "If you're looking for Valeria, she's out there."

Still holding a section of chestnut mane in his left hand, he used his elbow to gesture toward the pasture, where Valeria galloped along on the dappled gray, her blond curls loose, her white skirt billowing. Beside and slightly ahead of her was Alfonso whipping the ends of his reins from side to side to encourage his white stallion but, Sofia noticed, sparing the horse his spurs.

"My sister..." Sofia swallowed.

"And my brother," Beto said, finishing the thought, then adding, "I take it you don't approve."

"She's only fourteen. Besides, he's cruel to his horse. Not to mention hateful to you."

"I can handle it. I've been doing that all my life. But you have a point about the horse."

CHAPTER THIRTEEN

"I can't stand these tight stays!" Valeria moaned. "Why can't I wear my everyday stays?"

"Because your dress wouldn't drape right," Sofia said. It was June 30th. They had risen from their *siesta* and were standing in Maria Josefa's spare bedroom in Santa Fe, dressing for what promised to be the Wedding of the Decade—dashing Corporal Fernando Valdez de Guzmán's marriage to Isabella Gutiérrez, daughter of the richest merchant in *El Norte*, possibly the richest that side of Mexico City.

"Hold your breath a few more seconds, and I will make you the most beautiful woman at the ball," Camila promised.

"You *do* want the groom to notice you, don't you?" Sofia said, adopting a lighter tone. "Perhaps he will feel a pang of regret that he didn't break his engagement and wait for you."

Camila had already laced Sofia into her own stays and helped her layer her best linen blouse and finest petticoats over them and her chemise. Now, Sofia was hooking the bodice on her embroidered blue satin *robe à l'anglaise*. Gazing in the oval full-length mirror tilted on its stand in the corner, she fastened her mother's ruby earrings, noticing that their deep red precisely matched some of the tropical flowers embroidered on her dress. With their one-inch heels, her silk brocade dancing shoes felt reasonably comfortable.

"At least I can still breathe," Valeria said, inhaling and then exhaling. Sofia's earlier attentions with a curling iron had been more than satisfactory. Her sister's hair hung in golden ringlets, which Camila brushed lightly, achieving a more natural look. Using a tortoiseshell comb, she secured some of the shining honey-blond curls just below the crown of Valeria's head and turned her to face the mirror.

"What do you think?" Camila asked, hooking their mother's pearls around the girl's slender neck.

The yellow silk of Valeria's dress caught the afternoon sunlight. Except for the Brussels lace spilling from the sleeves and the back tucks where the bodice met the pleated skirt, the frock was absolutely plain. A delicate pattern of cutwork flowers decorated the hem of the petticoat revealed by the cutaway. The effect was breathtaking— unselfconscious innocence about to burst joyously into womanhood.

For the first time, Sofia regarded her sister without a hint of jealousy, only wonder, a fervent desire to protect her just as she was, and the sinking realization that she would inevitably fail to do so.

"You are radiant."

"Two more things," Camila said, holding in one hand a pair of tulle fichus, in the other two lace fans—one white, the other black—with matching satin ribbons to hang them from the wrist.

Handing the white fan to Valeria and the black to Sofia, she tucked one of the fichus around the neckline of Valeria's bodice, filling it in to just below the pearls.

"You are still young," Camila said, "not yet fifteen, am

127

I right?"

Valeria nodded.

"So you must be particularly modest."

Camila placed her right index finger to her lips, then announced: "As for you, Sofia. I believe you are twenty-one, so something more womanly would be appropriate."

After trying a couple of twists and knots, Camila arranged Sofia's thick brunette hair in a swept-back style that made her dark brown eyes look less deep-set, distracted attention from her aquiline nose, and accentuated her long neck—the one feature she shared with Valeria.

"And now," Camila said, "if you will allow me..." She tucked the second fichu into the neckline at the back of Sofia's bodice but brought the ends directly down into the front, revealing prominent cleavage only partially concealed by twin wisps of tulle.

As she spun Sofia toward the mirror, Camila looked satisfied. "You have to admit that your bosom is perhaps your best feature, especially when combined with your trim waist."

Sofia felt forced to concede that she was right. In fact, when Valeria snickered and teased, "All the lonely prosperous widowers will go mad for you!" Sofia didn't even react.

Instead, Sofia turned to Camila and thanked her for helping them dress. "Any duchess would be delighted to have you for a lady's maid, but don't you wish you were going to the wedding yourself?"

Camila laughed. "Oh, no. My parents have to go, because Papa is the groom's sergeant. And wait until you see him in his full-dress uniform and my mother in her evening gown. You won't recognize them.

"As for me, thanks to a recommendation from the *comandante*'s wife, the bride's mother has asked me to supervise the food service—the laying out and replenishing of the buffet, the passing of the *tapas*, even the flowers decorating the table with the traditional wedding fruitcake, which you should beware of, because it will have been soaking in rum for several days. The Gutiérrez family is paying me quite well for my service. But best of all, to direct the serving of the drinks, they have hired my sweetheart Santiago. Papa has given his permission for Santiago to walk me home after we clean the ballroom and put everything away. Although it will be quite late, Papa warned him that he will be watching from an upstairs window, and if Santiago does anything more than give me one kiss, he will come storming down the stairs."

Camila sighed happily. "But this situation will not last for much longer. The daughter of Señor De Soto—he's the silver merchant and jeweler—told me that Santiago has selected a ring, gold, with a small but perfect pearl. He is paying something toward it every month. As soon as he completes the purchase, I am sure he will ask my father for my hand and propose formally."

As Valeria and Sofia hugged her, Camila said, "Now, I must be off, to arrange the banquet tables. And you and my parents must be off to the church."

Descending the stairs into the cozy living room, Sofia gasped. There, next to the front door, was Sergeant Carlos Gomez, resplendent in his full-dress uniform—polished black boots, white trousers, a navy-blue coat with a high collar, shining brass buttons, and three small but bright medals arrayed across the left breast. His shoulders bore the insignia of his rank. In his white-gloved left hand was a folded bi-corner hat with a golden tassel at each end. His right hand cradled his wife's left elbow.

But this was Maria Josefa as Sofia had never seen her. Her glossy black hair was parted down the center into two braids, which were wrapped around her head like a crown. She wore an aquamarine teardrop in each ear and a full, long-sleeved dress of deep aqua taffeta, fitted only under the bust. In the late afternoon light, the rich color matched her eyes.

Maria Josefa broke the near-regal effect by laughing merrily and waving a finger at Valeria. "Valerita, my darling, you may stare, provided you can do so discreetly and with your mouth closed."

Then, with a courtly bow from Carlos, they bustled out the door.

Sofia looked at the jam of horses, carriages and flower-bedecked wagons creeping toward the entrance to La Parroquia. It was fortunate that the four of them had decided to walk the three blocks from the house to the church. From across the plaza, she spotted a gilt-trimmed carriage bearing Don Emilio, Doña Inmaculada, their children and a middle-aged woman who must be the widowed cousin. *The carriage has to be hers. I would have noticed if it had been stored in the stables at Rancho de las Palomas. Besides, it doesn't look suited to the rutted road between the ranch and Santa Fe.*

The entire garrison seemed to be in attendance, with the groom's fellow corporals arrayed in an honor guard flanking the church door, swords raised smartly, the privates at attention behind them.

"Carlos and I will find ourselves a place in the back pew on the groom's side," Maria Josefa said to Sofia as they dodged between two festooned wagons. "You young ladies should sit on the bride's side, behind Don Emilio's family but where the unmarried officers can get a good look at you. They'll be standing gallantly in the side aisles."

As they entered the church, Maria Josefa cast quick glances at the assemblage. "I wonder where Beto is?"

"Was he invited?" Sofia asked.

"Of course. Don Emilio is the first cousin of the bride's mother, and Beto is Don Emilio's acknowledged son. Formal etiquette would dictate that he sit immediately to Don Emilio's left, with Doña Inmaculada and their children to his right. But I suppose that particular custom is a bit outdated, except among the nobility."

Sofia imagined what the scene would have been like—a pew packed with adults and children, all squirming uncomfortably, Alfonso and Beto casting each other murderous looks, Doña Inmaculada's face frozen in icy hatred. Catching a glimpse of glossy black hair rising above a cluster of lieutenants and captains in the side chapel, Sofia smiled. *Smart fellow.*

The heat of the early afternoon still lingered in the church, and all the women seemed to be employing their fans. None too soon, a flourish of trumpets announced the procession—a gangly acolyte holding aloft a golden crucifix, four younger altar boys bearing tall candles, Father Antonio, unfamiliarly resplendent in shimmering white and gold vestments, and finally Fernando.

Over his corporal's dress uniform Fernando had draped a short cape of some sort of sheared white fur bordered in ermine. Embroidered on the back was the gold and crimson Valdez family crest that Sofia recognized from the groom's flirtatious attentions to Valeria during their caravan journey north.

On his head, Fernando wore a wig with a peruke and side curls turned up just enough to show a bit of his own brunette hair. The last time Sofia had seen a wig like that had been when she snuck into the gallery to watch her father in court.

Fernando stopped at the altar, turning gracefully as another fanfare blared forth. Down the aisle marched the bride—or more accurately, a white froth of satin, lace and tulle so voluminous that Sofia could see nothing of the person under it. The bride's father, however, was clearly visible, a middle-aged man with collar-length steel-gray hair, a neatly waxed moustache, and the fiercely erect bearing of a high-ranking military officer, although his black swallowtail coat and dark gray knee britches were clearly civilian attire. Across his chest was an emerald green sash secured at the shoulder with some sort of gold medallion. Was it the arms of Cuba? Santo Domingo? Sofia couldn't quite make it out, but the diamonds and rubies with which it was set glinted in the candlelight.

Without appearing to rush the ceremony, Father Antonio managed to move it along efficiently. Apparently, Señora Gutiérrez had requested a full wedding Mass, so given the crowd the distribution of Communion had been a logistical challenge. Nonetheless, Sofia noted with admiration, the final blessing came just an hour and a half after the first fanfare. She and Valeria waited politely for the families of the bride and groom and the elderly guests to leave and then filed out of the church themselves.

Directly across the plaza was the bride's family home, its ornately carved front doors open wide and flanked by young men in emerald green livery. Taking Valeria's elbow, Sofia steered the two of them into the foyer, where a broad pink marble staircase with white marble balustrades led to the next floor. Spilling down from above was a near din of conversation, laughter, clinking glass, and, comparatively faintly, music from an orchestra heavy on strings.

To Sofia's relief, no one was announcing the guests. They all just jostled their way through the arched entrance into the ballroom, which occupied the second level of an entire wing. Heavy golden ropes secured drapes in emerald green jacquard to the side of high arched French doors opening onto the terrace. Crystal teardrops glinted from four large chandeliers. Candles set in sconces along walls combined with late afternoon sunshine to lend a flattering glow. The floor was polished oak, rare in these parts but ideal for dancing.

The ten-piece band occupied a dais opposite the entrance. Tables to either side were piled with platters of dainty delicacies. Sofia couldn't make out the exact nature of the *tapas* from that distance, but she noticed waiters circulating with the platters, then setting them down to be refreshed. Other young men in black trousers and white shirts with bloused sleeves moved among the crowd with trays of champagne and red wine.

Valeria was agog.

"Remember what Maria Josefa told us," Sofia said. "It's all right to stare, but only with your mouth closed. Try using your fan."

Taking her own advice, Sofia surveyed the room, she hoped discreetly. Like Maria Josefa, most of the women middle-aged and above wore "round dresses" in jewel tones, some with spectacular necklaces Most of the younger women and several slender older ladies sported versions of *robes á l'anglaise*, including one severe-looking matron with a pile of silver-gray hair and a dress to match. She was listening intently to the bride's mother, who wore a dress of bronze taffeta apparently designed to show off the king's ransom of emeralds encircling her neck.

Men who were not in uniform tended to wear black or dark gray swallowtail coats with a military cut, as had been acceptable for at least a decade throughout the Empire. A couple of older men displayed rich brocade coats that might have been appropriate at the French court a quarter century earlier. On the heads of these gentlemen were large powdered wigs. Some of the young men wore wigs, as well. Others had obviously powdered their own hair before tying it at the nape with black satin or velvet ribbons.

Sofia spotted Don Emilio, Doña Inmaculada, and their party along the wall opposite the French doors, the men and boys standing, the women and girls sitting on small, ladder-backed chairs. Her hair piled atop her head and secured with a tall ebony comb inlaid with mother-of-pearl, Inmaculada wore a black satin-striped skirt and a matching peplum jacket buttoned to the throat.

How can she stand that, given the lingering warmth of the evening? Sporting a black matte silk gown nipped at the waist but at least with a neckline that hit just below the collarbone, her widowed cousin was bending over to say something in her ear. Consuela stared ahead awkwardly, the bodice of her light pink *robe à l'anglaise* so stuffed with tulle that her fichu hid her chin. Juan appeared even more awkward. Diego, Emilia, and Sebastian looked around furtively, as if hoping to see children their own ages with whom they could sneak outside to play.

Don Emilio, a sapphire blue waistcoat adding a festive touch of color to his otherwise somber black swallowtails and knee britches, balanced three plates of small delicacies as he steered his way toward Inmaculada and their children. A waiter followed with a tray of champagne and lemonade.

Turning from his family, Alfonso headed directly across the floor toward Valeria with long, determined strides. Sofia watched as a young lieutenant who had been walking in their direction apparently thought better of his target, paused and accepted a glass of champagne from a passing waiter.

"Good evening, ladies," Alfonso said, bowing deeply. He was wearing a powdered wig and smelled like he had bathed in that cloying cologne.

With a brief nod to Sofia, he offered Valeria his arm and invited her to the buffet table.

Despite the almost overwhelming aroma of florals, musky perfumes, beeswax candles, and rich and spicy food, a minute later Sofia picked up the scent of wild sage at her right shoulder.

"I thought you could use a Catawba ice," Beto said. "They're quite good, though one wonders what it must have taken to produce an iced confection here, in Santa Fe, in summer."

Dropping her fan and accepting the fluted crystal dish and tiny silver spoon, Sofia looked up. Despite herself, she stared. She had never seen Beto in anything but work clothes; and here he stood in a cutaway coat of high quality lightweight black wool, a high-collared ruffled shirt of fine linen, a gray silk ottoman waistcoat, a perfectly tied gray silk cravat, fashionably tight dark gray knee britches, white silk stockings and black leather shoes with silver buckles, both polished to a mirror finish. Combined with his height, the simple elegance of his attire made him one of the most imposing men in the room.

Giving her an impish smile, Beto said, "Samuel Steiner is a very accomplished tailor. He can make even me look like a gentleman. But perhaps I look more like the fellows in the etchings in one of my father's books—South Sea Islanders brought to Europe and dressed up for presentation to court as curiosities. By the way, what do you think of the hair?"

He bent over and turned his head from side to side for her perusal. "When I went to pick up this outfit, Señor Steiner showed me a broadside he'd just received from Paris. Apparently, men of quality in the European capitals have abandoned their wigs except for judicial proceedings, parliament and the like and have adopted the classical Roman look. He pointed out that since my hair was already short, and decidedly black, by merely feathering the edges a bit with my wet fingers, I could achieve what they call the Brutus, the height of masculine fashion."

Tossing his head back, he chuckled. "By contrast, you see, the groom appears to be sporting on his head a ferret in its winter coat. And my half-brother? Perhaps a weasel. What a pity, given that his own hair is gorgeous."

As Beto turned to hand her empty crystal bowl to a passing waiter, Sofia raised her black lace fan to her face to shield a laugh.

"That," Beto said, "is a silly affectation and not worthy of you. If you persist in concealing your face with your fan, I will have no choice but to fasten my gaze lower, and that could be embarrassing for both of us, given the cut of these britches."

Had he really said what she thought she had heard? Feeling a flush rise from her cleavage, Sofia closed her fan and rapped Beto on the forearm.

"Are you flirting with me, *señor*?" she asked playfully.

"I am a simple country stockman, *señorita*. I know nothing of this 'flirting.'"

Sofia noticed Beto glance toward the dance floor, where the members of the wedding party were finishing a reel. As the younger members and guests began to form themselves into squares of four couples each, Fernando nodded in Beto and Sofia's direction.

"The groom is inviting us to join him in the quadrille," Beto said, bowing briefly. "May I have the honor?"

Startled, Sofia asked, "Are you friends with Fernando?"

"Yes and no. As regards women, Fernando is a despicable dog, but he and I admire each other as horsemen. That bay gelding that he rides so well? I bred and trained that horse, and I sold it to him for a handsome sum."

"I don't know the dance," Sofia objected as Beto took her elbow and steered her toward Fernando and his bride.

"It's more like an athletic challenge, which is why the older guests are heading for the food and drink. The lead couple performs some sort of improvised step, which the other three repeat in turn, with whatever flourishes they choose to add. The lead then passes to the couple to the left, and the others repeat whatever they do. Each tries to outdo the other. Everyone will be watching."

Completing the bridal pair's square, Sofia gave them a quick curtsy, and Beto kissed the bride's hand. Isabella Gutiérrez y Valdez was plumper than Sofia had assumed, seeing her draped in layers of satin, lace, and tulle as she marched up the aisle on her father's arm. *So it wasn't all fabric.* The young woman's complexion was lovely, however, a pretty ivory and rose that rivaled Valeria's, and free of the wedding veil that had concealed it, the tall gold comb securing her chestnut hair glittered with an impressive array of diamonds.

The band struck up a lively tune that Sofia didn't recognize, and Fernando commenced dancing a hornpipe around Isabella, who picked up her skirts and hopped a bit side to side. As Fernando bowed in his direction, Beto took up the challenge, kicking up his long legs front and back as he circled Sofia, who got into the spirit by imitating the bride but hopping higher. The remaining two couples followed in turn, more or less admirably. The fourth fellow stumbled a bit but recovered nicely.

Leading next, Beto cocked an eyebrow at Sofia then lifted her by the waist and swung her around three times in a high circle, reaching the impressive level of his own shoulders. With an impish grin, he lowered her to the ground and whispered, "You are more substantial than you look."

The couple to the left managed the move, although the fellow swung his partner a bit lower, the next pair lower still. Fernando grunted audibly as he barely lifted the bride off the floor, shooting Beto an exasperated look. When the third pair assumed the lead, they limited themselves to raising their arms and clapping flamenco-style. The fourth simply twirled around each other.

As she spun, Sofia spotted Valeria two squares over. Alfonso had lifted her above his head, and she had her arms and legs spread as if she were flying.

Casting a quick look toward Inmaculada, Sofia was relieved to see Don Emilio blocking his wife's view. He seemed to be inviting Consuela to dance. *What a considerate man, to see that his twelve-year-old daughter didn't have to spend the ball sitting like a stick.*

The band struck up a minuet. Something slow and old-fashioned, Sofia noted, to give the older guests a turn on the floor and the younger ones a chance to recover from the exertions of the quadrille.

Beto led Sofia to the side. "I'm having altogether too good a time, but I have to be up at dawn to ride to my father's other ranch, Valles Caldera, and check on the progress of the cattle operation there."

With a smile and a brief bow, he headed toward the parents of the bride and groom. As Sofia watched Beto make his excuses to them, she wondered when he would return to Rancho de las Palomas.

Turning back toward the room, she noticed Maria Josefa and Carlos, beaming at each other as they spun gently to a sweet and vaguely familiar country tune. A man in a captain's uniform offered Sofia a gallant bow and an invitation to the next dance, which turned out to be a waltz.

His hair was almost as blond as Valeria's, and unlike most of the other dancers on the floor, he seemed adept at this recent Austrian import. Sofia wondered briefly if he might be from northern Spain, but her mind kept drifting to Beto—the smile in those gray eyes when he'd gazed at her, his unaffected pleasure in their banter, the giddy sense of weightlessness when he'd swung her so high during the quadrille, her last glimpse of those long legs as he left the ballroom.

No sooner had the waltz ended than a man who appeared to be around sixty begged Sofia's honor as his partner in a reel. He wore an enormous powdered wig, and his burgundy brocade coat would have been appropriate at the court of Versailles. On his right ring finger was a large oval-cut sapphire. *One of those lonely prosperous widowers Valeria keeps teasing me about.*

After dancing with another two older gentlemen, one with an apparently arthritic knee, plus three presentable-looking officers, Sofia excused herself from her last partner, saying she needed some air. She did, but what she needed more was food. The dainty delicacies remaining on the buffet table had been moved to one side and replaced by three roast suckling pigs, five racks of lamb, and a dozen bowls piled high with vegetables and fruit. The blend of tantalizing aromas made Sofia's stomach rumble.

As she made her way to the buffet table, Sofia looked around for her sister. Once again, Valeria was dancing with Alfonso, this time a lively *jota*. Occasionally, she danced with one of the young officers, but Alfonso's only other partners appeared to be his younger sisters. Admittedly, he seemed quite sweet with Emilia, guiding the nine-year-old playfully through a minuet.

Señora Gutiérrez smiled regally as she surveyed her guests from behind her silver and gold lace fan. *She deserves to be pleased. Everyone seemed to be having a good time.* The band played flawlessly, adroitly alternating the tempo between the sedate and the spirited. Granted, there were not enough partners for the young officers and soldiers, but as a result even the plainest girls and women were dancing.

Judging from the crowd around the buffet table, the cooks were doing a similarly fine job. Two corporals parted politely to give her access. One handsome young man in a ruffle-fronted shirt carved her a generous slice of roast suckling pig. Another cut her a chop from a rack of lamb, then raised an eyebrow. When she nodded, he gave her a second. Moving along to her left, she served herself a scoop of olives, some sugared carrots, and two dried figs.

Not wishing to appear as ravenous as she felt, Sofia ducked behind a tall potted fern set next to French doors leading to the patio. Taking advantage of one of the small ladder-backed chairs nearby, she sat down, spread the white linen serviette across her lap and began on the roast suckling pig, which she silently pronounced the best she ever tasted. To her relief, it was tender enough not to require a knife, since she had only been given a fork. The dried figs balanced the flavor nicely. The lamb chops were succulent, the olives sublime, and the breeze drifting in through the French doors refreshing.

Sofia was finishing the last of her sugared carrots when she caught a whiff of rich tobacco wafting in from the terrace.

"This is indeed an excellent cigar, Emilio," a melodious baritone proclaimed. "It goes beautifully with this fine *cavazos*. And if I am not mistaken, this cigar is from Havana, not Veracruz. Many thanks."

"You are one of the few men hereabouts who could appreciate the difference, *comandante*," she heard Don Emilio reply. "That is one reason it gives me pleasure to share such a cigar with you—that and our friendship, of course."

"For the sake of that friendship, please call me Estéban."

The garrison commander paused and took a long, audible puff on his cigar.

After exhaling, he said, "And also for the sake of that friendship, as well as our long business association, I hope you will forgive my broaching a matter of some delicacy."

"Of course, Estéban."

"As I reviewed accounts with my quartermaster last week, he pointed out that Rancho de las Palomas charges us about five percent more than market rate for our wool, meat, leather, and animals on the hoof. I understand and respect that the quality of Las Palomas meat and livestock is consistently high, that your tanned hides are always clean and supple, that your wool is tightly woven and the colors do not run. But I assume that since we are your biggest customer, you would charge us a few percent less than market, not more.

"The quartermaster even suggested that we might consider shifting a larger percentage of our orders to Las Golondrinas."

"Surely, there must be an error," Don Emilio said. His tone was one of shock. "At least since my father's time, Rancho de las Palomas has always charged the garrison five percent *less* than our civilian customers."

"I agree," the *comandante* said smoothly. "There must be an error. The question is on which side."

After puzzling briefly about the import of what she overheard, Sofia decided that it had to be a simple business misunderstanding, due to a bookkeeping mistake that Don Emilio would sort out once he had the ranch's records at hand.

A cheerful commotion arose from the ballroom proper, where the bride and groom stood beside the table with the wedding cake. Handing her empty plate to a passing waiter, Sofia made her way to the edge of the festive throng and peered between a tall woman in purple taffeta and a man in a major's uniform. The massive square fruitcake had to be three feet across. Gracing the top was the Valdez family crest executed in white icing and flanked by red and yellow roses and crosses. Someone passed her a glass of champagne, which she raised, joining in the toast.

Fernando prepared to cut the wedding cake with his sword.

CHAPTER FOURTEEN

Sofia watched as the serving staff finished slicing the cake and passed it around. Fernando fed Isabella a dainty piece, and she did the same for him. The band performed its exhausted best on a Bach concerto, signaling that nothing danceable would be forthcoming. The bride and groom bustled out of the ballroom under a shower of rice and rose petals. Guests followed, the younger men cheering.

Glancing around, Sofia spotted Carlos and Maria Josefa intercepting Valeria and Alfonso as they approached the archway. As she hurried to their side, she heard Carlos tell Alfonso, jovially but firmly, that *he* would be happy to walk the two "charming young ladies" home. Sofia also noticed the warning look Maria Josefa shot in Valeria's direction.

The cool night air refreshed them; but the moment they entered the cozy, welcoming house, Sofia felt ready to collapse. The clock on the mantle read one-thirty. How had the evening flown by so fast?

Valeria looked like she could have danced until dawn.

With warm thanks to their hosts, Sofia took her sister by the elbow and steered her toward the stairs.

"I'll be up in a few minutes," Maria Josefa said. "First, I must make my husband some coffee. He has vowed to stay up and wait for Camila."

Quickly undressing and washing, Sofia and Valeria climbed into the spare room's *cama matrimonial*, leaving the smaller bed for Camila.

"I think Alfonso may be in love with me," Valeria said. "He asked when I would turn fifteen. When I told him not until late July, he pouted—such a darling pout—and said that a month was so long to wait."

Sofia sighed as she recalled the angry words and hate-filled looks that Alfonso and Beto exchanged. And those were the ones she witnessed. How many other times in the previous weeks—or for that matter years—had the two half-brothers come close to blows? It seemed to her that Alfonso was the instigator, goading Beto to the brink of violence, as if hoping he would hit first. Could her beautiful, spirited sister ever be safe married to such a man?

Just as the sky started to lighten, Sofia heard the front door open and Carlos announce, gruffly but affectionately: "He kissed you *twice*. Santiago better hurry up and ask for your hand, or he'll answer to me."

When Sofia awoke again, it was past nine. She could hear Carlos snoring loudly in the room next door and Maria Josefa bustling around in the kitchen below. Still in the white skirt and blouse she wore the evening before, Camila sprawled face down on the single bed. Putting her finger to her lips and whispering in her ear, Sofia shook her sister gently.

"Wake up. Let's go downstairs but be quiet about it so that we don't wake Camila."

Maria Josefa greeted them heartily. "Don't worry about my husband and daughter," she said. "Even Gabriel's trumpet wouldn't wake them this morning."

She handed the sisters coffee. "Now you must tell me

how you enjoyed the ball. Carlos and I were so busy making sure the young soldiers had a good time—this is our duty, but also our pleasure—that we barely caught sight of you, Sofia, except for that quadrille with Beto. By the way, he looked truly elegant, don't you agree? And he clearly enjoyed your company."

Sofia found herself blushing. Maria Josefa smiled slyly before continuing.

"Valeria, of course, no one could miss. You were everywhere, with Alfonso. Every dance, you naughty girl."

"Not *every* dance," Valeria said.

Maria Josefa insisted on fixing the sisters "a proper breakfast" before they headed back to Rancho de las Palomas—eggs scrambled with potatoes and onions, plus bacon, beans, tortillas. As she smelled the simple *norteño* cooking, Sofia found herself ravenous once again.

When they had had their fill of Maria Josefa's hearty fare, the sisters tiptoed back upstairs to dress in their everyday skirts, blouses, and *rebozos* and pack their finery into their oversized saddlebags. Camila never stirred. Carlos continued snoring. As Sofia and Valeria reached the foot of the stairs, Maria Josefa hurried over to help them with their bags.

"When you unpack your gowns, hang them out to air for a day before putting them back in your trunks. And, as soon as you get home, put that necklace and those earrings back in Don Emilio's locked chest."

Although Sofia could tell that the afternoon would become hot, the air as they rode home retained some of its morning coolness. The brown gelding and the dappled gray filly transformed the journey into a pleasant Sunday outing. The aroma from the wild sage growing along the road reminded Sofia of Beto and prompted her to admit she had found him engaging company—not a bit arrogant or insolent and certainly not pompous.

They arrived back at the ranch in the middle of *siesta*. Inmaculada and her children were nowhere in residence, but Sofia noticed the stable boy combing Don Emilio's black stallion. The *patrón* must have ridden home ahead of his family and would probably be in his customary spot, his library. Leaving Valeria to hang their evening finery outside their room to air, Sofia dug into the saddlebag containing the pearl necklace and ruby earrings.

"I'm taking these to be locked back in the chest," she said, holding the red velvet bag aloft. "I'll be back in a few minutes to help unpack."

"Let me know if you run into Alfonso," Valeria said dreamily.

Announcing herself as she knocked on the library door, Sofia noticed that Don Emilio's invitation to enter was less hearty than usual.

"Good afternoon, my dear," he said as she walked in. Open on his desk were two large ledgers, one bound in red leather, the other in blue. Leaning against a leg of the desk were three more—one green, another black, the third brown. A fist-sized globe of garnet-colored blown glass secured a foot-tall stack of papers.

Don Emilio removed a *pince nez* from the bridge of his nose.

"Ah, I see that you have your jewelry to return to safety. I trust that you and Valeria enjoyed the wedding and the attendant festivities."

"Very much, thank you," Sofia replied.

Don Emilio sounded distracted. As he arose to unlock the chest, Sofia noticed that his movements were slower and stiffer than usual, as if this normally vigorous man had aged twenty years overnight. After securing the red velvet bag in its compartment, he crossed back to his desk and sank wearily into his chair.

"I am glad that you had a good time. And I have been meaning to thank you for the lessons that you and your sister have been giving the children. You have gone well beyond my expectations, which I admit were high. But now I have some pressing business I must attend to before my family arrives home."

As he gave her a sad smile, Sofia began to suspect that the conversation she overheard between Don Emilio and the *comandante* had exposed something more serious than a simple bookkeeping error.

The following afternoon, Sofia found herself once again at the brightly painted door of the library. Figuring that Beto must have finished reading José Cadalso's *Moroccan Letters*, Sofia decided to borrow the book from Don Emilio and, if possible, a volume of the writer's poems and the scripts of one or two of his plays. She hoped to compare them side-by-side and decide for herself whether, as Beto believed, Cadalso's passion for his young mistress had destroyed his mental abilities.

As she raised her hand to knock on the door, she heard angry voices and paused.

"I learned of the discrepancy because the *comandante* took me aside at the ball," Don Emilio said sharply. "His quartermaster brought to his attention that Rancho de las Palomas was charging the garrison five per cent more than commercial market prices. Five per cent more! How do you explain this, Alfonso?"

"That isn't so. The quartermaster's records must be in error."

"Since your grandfather's day and probably before, Rancho de las Palomas has charged the garrison five per cent *below* market, both because they are by far our largest customer and we need to keep them and because it is our duty to support the army that protects our lives and property."

Sofia heard the rustle of papers and the thump of a heavy object, perhaps the paperweight.

"These invoices tell one story," Don Emilio said. "These ledgers tell another. I've organized the invoices by date. You can see that the dates and descriptions of goods sold agree, but the prices do not. In every case for the past year—*every case*—the invoices are ten and a half per cent higher than the amounts you recorded. I must admit that you've been very meticulous."

Sofia heard Alfonso cough, then stammer something she couldn't make out.

"So you admit it?" Don Emilio said, his tone icy. "I trusted you. I've trusted you to manage the ranch's business affairs for the three years since you returned from university in Mexico City, but you betrayed my trust. I've mistakenly assumed that you were an honorable man. I've never questioned your frequent trips to Santa Fe. I've always believed that you were conducting legitimate business on behalf of the ranch and that you deserved to stay for a bit of pleasure afterwards."

Sofia thought she should turn away. This was, after all, a serious private matter between Alfonso and his father. But then she remembered Valeria saying that she thought Alfonso was in love with her, and he had complained about having to wait for her fifteenth birthday, less than four weeks away, to court her formally. This scoundrel who had stolen from his family—because that was what Don Emilio's meticulous review of the ledgers and invoices had apparently revealed—wanted to marry her sister. Her duty toward Valeria demanded that Sofia learn all she could about the matter so she kept her ear to the door with its incongruously cheery carved and painted pattern of doves and flowers.

"What you allot me of the ranch's profits does not permit me to present myself as a gentleman in Santa Fe," Alfonso said.

"In that case, you could have come to me for a reasonable increase. But we are talking about the equivalent of ten thousand gold *escuchos* here, maybe more. That is way in excess of whatever you would need for a couple of fine suits of clothes and the occasional bottle of port to share with your friends. Where did the money go?"

"Speaking as one man to another, I must admit that I am a patron of Madame Le Ferrier's."

"The fanciest brothel in *El Norte*," Don Emilio said.

"Surely you wouldn't want me to resort to one of the lesser establishments. At Madame Le Ferrier's, my fellow customers are high-ranking officers and Santa Fe's top businessmen. The garrison surgeon inspects the girls every week for disease."

"I have news for you, my son. The garrison surgeon inspects all the girls in all the houses on the same schedule. The army can't afford to have soldiers of any rank disabled by the clap or the pox."

Don Emilo cleared his throat. "But you couldn't possibly have spent all this money on whores. Even if you were keeping a mistress—and I certainly would have heard if you were..."

"Madame Le Ferrier also has tables. Some of us relax over games of chance before or after spending time with the girls. There is a card game called *bassette*, newly introduced from France. It is considered especially appropriate for gentlemen. Others can't afford it, so being seen in a *bassette* game confers a certain prestige, to a fellow and to his family."

"I suspect that others can't afford it because the stakes are high and the odds heavily favor the house," Don Emilio said. "And being seen to lose heavily with good grace suggests that you have a lot of money."

For what was probably a minute but seemed like five, not a sound came through the door. Then Sofia heard Don Emilio say wearily, "When I learned of your theft—and that was indeed what you have done here—I considered disowning you, Alfonso. But that would break your mother's heart, perhaps more than your betrayal has broken mine. Plus, it would create a scandal that would destroy our family's good name. Instead, I have decided that you will continue in your current role, with the exception that I will check every entry that you make. Consider me as following along behind you—with a magnifying glass. Once a week, you and I will meet here, in my library, for however many hours it takes, and you will report to me on any business you conduct on behalf of Rancho de las Palomas, whether those exchanges are formal, in writing, or merely discussions of future transactions.

"Am I clear?"

"Yes, Father."

"To help mend the damage inflicted on our largest and longest-standing customer, and by extension the Crown of Spain, I will meet privately with the *comandante* and tell him that, as he suspected, we have made an error in bookkeeping. I will apologize profusely, I will thank him for bringing this grave mistake to my attention, and I will offer him a *ten per cent discount* on all orders for the next twelve months, at which point the discount will return to the customary five per cent."

"But, father, surely this is excessive."

"Rancho de las Palomas will survive a year of reduced profits far better than we would survive the loss of the garrison's patronage—and our reputation."

Don Emilio coughed, then continued. "You understand, of course, that a reduction in our profits will mean a reduction in your personal income—yours and Beto's?"

"Yes, father."

"I have been thinking of how to make this up to Beto, perhaps in my will."

Alfonso's tone, which had been contrite and respectful, suddenly shifted. "If you leave him *anything* beyond a horse or two, I will contest it in court," he said, his tone hard. "You may have acknowledged that half-breed legally, but I am confident that any judge in New Spain would see my claim as your oldest son, your *legitimate* son, as stronger."

"You have a point. However, during my lifetime, I am free to dispose of any property to which I hold clear title in any way I wish."

"Rancho de las Palomas is a family asset," Alfonso said

hotly. "On behalf of my mother and my siblings, I would challenge any attempt to give away any part of it."

"True," Don Emilio replied smoothly. "However, I inherited Rancho Valles Caldera directly from my mother. The deed is in my name alone."

"I will see that bastard dead before I see him own an acre of Chavez land!"

Hearing the sharp rap of Alfonso's heels and the jangle of his spurs, Sofia fled down the stairs and headed for her room.

For a full day, Sofia tried to put the confrontation out of her mind. Gradually, she allowed it to intrude. When she considered the exchange coolly, rather than a furious dispute between a man she admired, a man who deserved her gratitude, and a scoundrel who had as much as declared his intention to seek her sister's hand, Sofia recognized that Don Emilio had come up with a wise solution for preserving his family's honor. As to his mention that he was considering making a gift of his mother's ranch to Beto, Sofia decided that this was simply a ploy to bring home his point, not dissimilar to his saying that he had thought of disowning Alfonso.

Five days later, Sofia was straightening up after morning lessons when she heard jovial shouts of welcome and the clatter of hooves. Looking out the refectory door, she saw Don Emilio striding across the stable yard as Beto stepped down from his paint mare. Clapping him on the shoulder, the *patrón* declared warmly, "I have never been happier to see you, son."

"Father!" Beto said with equal affection. "I suspect you have missed our games of chess and are feeling confident that you can beat me this evening. And of course, you will want my report on developments at Valles Caldera, which are quite positive."

"To be sure," Don Emilio said, his tone turning sober. "But I also have something important I need to tell you. Before I give you this information, you must promise me that you will keep it in strictest confidence—and that you will take absolutely no action on it."

"Of course, Father," Beto said, sounding puzzled.

Sofia watched as the stable boy took the mare's reins, and Don Emilio, his hand still resting on Beto's shoulder, led him toward the stairs to the library.

CHAPTER FIFTEEN

On Sunday morning, Sofia sat at the back of the chapel so she could leave the moment Doña Inmaculada concluded the prayers. These seemed especially long and slow that day. When the last amen finally came, Sofia squeezed Valeria's hand and ran out the door. Valeria would enjoy the day sketching on her own.

The wildflowers in the meadow by the mill pond were in full bloom. In the coming week the girls would find plenty of inspiration there for the altar cloth they were designing. Although Sofia was no artist herself, she could draw well enough to rough out the landscapes where she would bring the boys later to do their topographical schematics. Ever since the mock staging of the Battle of Cartegna de las Indias, several of the boys asked to borrow some of Don Emilio's military histories, and their reading skills had improved substantially as a result.

Dashing into the kitchen, Sofia picked up a round loaf of bread and a four-inch wedge of goat cheese. As she wrapped these in a muslin cloth, she wondered why her heart raced. It was probably just exhilaration at the prospect of getting away from the *hacienda* and out into the countryside. The early July weather was pleasantly warm, but it might be hot by afternoon, and the sun would be intense. Sofia stopped briefly at her room to shed her *rebozo* and pick up her straw hat with the faded lavender ribbon. Almost as an afterthought, she tore four blank sheets from Valeria's sketchbook and grabbed a couple of soft lead pencils.

Beto was waiting in the stable yard with her dark brown gelding already saddled. Sofia was struck once again at how handsome the horse was. Beto's own paint mare pawed the ground with her right front hoof, as if eager to be on their way.

"You brought food," Beto said, gesturing to the muslin-wrapped package in Sofia's right hand. "That's good. We may not be back before late afternoon. There are three spots that I think would make good military landscapes. The terrains differ, so it will take some riding to see all three."

He seemed more cheerful than usual. As he took the food and drawing materials from Sofia's hands, he looked her in the eyes and smiled. Even through his work glove, she could feel the warmth of his hand as he helped her into the saddle.

When they arrived at the gate leading to the back pasture, Beto leaned over to unhook it. Sofia was impressed that he could reach the latch without dismounting. *He has such easy balance.* As he shut the gate behind them, he said, "First let's ride over toward the south. There's a spot on the other side of the river with some promising features."

Beto nudged the paint mare into an easy lope, and Sofia's horse pulled beside his as they crossed the pasture, the river, and the field beyond. Sofia couldn't remember when she had felt so free.

After a quarter hour, Beto pulled his horse to a halt and turned in the saddle to face her.

"Look over there, toward where the river loops back

toward us," he said with a sweeping gesture. "The defenders of the *hacienda* could hide among those cottonwoods, even camouflage themselves with branches. Then, when the enemy came over that rise behind us, the defenders could ambush them."

This would indeed be a good spot to bring the boys for their landscape drawing, Sofia acknowledged. It had plenty of features for them to practice on—the river, the trees, the bluffs. And imagining a battle would motivate the students to be precise.

"Can we dismount so that I can do a rough sketch, to help me find this spot again?" Sofia asked.

Sliding nimbly from his horse, Beto helped her down, in the process placing a hand on her thigh—unnecessarily, but not unpleasantly.

"If I turn my hat upside down, the brim might provide a surface for drawing," he said.

Although the hat left something to be desired as an easel, it sufficed. After Sofia completed her quick sketch, Beto helped her back on her horse, cupping his right hand under her left buttock. An all-too-innocent look crossed his face.

"This next place I think you'll like," he called back as he took off at a canter.

Topping a rise, Sofia saw nothing but buff-colored hills rolling off in three directions. Purplish-blue mountains jutted in the far distance, but everything in between seemed so similar as to be disorienting.

"These hills will present a real test of perspective," Beto said, dismounting. "And you can imagine a band of Mescaleros, lying in wait on the other side of any one of them."

As she took his hand to swing down from her horse, Sofia realized that she was getting into the spirit of the game. This must have been what Camila had meant several weeks before when she had said that Beto could have a sense of humor.

He pulled off his work gloves and tucked them under the back of his saddle. Reaching into his left saddlebag, he extracted the muslin-wrapped bread and cheese.

"There's a little spring just down that draw," he said. "The horses could use some water, and so could I. We could also use some of this food."

Showing Sofia how to hold the reins loosely, so that the dark brown gelding would understand to follow but be able to maintain his footing, Beto cautioned her to mind her own step. Shortly, they reached a shaded slab of sandstone beside a clear stream no more than six inches wide.

"How did you ever find this place?" she asked.

"When you herd sheep or goats in land as arid as this, it pays to know every source of water. Your life often depends on it."

He tore off a piece of bread and handed it to her, then drew a hunting knife from a sheath at his waist and cut her a generous wedge of cheese. Sofia noticed that his hands were clean, the nails well-trimmed, and she could smell his blend of sweat and wild sage, intermingled with the scent of horses.

"I have a question," Beto said, surprisingly polite. When she nodded in encouragement, he asked, "Where did you learn to argue? The girls I know who went to convent schools wouldn't think of challenging me or any other man, or an older woman for that matter, even if anyone could see that we were wrong."

The question was so unexpected that Sofi burst out laughing. She had to hold her hand in front of her mouth to keep from spitting out the bread and cheese.

Taking off her straw hat and placing it beside her, but not between them, she said, "My father was a lawyer. When he had a case coming up in court, he would rehearse it over supper. He would have either my mother or me pretend to be the opposing counsel. The other one of us would be the judge. At the time Valeria was too little to join in, but she would sit there looking from one of us to the other, smiling that adorable, dimpled smile of hers, not understanding the game but enjoying it completely."

"Did he like it when you really argued with him, not just then?"

"Yes, but I had to make my case reasonably. If I cried or stamped my foot or threw anything, even my doll, I lost the case."

"I like the way you argue, too," Beto said, rising. "Most of the time."

As they made their way up from the spring, Sofia could see Beto scan the sky. It had been a clear, intense blue when they left the *hacienda*. Now there were a few fluffy clouds scattered across it like a herd of white sheep.

"The next place is the best, but it's about an hour's ride…just in case you need to relieve yourself," he said.

Taking advantage of the information, Sofia ducked behind a clump of small junipers. When she emerged, Beto was standing at the edge of the bluff with his back to her, appearing to be gazing at the view while simultaneously tucking his shirt into his pants. They exchanged embarrassed smiles.

This time, he waited to put on his gloves until after he had helped her onto her horse. After boosting her into the saddle, his hand cradled her left buttock briefly. Feeling a tingle run up her side, Sofia pretended to be intent on tying the ribbon of her hat under her chin.

After an hour riding northwest, they could see, another mile distant, a mesa that sloped away from a clear but steep riverbank. The air darkened briefly as a cloud crossed the sun. Looking up, Sofia saw a tall black cloud, shaped like an anvil, advancing from the east. A separate, lower line of clouds, not as tall, but boiling like a thick gray soup over a hot fire, approached from the west.

A sharp wind hit them with the strong scent of wet grass.

Pointing to a ravine cutting through the mesa, Beto shouted over the first crack of thunder, "I think we'd better head there. These summer storms can be ferocious."

"To those cottonwoods?" Sofia shouted back.

"No, we don't want to be down in the arroyo. We could be washed away. But the trail up this side of the mesa starts by those trees, and there's a place just below the top where we can shelter."

CHAPTER SIXTEEN

As Sofia and Beto galloped for the ravine, hard drops of rain began pelting them. Their horses splashed through the river, Sofia's gelding stumbling once on the slippery bank but quickly regaining his footing. In the ten minutes it took to reach the cottonwoods, Sofia found herself soaked through.

The steep path up the mesa was still reasonably dry, so the horses managed well. Twenty feet from the crest, the face of the wall cut in, and a stone ledge jutted out above. Sofia could see that someone had reinforced this shallow cave with cedar posts and crossbeams and had added a fenced pen where the roof slanted down into the cliff. Sheltered from the rain, the little corral afforded space for two or three horses.

Beto led their horses into the makeshift stable, unsaddled them, and hung the saddles, blankets, saddlebags, and tack on the fence.

"This is where the herders sometimes stay when the sheep are in the spring and fall pastures," Beto said. "Occasionally, I spend the night here myself. It's high enough above the stream to be safe."

Swinging his legs over the fence and into the main shelter, Beto removed his work gloves, then his shirt. "We need to get out of these wet clothes," he said. "Otherwise, we'll get chilled."

Sofia pulled off her hat, which was a sodden mess, and brushed back a curl dangling over her right eye. She noticed that Beto's chest was smooth but that where his trousers rode on his hipbones, a thin line of black hair descended from his navel, like an arrow pointing downward.

"Aren't you going to turn your back?" Sofia asked, reaching across herself to pull her blouse over her head.

"No. But I'll help you."

She gasped briefly but didn't resist. Under the layers of clammy muslin, a tingling sense of warmth spread across her body. Beto fumbled a bit with the ribbon securing her stays but seemed to have no trouble with either of her petticoats. Sofia felt her nipples harden and realized that he could see them clearly through the thin fabric of her chemise. Raising it, he nuzzled first the right, then the left. Using the same hand with which he cast her chemise aside, he grabbed two horse blankets from the rail and spread them on the dirt floor. With his left hand in the small of her back he lowered her down softly, then undid his trousers and entered her. After the briefest hesitation, he slid in and out of her as if buttered. She lifted her hips to meet him, suddenly giving a cry that mingled with a clap of thunder. With a few more thrusts he shuddered, arched his back, and rolled gently to the side.

Reaching over and drawing her toward him, Beto ran his finger from her right knee up her thigh, pausing briefly between her legs, then stroking along her hip bone and up to her right nipple, which he flicked gently. "I hope I didn't hurt you," he said with a note of concern. There was a small smear of blood on his fingertips.

"No. I felt a brief twinge when you entered me, but all the sensations after that were pleasant—at the end very pleasant."

"So this was your first time?"

She nodded.

"You don't make love like a virgin," he said, turning on his side and propping his head on his hand. "You make love like a woman who knows what she wants." Then, raising his eyebrows slightly, he added, "Besides, my father told me that you had been engaged, to a professor of medicine who died like your parents, sadly, of *la vomita*. I thought that in Veracruz, once a man and a woman had made their wedding plans public..."

"Ah, yes. In the Sodom of the South, it is not uncommon, once the betrothal is announced, for a couple to celebrate their wedding night, often a number of times, in advance of the marriage ceremony. But Mateo never suggested this to me, either in his words or in his actions. The farthest our physical relationship went was the occasional brotherly kiss."

"Perhaps he was one of those men who prefer his own sex."

Sofia shook her head. "Several of my parents' friends were of that inclination, middle-aged men who had never married and seemed happy to escort widows and spinsters to parties. These gentlemen often had exceptional charm and wit, so they were always welcome guests. I asked myself whether Mateo might have similar tastes and wanted to marry for form's sake, but I finally decided that he was simply one of those people who prefer to live in their minds." She sighed. "And in me he found a soulmate."

"Ultimately, this would not have satisfied you."

"No, I suppose not."

With a start, Sofia realized that she had never been able to talk to any man this freely, even Mateo. And she realized that being so open with Beto felt comfortable, like the most natural thing in the world. This man whom she had considered arrogant and insolent...

"I sometimes enjoy dwelling in my mind," Beto said, "for example, discussing books with my father. But as a rancher, I live mostly in my body. Otherwise, I couldn't do my work, with these arms and these shoulders and these legs. To be a good foreman, I can't just direct the ranch hands to do this or do that. I have to get in there with them, to perform the physical labor alongside them. Otherwise, they wouldn't respect me, and the young ones might do something wrong and get hurt. As with Tomás, they may get hurt even when they do nothing wrong, but at least I can be there to help."

He paused and toyed with one of her curls, wrapping it around his index finger, then unwrapping it. He went on to nuzzle the side of her neck, sparking a sensation that she found delicious.

"My true calling is as a stockman," he whispered to her right ear. "To see the result of two fine, strong animals bred to each other successfully gives me enormous satisfaction."

"Like with the little lamb that was born on our journey north?"

"Exactly."

"And that is why you were so protective of her, and so rude to Valeria and me."

"I figured that you and your sister and your bedding would be fine. By the way, the lamb is doing well—still nursing, but her mother will let people and the gentler dogs near her. So if Valeria wants to come to the pen and pet her..."

"And what happens if *I* get pregnant?" Sofia asked, voicing a concern she had been too absorbed in pleasure to consider.

"Either we will get married or you will go into a convent." Beto shrugged. "I would greatly prefer the former."

Stunned, she asked if he had brought her up here and seduced her in order to manipulate her into marriage. Her mother had warned her that unscrupulous men sometimes exhibited the opposite behavior, using the expectation of marriage to seduce naïve girls; but she had never heard of what she now suspected.

Looking over at her with a knowing smile, Beto

admitted that first, when he recognized he desired her, as he had never desired a particular woman before, he began to fantasize, or perhaps to scheme or a bit of both, of ways to get her alone and seduce her—where it would be, what they would do, what pleasing arts he would use to persuade her to repeat the experience. Then he reminded himself that he was an honorable man. What would happen if he succeeded in his seduction and she became pregnant? He reasoned that this would not be so bad, because there would be no impediment to their marrying, that she wasn't another man's wife or a servant in the *hacienda*. An employee, yes, but not a servant—an employee reporting to Don Emilio and Doña Inmaculada, not to him. Nor was she the daughter of a ranch hand.

In fact, she would be exceptionally suitable. She was intelligent, so she could manage the household efficiently, see that merchants didn't cheat them or that petty jealousies didn't disrupt the organized running of things. The women of the *hacienda* would respect her because of her intelligence, strong character, and fairness, not because she put on the airs of a grand lady. She had natural authority.

Plus, she would make him a good companion. They could talk about books and ideas, and she would argue her points when they disagreed, so that he wouldn't feel like he was hearing an echo. She would not hesitate to give him sound advice, as she had when she recommended that he treat the workers as well as he treated the horses. And they would give each other great sensual pleasure, of course, he added, nuzzling her again. Furthermore, he continued, she seemed strong and healthy and had broad hips and fine, full breasts, perfect for bearing and nursing children. And she clearly didn't entertain any stupid pious ideas about sex.

"Then, a voice seemed to whisper to me that my thinking had been upside down. I knew that I wanted a family. I hadn't really had one myself growing up—not a proper one. It was time I took a wife. What if in pursuing my growing carnal desires, I could also secure a good mate?

What if I could seduce you and give you so much pleasure that you would then agree to have me for a husband?"

Sofia stared at the ceiling beams, her head reeling.

Beto went on to remind her of his positive attributes and his prospects.

"I am a very good horseman," he said, his tone growing increasingly earnest, "and, I think you will agree, an astute animal-breeder. I am big and strong enough to protect a woman and children from any physical threat. Also, I have money—not a lot, but some. My father gives Alfonso and me a portion of the ranch profits. I do not have any expenses— and few vices. I have never seen the pleasure or profit in gambling, so I save most of my money, and when I have enough, I buy a small silver bar from Señor De Castro in Santa Fe. He is kind enough to keep these for me in the safe at his shop.

"So there is my case," Beto concluded. "And if I have impregnated you, that will only strengthen it."

Sofia could feel blotches of irritation blooming on her cheeks.

"If that was a proposal of marriage, it was certainly the bluntest I've ever heard." She paused, her face hot. "I feel like a mare you're evaluating for breeding."

Pushing him away and sitting up, she asked, "What about love?"

"Romantic love? That's just a silly myth. Think about José Cadalso. He was a brilliant military officer and writer. Then he fell in love with that actress and started writing honey-sweet poems to woo her and even plays in which she could star. In short, he lost his mind. And, besides, you told me yourself that you agreed that such passion was a dangerous delusion."

Before Sofia could frame a response, Beto brushed her belly again. Weaving his fingers gently through her thick thatch of pubic hair, he eased his hand between her legs, first gently pulling on her clitoris, then probing inside her to a spot that convulsed her with delight.

"You are not a mare," he said softly, "but I can make you whinny. Let's give this another try. I call tell you want to and," looking down toward the base of his own belly, "you can see that I am ready. Why don't you sit on top of me this time? I understand that this gives a woman more control over her own pleasure."

Straddling his narrow hips with her knees and bracing her hands on her thighs, Sofia settled onto him, at first receiving only the point of his penis inside her, then making a slow circular motion before taking him into her fully. She repeated the motion twice more, watching Beto's mouth go slack with wonder. He moved his hands from her hips to her breasts, which she had arched toward him. She now moved faster, directly up and down. His breath came in gasps.

"Stop for a moment," he whispered pleadingly. "I don't want to finish too quickly."

But she was already there, ahead of him.

Afterwards, Beto sat up, tugged off his boots and socks, then wrenched off the pants bunched around his ankles. He glanced over at Sofia, who lay on her back, her knees up, wearing only her own short brown riding boots and her spring green stockings. "I have to admit that I find the effect arousing," he said, sweeping a hand above her, from her breasts to her feet. "But we need to give these things a chance to dry." He drew off her boots and stockings and rose to arrange their clothes over the beams of the lean-to.

Viewing Beto's body from this angle, Sofia found it exceptionally appealing despite his disproportionately long legs. His buttocks were compact and tight, with endearing dimples. His back angled up to shoulders broadened by demanding physical labor.

As he hung up her stockings, he turned to her with a sly smile.

Sexually, he was well endowed but not so large as to be alarming. Sofia had been surprised at how well they fit together, considering the difference in their heights.

"Now who is looking at whom like a horse?" he asked.

"Would you bid for this stallion at auction?"

With an appraising pout, she cocked her head to one side. "Yes, but only until the bidding got high."

Returning to the blanket, Beto lay down, propping his head on his left hand, and stared down into her face.

"You seemed so attuned to my pleasure," Sofia said. "You must have had a lot of women."

"Some, but only casually."

"Do you patronize the same brothel as Alfonso?" she asked. "I hear that it is quite elegant."

"No. As a *mestizo* I would not be welcome at Madame Le Ferrier's. By the way, she herself is a quadroon from New Orleans, not, as she pretends, the daughter of a famous Parisian courtesan and a French count."

"But the girls of the house you do patronize, they provide you with sufficient satisfaction?"

She turned toward him, brushing back a straying strand of hair. Again, she was struck by the sense that she could ask this man anything, without embarrassment, and he would favor her with a candid response.

"I have thought about this some," he said. "For a man, there is a regular occurrence of sexual tension, I gather more frequent in young men than in old. This any man can relieve on his own. If he is a monk, for instance, and forbidden this conscious release, the tension will resolve itself in a dream. But sometimes that is not enough. At such times, a man wants a woman, and his own hand will not suffice. Some men with poor judgment turn to the girls around them, the servants. Even before my voice changed, Don Emilio cautioned me against this, and I think he did the same with Alfonso. The girls who accommodate the *patrón*'s sons, and possibly these girls' parents, will expect favorable treatment, which will cause discipline at the *hacienda* to deteriorate. The wiser approach is to find a decent brothel, a well-run house where the girls are clean and pleasant-natured and may even show some enthusiasm for their work—although I expect this is usually play-acting. Also, one where the girls change frequently, so that no one gets attached to each other. It is fine to be a favorite customer of the house, but never of any one girl."

Reaching over to stroke her hip and thigh, Beto asked: "And how is it for women?"

Sofia frowned in thought. "Sometimes there is a vague restlessness, which can often be quieted through physical activity or, for me, playing a piano piece *forte*. Occasionally, a woman will pleasure herself or wake up from a dream to find her nipples erect and her hand between her legs. But this changes when she wants a particular man."

"It changes also for a man, when he desires a particular woman," Beto said. "Then no other woman can satisfy him. With even the prettiest girl in the brothel, he may find himself unable to perform. And yet, with the woman he wants, he can copulate to exhaustion."

He eased himself down to kiss her, first brushing his lips lightly across hers, then probing her mouth with his tongue, running the tip along the roof of her mouth, setting in play a tingle that radiated down her spine. Disengaging, he transferred his attention to her nipples, sucking each teasingly in turn. He continued his journey south, licking the soft down along her belly and—at last—revealing her clitoris with his fingertips and flicking it with the tip of his tongue. Just as this artful attention brought her to the brink of a pleasure almost unbearably intense, his tongue began to explore inside her, finally reaching the spot that convulsed her in a paroxysm of sensation.

She must have screamed or at least howled, because she heard the horses neighing and clattering their hooves in alarm. The cause couldn't have been the rumbles of thunder, which sounded ever farther off. The rain had stopped, although occasional drops splattered down from their shelter's beams.

"So you brought me up here to seduce me," she said,

still glowing but feeling her heart return to its accustomed rhythm. She lifted her arms over her head in a languid stretch.

"I confess that was part of my plan, but it was only one scenario. I had several ideas for getting us alone together, hoping that sooner or later you would allow me to make love to you. Each scheme was based on some help it could give you with your teaching, of course. Today, for example, I think you will agree that every spot I showed you would provide an excellent landscape for the boys to draw."

Sofia nodded but pointed out: "This shallow cave and the stream below wouldn't make a realistic setting for a battle plan."

"But viewed from the other side of that little river, from the stretch where we were before it started raining, the landscape would be excellent."

"And if it hadn't begun to rain, would you have brought me to this spot?"

"Oh, yes. My plan was to have you make your sketch, then for me to say that I wanted to show you my favorite spot on the ranch. I would bring you up here, and maybe you would let me sit close to you, because you would be relaxed and happy from our fine ride. As we listened to the breeze in the pines and the cottonwoods, and to the sound of the little stream below and maybe a bird calling to its mate, I would tell you how I sometimes sleep up here when the sheep are in pastures nearby. And then maybe you would begin to think that you might enjoy spending the night up here sometime. And then maybe you would let me do this." He stroked the back of her hand lightly. "And if you let me do that, maybe you would let me do this." He kissed her lightly. "And if you let me do that, maybe you would let me do this." Extending his right hand, he cupped her left breast.

"So that drenching rainstorm spoiled your plan."

"That drenching rainstorm was literally a gift from heaven," Beto said with a grin.

Sighing contentedly, in fact a bit smugly, he rolled over on his back and soon began snoring lightly. The sound was soothing, not at all unpleasant.

Sofia dozed off as well. The next thing she was aware of was the sensation of his fingertips tracing the lines of her face—her too-long nose, the brows above her too-deep-set eyes.

"My desire is strong," Beto said, "but my friend here is a little tired."

Following his gesture toward his penis, she saw that it was half-tumescent, though twitching bravely as if rousing itself.

"Perhaps some attention from your lips and your tongue would help."

Softy stroking the back of Sofia's head, he directed it downward.

"Hold me around the base with your thumb and forefinger," he said. "Then run the tip of your tongue along that vein on the outside. When you get to my foreskin, push it back gently, then suck just a bit. You only need to take a few inches into your mouth."

As he spoke, Sofia did as he directed, finding the musty mingling of their flavors unlike anything she had tasted before.

Suddenly, Beto pulled her up, turned her onto her back, and entered her.

"My God, you do that well," he said, "but I want to finish inside you."

Although she would not have believed it possible, Sofia found herself rising once more to his thrusts, meeting his pleasure with her own.

By the time Sofia and Beto recovered, the storm had moved off to the south, but the water rushing through the arroyo was louder than ever. Pulling on his pants and boots, Beto went to scout the trail.

"There's a tree blocking the way a hundred yards down," he reported. "That little stream is now a river, and God only knows what the river is doing. Our surest course will be up over the mesa. It slopes gradually to the west, and we should be able to find a low spot to ford. In actual distance the route is longer, but it will be safer."

Casting a longing glance at her supine form, he said, "We had better leave now, or I'll be after you again, and you'll be too sore to ride."

Raising herself gradually from the saddle blankets, Sofia licked her lips, which were swollen with Beto's kisses. She swayed slightly as she stood, groggy with sex.

"Are you going to be able to grip with your knees, or will I have to tie you to your horse?"

CHAPTER SEVENTEEN

For the next two weeks, Sofia did her best to avoid Beto, but it seemed that everywhere she went he was somewhere nearby, crossing the stable yard toward the sheep pen, descending the stairs from his father's library, checking up on Tomás. Always, there was that spicy scent of wild sage mingled with sweat. Although he might favor her with a fleeting smile or a touch of his hat brim, he would turn back quickly to whatever he was doing.

When her period came, exactly on schedule, Sofia felt a mix of relief and disappointment—mostly relief. Despite his clumsy proposal of marriage, she concluded that their afternoon of lovemaking may have been all that Beto wanted. She determined to regard it in the same way. She told herself that her curiosity about sex and about this enigmatic stockman had been satisfied. Their afternoon tryst had been pleasurable. Beto had been a gentle and attentive lover, so even if she never felt those exquisite sensations again, she could go to her grave secure in her memory of that one experience.

Valeria babbled on happily about Alfonso at every

opportunity. Didn't Sofia think that his hair was like an angel's, that his perfectly shaped nose was noble, that his physique put one in mind of a Greek god? And there was no longer any question that he fancied her.

"See? On his last trip to Santa Fe, he bought me this gold locket shaped like a rose. I will never take it off."

For fear of embarrassing Don Emilio, Sofia kept her silence about Alfonso's embezzlement, restricting her responses to vague cautions.

"You are still very young," she said one afternoon when Valeria had been particularly effusive. "You won't even be fifteen until next week. Why not let Doña Inmaculada spread the word around town that you are now of an age to entertain suitors and see if some of those handsome young men you danced with at the wedding come forward? You could have your pick."

Valeria sighed as she gathered her honey-blond hair behind her neck and tied it with a red satin ribbon. "None of those others were as handsome as Alfonso. Besides, Doña Inmaculada would never cast a matrimonial net around Santa Fe on my behalf. She wants me for Alfonso."

"I'm afraid you're right. *La patrona* looks at you and thinks what fine, blond grandchildren you and Alfonso would make."

"And what about you?" Valeria asked. "I know that she is somewhat cool toward you, but she might see the advantage of your marrying one of Santa Fe's well-positioned widowers, a gentleman appropriate to your own age."

Those lonely, prosperous widowers again.

Valeria smiled impishly, but Sofia let the comment pass. At least her younger sister didn't seem to have any idea about her adventure with Beto.

That Tuesday afternoon, as Sofia was at her piano, Emilia walked gingerly up to her and cleared her throat. "Señorita

Sofia, would you teach me how to play the piano?" she asked timidly. "I am only nine years old, and my hands are still too small to reach across many keys, but I am willing to work hard and to practice every day. I asked my father if I could ask you, and he gave me a big *abrazo* and told me that it would please him very much if you taught me to play."

"Of course," Sofia said. She noticed that the child's eyes were the same gray as Beto's—and Don Emilio's and Alfonso's, as well—but there was a clear innocence to their expression.

"I would be delighted to teach you. I have some beginners' pieces here." She reached for her portfolio of sheet music. "I know you can read music a bit, but today let's start with reviewing the scales."

Emilia smiled beatifically, her shoulder-length brunette curls bobbing. This was the most animated Sofia had seen her.

"I do so much want to learn to make music," the little girl said.

They spent the next half hour going over scales, first vocally, then on the piano. When it seemed that Emilia had the notes down, Sofia sent her along, promising that they would try a pretty tune at the next lesson, Thursday.

Once Emilia had skipped off, Sofia became so engrossed in Domenico Scarletti's "Sonata in B Minor," struggling to master the distinct parts for each hand, that she recognized Beto's wild-sage-and-sweat scent without hearing his footsteps until he was directly behind her. He bent over and nuzzled the left side of her neck, sending a delicious sensation down her shoulder to her fingertips and reminding her of their afternoon above the arroyo. Gently but firmly, he lifted her hands from the piano, closed the lid, and slid his fingers into the top of her blouse, where he cupped her breasts and flicked her nipples playfully with his thumbs.

Sofia stood, a vague thought of protest crossing her mind but departing just as quickly. Her own body was putting the lie to any objection. As Beto raised her skirts and entered her from behind, she braced her palms on the piano lid and pushed back rhythmically with her hips, meeting each of his thrusts. After only a few strokes, she felt a surge of pleasure wash over her and shuddered. Although she expected him to reach his own climax shortly thereafter, instead he pulled back slightly, took a couple of quick breaths, whispered, "Let's see if you can do that again," and resumed his pulsing plunges. At the second wave of intense sensation, Sofia gave a soft cry, feeling her muscles clench and then relax as he released himself with a sigh.

Tucking himself in and settling down next to her on the piano bench, Beto said teasingly, "Maybe next time we should try that with me sitting in a chair and you astride me."

Sofia turned to face him. "You've been avoiding me for two weeks. I thought that despite your clumsy proposal, that one afternoon was all you wanted."

Beto shook his head slowly. "After what you call my 'clumsy proposal,' I thought you might need some time to think it over. Although you didn't say yes, you didn't say no. If I had talked to you, even on the most polite and trivial level, we would have ended up like this."

He cast a brief look at his crotch. "Besides, a part of me certainly wasn't ignoring you."

"What do you mean?" she asked.

"For such an intelligent woman, you do miss some obvious things. Haven't you noticed that whenever you're within a few yards of me, the women of the ranch sneak looks at the front of my pants and cover their mouths with their hands to hide their giggles? They notice that I'm starting to get hard. Marina is the worst. That toothless hag even points."

He sighed. "The ranch hands are almost as bad. In the past, when I have told them to do something with which they disagreed, they would say, 'Señor Beto, it might work better if we did it this way.' We would discuss the matter, and if their suggestion had merit, we would try their way. This rewarded initiative and was good for morale. Now, they just shrug and do what I tell them, but I have overheard them saying to each other, 'Poor Beto. Nowadays, he is thinking only with his cock.' How can I maintain my authority?"

"Fortunately, we women don't exhibit such obvious physical signs, at least not if we keep our *rebozos* draped modestly over our breasts."

"You think so?" he asked. "I can smell your desire for me from two yards away, and I am willing to bet that everyone else around us can, as well."

"By the way, I'm not pregnant," Sofia said.

"I knew that, too, from the way you smelled last week."

"You must be relieved."

"More like challenged." Beto snorted. "If you will not tell me yes now, I will simply have to work harder to impregnate you."

Unable to think of a response, Sofia raised the lid of her piano and attempted to resume the Scarlatti.

For Sofia, the following four weeks passed in a blur. To her relief, Doña Inmaculada never displayed so much as a breath of suspicion. *La patrona*'s cool indifference toward her, irritating at first, was proving advantageous. The wives and daughters of the ranch hands might giggle and gossip, but they would never feel comfortable passing along bawdy tales to the pious Inmaculada. And, Sofia reasoned, if Inmaculada were to sack her for immoral behavior, Valeria would have to go as well—along with any thoughts of a match with Alfonso. *Inmaculada will not start searching for secrets she cannot afford to find.*

The children were now learning at more or less the same speed as their age mates. Diligent about her piano lessons, Emilia had advanced to some of the simpler parts of a Mozart concerto. His leg now fully healed, Tomás seemed to delight in rolling up his pants and showing the other boys the scar and the little red spots where Marina had removed his stitches, but he had the good sense not to display them to

Doña Inmaculada the one time she stopped by at the end of lessons to approve the altar cloth that the girls were embroidering.

"Having so many birds and flowers strikes me as overly secular, but I suppose that Father Antonio will like them, given that he is a Franciscan."

Smiling at her oldest daughter, Consuela, *la patrona* added proudly, "I think Father Antonio will be happy to accept this for La Parroquia, and I will be honored to present it to him."

Then, with a disapproving glance at Tomás, who was striding toward the main refectory door without even a touch of a limp, Doña Inmaculada muttered something about witchcraft.

Two days after Valeria's fifteenth birthday, the children devoted their Saturday party meal to celebrating it. They presented her with small presents on which they had collaborated—a belt embroidered with flowers from the girls, a cane flute from the boys. Valeria thanked the children effusively, saying that she would always treasure their gifts. Sofia noticed that she had a new bracelet of turquoise set in finely wrought silver on her left wrist and that she was continuing to wear her hair pulled back, showing off Alfonso's gold locket.

Sofia also observed that the ranch operations seemed to be running exceptionally well. She watched Beto move about cheerfully, overseeing one project, consulting with the ranch hands on another. The men seemed to have regained any respect they may have lost for him. By tacit agreement, he focused on his work in the morning and early afternoon, and she attended to her teaching. Employing Maria Josefa's recommendations seemed to have reduced the friction between Doña Inmaculada's children and those of the ranch hands. The girls formed friendships across this divide, chattering and giggling and arranging each other's hair. The boys remained keen on military history and asked if they could re-enact Hannibal's crossing of the Alps, though they had yet to come up with an idea of what might serve as elephants.

One night as she was dozing off to sleep, Sofia mulled over her situation regarding Beto. She reasoned that the loss of her virginity was of little practical consequence. If she never married, who would care whether she was a virgin? She had no remaining family to embarrass, except Valeria, who seemed oblivious to Sofia's personal life. Even if their parents had been alive, they would have cautioned discretion but would not have been censorious. They were, after all, in the term currently in vogue, free thinkers. And the San Miguel chief's wife's explanation of Pueblo attitudes toward virginity had made a certain amount of sense.

Potential pregnancy was another matter, of course. Sofia recognized that Beto had been serious in his declaration that he wanted to impregnate her. She couldn't resist his advances. Her desire for him was so strong she felt her knees grow weak whenever she smelled wild sage, even if it was from one of the bushes in the field and he was nowhere around. And she had none of those women's troubles that might suggest that she was infertile.

So sooner or later, probably sooner, she would find herself carrying Beto's child.

He was right that when that time came, she would have two choices—retreating to the convent or marrying him. Sofia first tried to imagine her life in the convent. The vision was hazy. She saw herself playing the piano, both services and for pleasure, teaching children at the parochial school music and other subjects. But when she focused, she recognized that this would be her life only if she were to enter the convent now, as a novice nun or a respectable lay worker. If she came to the convent unwed and pregnant, she would be treated as a fallen woman, not allowed contact with children, perhaps even her own child, for fear that her vice would contaminate those innocents. The convent wasn't the *pueblo*. The nuns might not be as superstitious as Doña Inmaculada, but their approach to feminine virtue might well be as strict.

On the other hand, what if she were to accept Beto's proposal? She tried to imagine him as a cold, detached husband. She had certainly seen enough of those "companionable" marriages—and some not even companionable—among her parents' friends. He had told her flatly that he considered romantic love a dangerous delusion.

But she couldn't bring that scene into focus, either. What was that light in his eyes after they had made love? The gentle way he stroked her cheek? The warm way he laughed when she told him of her childhood misadventures? The open way in which he shared his? His sigh of satisfaction when he brought her sexual delight?

And all this talk of children—not just of impregnating her, which she supposed could be seen as a source of primitive male pride, but of raising them with her. One afternoon walking back from a secluded spot where they had enjoyed a particularly pleasurable hour of lovemaking, he stopped along the mill pond, picked up a flat rock, and sent it skipping across the surface.

"There's a bit of an art to that, which I will teach our sons," he said. Then he pointed to a patch of white daisies with butter-yellow centers. "I will bring our daughters here, too, and we can pick flowers to make you a bouquet."

Suppose I could be content with whatever it was that Beto feels for me. What of my own feelings? After losing my soulmate Mateo so suddenly and terribly, could I ever open my heart to another man?

And yet, always there would come a moment when Sofia would catch the spicy scent of wild sage and sweat, and Beto would pass her a quick note saying where he wanted to meet late that afternoon. Often, it would be the soft grassy bank a hundred yards downstream from the millpond. Surrounded by cottonwoods, this spot was sun-dappled yet cool, and Beto had assured her that no one else on the ranch knew about it. They would go there separately, five or ten minutes apart, make love at least once but sometimes twice, and talk. Sofia continued to feel free to speak whatever was on her mind, and Beto seemed to feel the same.

One warm early August afternoon, Beto announced that they should take off their clothes, instead of just pushing them aside to give him access.

"I have not seen you nude since our afternoon above the arroyo. The sun is warm, and this place is private. I want to admire your body before I enter you and to feel your breasts against my chest when we make love."

Taking off his loose muslin shirt, he pulled her ruffled blouse over her head. "You are much better than I am at removing those stays." Beto went to work on her petticoats.

"We will leave your shoes and stockings," he said and began gently sucking her nipples.

They reached climax almost simultaneously. As Beto settled himself on his side with a contented sigh, Sofia decided that it was time to ask him something that she had been wondering.

"As you know," she said, "I am completely without sexual experience. You must tell me if there is anything I can do to increase your pleasure."

Beto leaned back and laughed. "You make love as artfully as the most accomplished courtesan, at least for my taste. Please do not change your approach." Then he asked, "Do you want to know what gives me the most pleasure?" He smiled down at her.

"Yes. Tell me."

"It is when you are about to reach your peak, and your muscles begin to clench around me rhythmically, and you emit little—or sometimes big—cries. At that point, I become consumed with delight simply from the sensation. Also, I feel great satisfaction and pride as a man. So do not try to invent ways to please me. You will please me most by allowing your body and your mind to respond to me, as they clearly do."

Beto paused and took to stroking her left arm softly with

his fingertip.

"I also have a question for you, but I am not sure how to frame it without coming across as the insolent fellow you have accused me of being in the past."

"Go ahead. I will take whatever you ask not as insolence but as candor—just this once."

She felt herself smiling. The afternoon sun glinted off Beto's glossy black hair.

"You never deny me," he said thoughtfully. "You never tell me that this is not a good day or that you must go do such-and-such rather than meet with me like this. I understand that such coyness is a common feminine reaction."

Sofia raised her eyebrows in mock dismay.

"Ahhh. So you would prefer if I told you no twice for every yes? Perhaps I am depriving you of the excitement of the chase?"

"No! You must not do that. There is not a moment of the day when I wouldn't prefer to be here, or some other pretty, private place, making love to you than doing whatever it is I am doing. But I can go about my work with good cheer knowing that in the late afternoon I will be inside you, probing every delicious spot—perhaps even with the result that nature intends."

For a man who is such an artist at the techniques of lovemaking, Beto is clearly naïve when it comes to understanding women.

"I, too, look forward to our time together," Sofia said. "In the mornings when I'm teaching the children, even when I'm playing the piano, I have to imagine that I am placing my anticipation in a box and locking it. Only when you let me know when and where to meet do I take out my imaginary key and unlock it."

She looked up at those clear gray eyes.

"But you must understand that I am not like most women. First of all, my parents were people of the Enlightenment, so Valeria and I were raised to be respectful of common social mores but not to be bound too strictly by them. We were taught to avoid creating scandals or acting in ways that would hurt others, yet to understand and follow our own minds and hearts. Second, you give me intense sensual pleasure, but you treat me with respect, at least as regards our personal relationship. I do not think of myself now as a fallen woman, and I am quite sure that you don't think of me that way, either. Why would I want to play little flirtatious games that would deny me the pleasure of your body? Third, I enjoy your company. As a stockman, and a rancher, and a man who reads widely but differently from me, you have a perspective that I enjoy and value. Finally, I am twenty-one years old, on the verge of being an old maid. Times like this with you may be my only opportunity to experience sexual delight. When Mateo died, I decided that I would never marry, although I kept that to myself. Now, although I may die a spinster, I will not die a shriveled-up virgin."

"But when you anticipated dying a spinster, you did not count on this big Indian." Beto thumped himself on the chest in a parody of self-importance.

"No, I did not count on this big Indian," Sofia said and allowed herself to slip into contented drowsiness.

Having no sense of how long she slept, Sofia awoke to the light sensation of Beto's finger gently tracing her full eyebrows and brushing down the ridge of her long nose. Opening her eyes, she saw his face no more than a foot from hers, a faint smile on his lips.

"If I didn't know better, I would say that you were looking at me tenderly," she whispered.

Beto drew back as if startled.

"Of course, I am looking at you tenderly. I feel great tenderness for you in my heart."

Now it was Sofia's turn to be surprised.

"Furthermore," he said, "when a man wants a woman to bear his children, it behooves him to show her tenderness. If he is rough or cold toward her, she will not trust him with their children. She will behave like many other mammals and make this male keep his distance. But if he treats her tenderly, she will think, 'This man will be a fine father. He may be firm, but he will be gentle. The children will feel protected *by* him, not *from* him. I can let him play with them and give them rides on his shoulders, and I can be certain he will never hurt them.'"

Sofia sighed, recognizing that this physically imposing, hot-tempered yet gentle man was not going to abandon his campaign for her hand. She stood and began to dress.

"Let's walk back together this time," Beto said. "I can pretend to be showing you where I plan to expand the sheep pens. Maybe the theme for your lessons next week can be sheep."

Sofia had to admit that that wasn't a bad idea. There was plenty about sheep and shepherds in the Bible, both New and Old Testament, which should satisfy Doña Inmaculada; and the children could learn about the biology and habits of sheep firsthand.

Halfway back to the *hacienda*, Sofia noticed a pair of roadrunners. She stopped and pointed for Beto to look. One of the birds was dashing manically around two *chollas* bristling with thorns. The roadrunner would circle one several times, then move over to the other and repeat the performance, all while the second bird crouched unmoving, looking on.

"What are they doing?" Sofia asked.

"The male is showing the female that he has found a fine, safe place to nest—two, in fact," Beto explained. "He has asked her to choose which one she prefers and to accept his proposal that they mate. See? She has turned to face the first *cholla*. Now he's bringing her a fresh lizard. When she opens her mouth like that and fluffs her wings, and gives that sharp cry, she is telling him yes. As he mounts her, he drops the lizard into her mouth."

Turning back to the path, Sofia and Beto walked on another twenty yards, reaching the back wall of the refectory.

Shyly, he took her hand in his and stopped again.

"As you know, I sleep at the stable master's," he said, "in the same room I have had since I was a boy. But if you marry me, I will build us a comfortable little house, with an extra bedroom for the children." He paused, then added: "Maybe two extra bedrooms, one for the boys and one for the girls."

Feeling a familiar prickle of irritation, Sofia dropped his hand. "I am not a roadrunner, just as I am not a mare!"

She wasn't sure what she wanted from this man. Perhaps, she admitted to herself, she wanted to be courted, rather than have the practical advantages of a match laid out like a business proposal.

Beto looked baffled, too. "Oh," he said, as if an afterthought, "your broad hips and your full breasts are not just well-suited for childbearing. They are beautiful to my eyes—and to my hands and to my other parts."

This, she thought, came closer. Beto pulled her toward him and kissed her deeply, running the tip of his tongue along the ridge of her palate. Lifting her gently, he braced her shoulders against the white stucco wall and with what seemed like a single gesture, raised her skirts, unfastened his pants, and slid inside her. Sofia tried to suppress her cry of pleasure but let out a brief yelp despite herself.

As Beto lowered her to the ground, he whispered, "As I told you earlier, if you keep avoiding my proposals of marriage, I will just have to work harder to make you pregnant."

"It would be scandalous to get married and then have a baby only seven or eight months later," she whispered in return.

"Infants born as little as half a year after a wedding are common here, the famous early babies of *El Norte*. Remarkably, these 'premature' infants come into the world full-sized and healthy. Doña Inmaculada would say that these babies show that Las Palomas is particularly blessed by God."

CHAPTER EIGHTEEN

Shortly after the wake-up bells the next morning, Sofia overheard Jimena's baby, Julio, emit a hungry cry and felt her own breasts ache. She also noted that her period was more than two weeks late. Suddenly nauseated, she ran outside quickly, getting as far as she could before vomiting behind a rose bush. After rinsing her mouth with water from the pump, she made her way a bit unsteadily back to her room. Valeria, who was brushing her hair, asked if she was ill.

"I feel much better, thanks. Probably something I ate last night disagreed with me."

Two mornings later, as Sofia was dressing, Camila bustled in bearing a mug of *atole* so thick that Sofia wondered if she should eat it with a spoon. Valeria had already dashed off to set up the classroom.

"Marina told the cook that she should make this special *atole* for you now and that you must drink it first thing every morning," Camila said with an impish smile. "That way, both of you will be strong."

Both of us….

"Also, you must not stand too long in one position, and if you experience cramps or little spots of blood, you must go to her immediately, and she will make you a special tea. Oh, and you and Beto should continue to enjoy each other, but don't allow him to be rough."

Sofia was flabbergasted. She had only just realized herself that she might be pregnant.

"Does everyone at the *hacienda* know?" Sofia asked.

"Only the women, and only a few of them."

"But everyone knows that Beto and I are…?"

"Lovers? Pretty much everyone, except *la patrona*, who is so focused on your sister and her precious Alfonso that she hardly notices you at all. As for the rest of us, we may be simple country people, but we are not blind."

Late Saturday night, Sofia heard voices raised across the courtyard from her room. Once again, it was Don Emilio and Doña Inmaculada. They were clearly arguing, though not as violently as on the previous occasion.

"This is a concession that you can make easily," Doña Inmaculada said. "You owe it to me and to our family."

"But it is a clear conflict of interest. Valeria is my ward, at least unofficially, and Alfonso is my son. Who will protect her interests in this matter?"

"She doesn't need protection in this. She has no dowry to speak of, only her beauty, her breeding, and perhaps her artistic talents. So there won't be much for Alfonso to lose at cards. Besides, with a lovely young wife to show off in Santa Fe, Alfonso will surely settle down and give up gambling."

"I have to admit that they appear to fancy each other."

"And think of the beautiful grandchildren they will make for us," Doña Inmaculada said triumphantly.

Sofia had to restrain herself from dashing across the courtyard and objecting. Valeria had just turned fifteen.

Given her beauty, vivaciousness, and generous spirit, she would be a wonderful catch for any of the most eligible young men in the region. She should be allowed a year or two to entertain a range of suitors and enjoy being courted ardently before choosing one.

Besides, Alfonso was not a man of honor, and Valeria deserved a husband whose reputation and demeanor were above reproach. Furthermore, he was cruel to that fine white stallion. Mightn't he turn cruel toward Valeria as well?

But Sofia realized that she had lost the argument without having even entered it. Valeria was obviously mad about Alfonso, and he seemed to be besotted with her. Clearly, he understood how to woo her, with expensive little gifts and probably words that were just as pretty.

As Sofia was exiting the chapel after Sunday morning prayers, Don Emilio strode up to her and bowed briefly.

"My dear, I would greatly appreciate your following me to my library," he said. "There is a matter of importance that we should discuss."

As the *patrón* opened the brightly painted door, with its artful design of doves and flowers, Sofia saw that Alfonso was already present, pacing back and forth across the room, his sideburns perfectly trimmed, his auburn curls glistening in a ray of sunshine. *He is indeed handsome, one of the handsomest men I have ever seen.* Like his father, he was tall, although not quite as tall as Beto, and he carried himself with the confident air of privilege.

"My son Alfonso has asked my permission to court your sister," Don Emilio said gravely. "This presents something of a conflict of interest for me, given that Valeria is *de facto* my ward. I wanted you to know that my wife and I have discussed this matter at length, and I have decided, after considerable thought, to give my consent."

"But I am her nearest relative, in fact her only surviving relative, and I do not give mine. I am of age and can speak for our family."

"You may be Valeria's nearest relative, and you

yourself may be of age, but as a woman, you have no legal standing in this matter," Alfonso said with a cruel twitch to his smile.

"Be quiet, Alfonso!" Don Emilio said. "This is your future sister-in-law. You must treat her with respect."

Bracing his hands on his desk, Don Emilio fixed Sofia with a direct gaze. "Please be so good as to reveal to both of us, here in each other's company, the grounds for your objection."

Sofia paused. She dared not give her strongest reasons—Alfonso's compulsive gambling and his embezzlement from the ranch—because to do so would entail confessing that she had overheard the confrontation between Alfonso and his father. So she had to go with her weakest argument.

"My sister has only just turned fifteen," Sofia said, struggling to keep her voice calm. "I think you will agree that she is a true beauty and that she possesses a lively, engaging, and generous spirit, not to mention that she is accomplished in art. I also understand that here in *El Norte* her having been born in Spain significantly increases her desirability."

"And those are precisely the reasons that my wife and I would welcome her as a daughter-in-law. I might be inclined to grant your wish that Valeria be allowed a year or two as what the French and English call a debutante; but, frankly, we believe that she has already made her choice."

"Anyone can see that she fancies me," Alfonso said, "and that I fancy her."

Sofia felt her prickle of irritation rise toward anger. Fearing that she would soon lose her composure, she faced Alfonso. "Sir, I am not convinced that you are either a man of kindness or a man of honor. My sister deserves both."

With that, Sofia excused herself and rushed from the room.

Stopping briefly to grab her straw hat, her thin leather riding gloves, and a goatskin water sack, Sofia went to look for Beto. She found him lounging on the old saddle by the stable yard wall, reading Marcus Aurelius. If it was true, as Camila said, that everyone knew they were lovers, there was no point in their avoiding each other in public.

"I won't be able to meet you this afternoon," Sofia said softly. "I must go to Santa Fe."

"Why?" Beto asked, looking startled.

"Alfonso has asked Don Emilio's permission to court Valeria. I want to seek Father Antonio's advice on what could be done to prevent such a marriage. Your half-brother is a scoundrel totally lacking in honor. He is a compulsive gambler. He is cruel to his horse…"

"And somehow, you have learned of his embezzlement," Beto whispered, completing her thought.

She nodded.

"I thought that Don Emilio and I were the only ones who knew. My father only told me because he considered that my position as ranch foreman necessitated it. I kept my vow not to reveal this to anyone, so how did you discover this?"

"One day, as I was about to knock on the door of the library to borrow some books, I overheard your father confront Alfonso."

Beto raised his brows and nodded in appreciation. "So you intend to ask Father Antonio to hear your confession and then seek his advice under that cloak of secrecy."

"Exactly."

"To make a full confession, you will have to tell him about our lovemaking. Please refrain from going into detail. After decades of celibacy, the good father's heart might not be up to the excitement."

Using her hat, Sofia swatted Beto's knee playfully.

Turning serious, Beto said, "You must let me accompany you."

"Thank you, but I don't think that would be a good idea. If we were both gone from the ranch for an entire afternoon and evening, people would wonder why. I will be fine riding there alone."

Rising from the old saddle, Beto scanned her face. "At least you must allow me to ready your horse. And you must promise me to be careful on the road."

As if he had been looking forward to an opportunity to run, Sofia's dark brown gelding eased into a comfortable canter, his black mane and tail flying. By one o'clock, she found herself in front of La Parroquia. Dismounting and hitching her horse to one of the iron rings set for the purpose, she knocked on the door of the modest residence connected to the church. After her second knock, she heard a shuffling, and a woman of indeterminate age opened the door.

"May I help you?" the woman asked, flicking an end of her coal-black *rebozo* over her shoulder.

"I would like to see Father Antonio, *señora*," Sofia said politely. "Please tell him that I am Sofia, one of the teachers from Rancho de las Palomas, and that I seek his advice concerning a serious matter."

"Father is just finishing his dinner, but I will let him know that you are here. And please come in. After your long ride, you must want some dinner yourself."

"Thank you, but no. Perhaps just a bit of bread…"

Sofia heard footsteps coming from the adjacent room.

"Who is here?" Father Antonio asked. "Sofia? Welcome, my child. What a pleasant interruption to an otherwise dull afternoon."

"I wish that the reasons for my visit were truly pleasant," Sofia said as the priest emerged, wiping his hands on the skirts of his brown habit. "I hope that you will consent to hear my confession."

"Ahhh. All these months I had taken you for a skeptic."

"Even skeptics sometimes need to confess," Sofia said, suddenly recognizing that this was true.

"In that case, please follow me into the sanctuary."

His steps were strong and firm, giving lie to his thin gray

hair and the bald spot that was at least twice the size of the expected tonsure.

"Father, if we were to sit facing each other, rather than divided by the screen of the confessional, would the secrecy of the confessional still apply?"

"The confessional is wherever you and I decide it to be," he said, settling onto a front pew and patting the space beside him. "Let us first go through the preliminaries. That way everything we say from then on will be a sacred secret."

Relieved, Sofia sat down, searched her memory, and began, "Bless me, Father, for I have sinned. My last confession was more than a year ago."

Father Antonio nodded. "Do you want to make a true confession, or do you simply want my advice?"

"I guess I want both, although I haven't given that much thought." Taking a deep breath, she said, "I think I am guilty of wrath."

Beginning haltingly, Sofia described her feelings toward Alfonso—from her distaste at his pretentious manners to his gambling and, finally, his embezzlement. She concluded with her distress at the thought that he might marry her sister.

"Father, surely there is something that can be done to prevent such a marriage."

After appearing to be deep in thought, Father Antonio said, "Unless Don Emilio is willing to bring charges against his eldest son, there is nothing that the Church or the civil authorities can do. I take it that Valeria has never married before and that she is a baptized and confirmed Catholic, as is Alfonso?"

Sofia nodded.

"Your own judgment that Alfonso is not a man of honor or kindness and is therefore unworthy of your sister will make a difference only if you can convince Valeria to reject his suit."

Sofia smiled wryly. "That will never happen. From the moment she first set eyes on him, she has gushed about how handsome he is. Even before her fifteenth birthday, he gave her a golden locket, which she never removes. On the occasion itself, he presented her with an expensive bracelet. Even as we speak, he is probably plying her with honey-sweet words. All she talks about is Alfonso, Alfonso, Alfonso."

"He must fancy her, as well, considering these attentions. And Doña Inmaculada—I imagine she is delighted at the prospect of having a Spanish-born blond, with both beauty and breeding, as the mother of her grandchildren."

Sofia sighed in assent.

"I imagine that *la patrona* and that widowed cousin of hers are already planning an extravagant wedding. My dear friend Emilio would do well to tighten his purse strings."

Sofia sighed again. "Valeria could have her pick of the most eligible young men within a hundred miles. Why does she have to settle for this one?"

"Now, my child, for my advice," Father Anonio said gently. "You must put aside your anger and, yes, your self-righteousness and work to identify Alfonso's positive qualities. Given your own character, this will be hard for you, but you must do it."

Sofia nodded reluctantly.

"And now, you hinted that you might have something else to confess."

"Beto and I have been lovers," she said. "I cannot tell you how many times."

"Has his desire been so powerful that you haven't dared to resist?"

"On the contrary, Father, he gives me as much pleasure as I seem to give him."

"So he has not forced you or intimidated you? You have been a willing participant?"

"Yes."

"And from your tone and the flush in your cheeks, I surmise that you *are* lovers, not just that you *have been*."

After a brief pause, Father Antonio continued. "Tell me, my child, has he mentioned marriage?"

"He is *always* mentioning marriage, beginning with our first time together, when he laid out his prospects very candidly and said that if I became pregnant, I would have to choose between the convent and marrying him and that he would far prefer the latter. He even confessed that he determined to seduce me not simply out of carnal desire but to persuade me to become his wife. He has a high opinion of his skill as a lover, perhaps justified, and he constantly slips the issue of marriage into totally unrelated conversations, describing how he will teach our children this or that, how he will build us a house, and even how he will keep trying to make me pregnant, in order to strengthen his case."

At this, the gray-haired priest laughed and slapped his knee.

"And you, I gather, have neither accepted nor declined."

Sofia nodded and brushed a strand of hair behind her right ear.

"What are you waiting for?"

Looking down at her hands, Sofia said, "Beto keeps laying out practical reasons why we should marry. He approaches the matter as if he were evaluating us for breeding. He has said that he considers romantic love a dangerous form of madness, and he knows that I distrust the concept as well. But a sweet word from him now and then might be welcome."

Father Antonio leaned back in the pew, as if preparing to tell a story. "I will speak to you now not as your priest, but as a widower who loved his wife with all his heart," he said.

"Will whatever we share still be covered by the secrecy of the confessional?" Sofia asked.

"Yes. Let us say that I am counseling you on your spiritual and moral life."

Sofia nodded agreement.

"When I fell in love—and I must admit, I experienced a heady sensation akin to falling—I was a cavalry officer, and that is how I approached everything—like a cavalry officer," he said. "If you want something, you define your objective, develop your strategy, and assuming you have enough troops and materiel, you will win the day."

He turned to face Sofia directly and clenched both fists in a parody of military confidence.

"Now in those days, as today, a young lady could have more than one suitor. As long as it wasn't too many and the family approved of each of them, she could consider them all and make her own choice. I had my heart set on this girl, so as soon as her father gave his permission, I brought out what I considered the heavy artillery of courtship. As she and I sat together in the courtyard of her home, I told her that I was from a prosperous family and had a modest independent income, which combined with my captain's salary would allow us to live comfortably. I told her that I had considerable prowess as a swordsman—this was an important skill back then—and could defend her against anyone who attacked her person or her honor. I told her that my family planned to give me a nice little plot of land at the edge of town, where we could build a house."

Smiling ruefully, he continued. "This beautiful young woman, on whom I had my heart set, would listen patiently and occasionally let me touch her hand, but she would neither accept me nor give me a flat no. I was going out of my mind trying to figure out what more I could offer her. At the time I was not a religious man, but I even prayed for guidance in the matter."

"Then what happened?" Sofia asked, recognizing that she'd been holding her breath.

"Ahhh," Father Antonio replied, shifting his cowl and the skirt of his brown habit. "One night at the tavern, I overheard this fellow bragging to his friends. They were rather drunk, so their voices carried. He was saying that he was certain that this girl we were both courting, on whom I had set my heart, would accept his proposal within the following week. His companions asked how he had won her.

One of the bolder ones remarked that his prospects were only moderate, his accomplishments so-so, and his looks no better than average. 'It wasn't that difficult,' my rival said, causing me to feel around for my sword, forgetting that the rules of the house had required me to hang it at the door. Then this rascal went on to explain to his friends that he had told this excellent young woman, perhaps the most eligible in town, that her cheeks reminded him of roses in the moonlight, that if she refused him, he was of a mind to kill himself, and other pretty words along that line. And he had recited poetry to her, sonnets by that English fellow Shakespeare, translated somewhat infelicitously into Spanish. The other fellows chuckled and said they would bear his example in mind."

"What did you do?"

"Well, I stormed out of there. Frankly, I might have tried to kill the fellow, or at least started a brawl, if I had stayed. Grabbing my sword from its hook, I barged out the door and over to the young lady's house. It was quite late, almost midnight, but I didn't care. I banged on the door with my fist. The maidservant who opened it took one look at my face and screamed. My beloved's father clomped down the stairs, loudly demanding to know what was going on. The girl and her mother were close behind him.

"I assure you that I was not drunk, but my temper was high. I shouted to my beloved that no one on earth could love her as much as I did. After taking a couple of breaths to calm myself, I got down on one knee, although the sword made assuming this posture a bit awkward, and asked her once again to be my wife. Looking first at her father, who nodded his permission, she said, 'Yes. Of course.' Her father, the old scoundrel, bellowed, 'It's about time, you idiot! I was afraid that I was going to have that fool of a horse-broker for my son-in-law.'"

Sofia glanced down at her hands. She could feel a blush rising from her neck to her cheeks. "So just as you were thinking like a cavalry officer, Beto has been thinking like a stockman."

"Exactly. Also, I suspect that he is somewhat afraid of his feelings for you, as well. His father's passion for his mother caused great disruption and came close to destroying one of the most respected families in *El Norte*. Beto knows that he has a similar temperament, so naturally he would try to deny that he wants what he wants most in the world—your love."

Sofia sighed and met the priest's warm brown eyes. "I, too, have been confused about my feelings. When my fiancé Mateo died of *la vomita*, I lost my true soulmate. Combined with my grief over my parents' deaths in the same epidemic, the pain was so terrible that I am frightened of feeling that deeply about anyone again. Also, among my parents' friends I have seen passionate couples who were left with nothing but resentment or contempt for each other when the first fires of passion died."

"But this would not be the case with you two," Father Antonio said. "Unlike Beto's father's situation, you and Beto are free to marry each other. You also share all the things he has pointed out, however clumsily. This includes not only companionship but also the physical pleasure you take in each other.

"As for the pain of losing one you love deeply, I speak from experience when I say that the joy of that love more than balances out the suffering."

Now it was Father Antonio's turn to glance down at his hands, then up at the simple wooden crucifix above the altar. "The Pope might disagree with me on this," he said, "but I do not consider your lovemaking and the joy that you and Beto take in it the Deadly Sin of Lust. Human beings have been around a lot longer than Holy Mother Church. I think that the pleasure you experience together reflects God's plan for forging a bond between a man and a woman that is so strong that it can withstand life's inevitable challenges and griefs—even," he sighed, "the illness and early death of one or the other."

Regaining his composure, Father Antonio continued. "I

am quite certain that even if I required that you regret your actions and vow not to repeat them, you could not do so in good faith. So I will ask you instead to make a sincere act of contrition for indulging your judgmental wrath toward Alfonso, which I really do consider a sin. Then say three Hail Marys, return to Rancho de las Palomas right away, and accept Beto's proposal. He truly is a fine young man, you know."

With another quick glance at the crucifix, Father Antonio made the sign of the cross and recited the Latin words of absolution.

"One more thing," the priest said as he rose from the pew. "Please tell Don Emilio that I would be grateful for his hospitality day after tomorrow. I should counsel you and Beto, both together and separately, before posting the banns. Also, *la patrona*'s cousin has said something about Inmaculada's bringing charges of witchcraft against the ranch's midwife. I don't know what century she thinks we're in, but there is probably some leftover piece of civil or Church law that might allow Inmaculada to bring such a charge, however frivolous. It would be best if I put a stop to this nonsense before it goes any further. Also, please tell my dear friend that I am eager to beat him again at chess."

As Father Antonio opened the church door to usher Sofia out, they both looked up at the sky, covered more than halfway by a roiling black cloud. A bolt of lightning struck a peak to the northeast. After the clap of thunder had died, the priest said, "On second thought, perhaps you should spend the night with your friend Maria Josefa. Besides keeping you safe from the coming storm, she has considerable knowledge of the human heart."

Untying her horse, Sofia rode to the modest adobe house two blocks south of the plaza and knocked on the blue wooden door. Maria Josefa's face lit up when she recognized her.

"I had no idea you were coming to town. Whatever

brings you to Santa Fe, you must spend the night here. Carlos is away for a few days taking his men on maneuvers. He will be sorry to have missed you, but I certainly welcome your company. Besides, that sky looks wicked. Settle your horse in the stable out back and then come in, and we will have some chamomile tea."

The living room was small but cheerful, with two wooden armchairs, a sturdy seating bench strewn with pink and blue and red cushions, and a piñon fire crackling in the corner. Settling herself on the bench, Sofia felt a sudden wave of nausea. Looking concerned, Maria Josefa quickly fetched her a broad basin from the kitchen.

"When is the baby due?" she asked as she offered Sofia a blue bandana to wipe her chin.

"How could you tell? I have only missed one period."

"To be honest, I guessed when I opened the door. Your skin has a flattering glow that I associate with a woman happy to be expecting."

"If my calculations are right, sometime around Easter," Sofia said. "But I worry about throwing up so much—and not just in the morning. And my heart is torn as to what I should do."

Maria Josefa smiled warmly. "This vomiting is unpleasant and perhaps embarrassing, but it is a good sign. It means that your body is adjusting to this change. In a few more weeks, this occasional nausea will pass, and you will feel better than ever."

Maria Josefa rose and returned with two earthenware mugs, the kettle, and a box of chamomile. Dropping a few pinches of the dried leaves and flowers into each mug, she topped it off with hot water.

"Does Beto know about the baby?"

Watching her tea swirl and then settle, Sofia shook her head. "I don't think so."

"And has he asked you to marry him?"

"He is always asking -- to the point of being tiresome."

"Then why haven't you accepted?" Maria Josefa asked.

"I guess you know that no other man will come forward to marry you, except maybe, years from now, a widower looking for someone to take care of him in his old age. Remember what I told you about your reputation."

Sofia responded that she had intended never to marry, which was one reason she had indulged her desire for Beto—and her curiosity about sex.

"He has said everything except that he loves me," she said. "He considers romantic love a particularly destructive form of madness. I must admit I can see his point. But I also am certain that I don't want to spend the rest of my life with a man who doesn't love me. I might be happier in the convent."

"True, given the circumstances of his own birth and early childhood, Beto might well be suspicious of passion," Maria Josefa said, stirring the tea and handing Sofia a cup. "But your situation is entirely different from his father and mother's. You are both free to marry, and doing so will hurt no one. You are close to the same age. You both appear to be in good health. You are both intelligent, and although your social standings are certainly not ordinary, they are similar enough. From what my daughter Camila tells me, when you disagree, you stand up to each other but with respect. And everyone around you can see you both are enthusiastic about the physical side of marriage.

"Except perhaps for Alfonso and Doña Inmaculada, everyone on the ranch seems to like and admire Beto, despite his temper, which I suspect you are helping to corral. A man his age who does not have his own woman is bound to be snappish."

Maria Josefa undid her long braid and began to comb it. She seemed to be awaiting Sofia's answer as to why she hadn't accepted Beto's proposal.

"I'm not exactly sure what I am waiting for," Sofia said thoughtfully. "Perhaps some indication that he loves me, or even a message from my own heart that I love him."

"From what Camila tells me, everyone on the ranch can

tell that Beto loves you passionately. At the wedding party of Fernando and Isabella, I noticed he danced one quadrille with you and then excused himself to their parents. He may have used the pretext that he needed to rise early the next day to travel to Rancho Valles Caldera, but it was clear that he didn't want to stay and see you dancing with other partners on the one hand or to play his card too soon by monopolizing you on the other."

"But that doesn't mean that he loves me. If he merely desired me, he might not want to see me in the company of other men."

Maria Josefa sighed. "I suspect that you are hiding from your own heart. Would you like me to teach you how to peek around that curtain?"

"Yes. I would be grateful."

"All right," Maria Josefa said gravely. "First you must close your eyes, take three deep breaths and empty your mind of all thoughts."

Sofia complied, although she had some difficulty with the last requirement.

"So, you believe that you are free to choose between two options now that you are with child—the convent and marriage to Beto. Imagine that you elect the convent. Open your mind and tell me how you see your life there. Relax and let yourself really see it. Then tell me."

To her surprise, Sofia saw the scene clearly. Unlike the hazy images that had floated through her mind during her previous musings, it was as if she were standing at her own shoulder.

"I am dressed all in gray," she said, "a gray apron over a gray dress, a gray scarf covering my hair. I am on my knees scrubbing the gray stone floor of a long corridor—for penance. I would have less tedious work if I weren't being punished for my sin."

"Where is your baby?"

"My baby is in a nursery, with other children born out of wedlock, also children who have been abandoned or orphaned. The novice nuns who serve as nursemaids keep the children clean but do not cuddle or play with them."

"And how often do you yourself see this baby?"

Sofia felt her fingers and toes tingle, as if she were in some sort of trance.

"Four times a day. Only for feeding."

"And what of Beto? And Don Emilio?"

Sofia gasped. She felt tears gather in her eyes.

"I see them sitting in Don Emilio's library. They look grief-stricken, as if someone close to them has died. Beto is weeping. Don Emilio is patting Beto's knee and weeping also."

"Come back to me now," Maria Josefa said gently. "Now you know that your heart understands that this baby is not just yours. This baby is also Beto's and, in a way, Don Emilio's. If you retreat to the convent, you will be taking this child from them."

Sofia wiped her eyes with the back of her hand. Maria Josefa refreshed their tea and gave Sofia a gentle look.

"Now, I want you to go back into your heart again."

"No, please!" Sofia pleaded. "That was too painful."

"This will not be painful. I promise."

When Sofia nodded her assent, Maria Josefa said, "Imagine that you and Beto marry. What do you see?"

Sofia closed her eyes again, took a shuddering breath, and straightened her back. The mug of tea felt warm in her hands.

"It's evening and snowing outside, but the room is warmed by a crackling and aromatic piñon fire. I am sitting on a cushioned bench facing the fire, nursing an infant, a baby girl. Beto is standing between us and the fire, his legs apart, his right hand raised to his brow, pretending to search the horizon for something. He turns this way and that. A young boy, perhaps two and a half years old, hides behind his left leg but giggles and stamps his little feet in excitement. Pretending to be surprised, Beto swoops down and lifts the child to his shoulders. The boy squeals with delight and hangs onto Beto's ears as he dances around in the firelight."

"What happens next?"

"Beto sets the child down and hobbles over to me, with the little boy hanging onto his leg. Beaming, Beto sits down and puts his left arm around me. With his right hand, he tousles the child's auburn curls. He kisses the top of my head."

"And how do you feel?"

"Completely contented and..."

"And loved."

"Yes, loved, and cherished." Sofia opened her eyes and smiled. "Then he nuzzles my neck and whispers suggestively that it's time we all went to bed."

Maria Josefa chuckled fondly. "Yes, as a husband, Beto will always be incorrigible in that regard. I recommend that you nurse your babies for the first two years. That will make it less likely that you will get pregnant again immediately."

"Did you put something in my tea to induce a trance?" Sofia asked.

"No, not at all. I just showed you something my mother taught me, a simple path to your own heart. With some practice, you can do it yourself. No one can read the future because it doesn't yet exist. But often our own hearts have a good idea of what will happen if we choose one path or another."

Maria Josefa shook her head back and continued disentangling her waist-length hair. "If you like, I will explain some more obvious ways to tell if you love Beto and if he loves you."

"Please do."

"When a woman loves a man, she exaggerates his good points and diminishes or even makes endearing his flaws. Some people are so favored by nature that anyone would agree that they're beautiful," she continued. "Take Alfonso. Anyone, women but even men, would say that he is uncommonly handsome. Or Fernando, who is not quite so favored but almost and who knows how to make the most of what he has."

She paused. "But Beto? The various parts of his face don't seem to belong together. Some people would even say that his broad nose was ugly and that his legs were too long…"

"But those high cheekbones give his face a proud nobility, and his wide shoulders and narrow hips…"

"You see what I mean," Maria Josefa said. "Now, to look at the matter from a man's point of view, anyone would admit that your sister, Valeria, is beautiful."

Feeling a familiar frown of envy beginning to creep across her forehead, Sofia nodded. Maria Josefa went on. "All the men, from the oldest grandfather to young boys, follow her with their eyes. How does Beto treat her?"

"He is polite and appropriate. He says 'Good morning' or 'Good afternoon.' But he neither stares at her nor looks away flustered."

"And how does he look at you?"

"He always seems to be following me with his eyes, or else he turns away abruptly as if he has to attend to some important task."

"And when you are alone, does he comment on your appearance?"

Sofia sighed. "He praises my hips and my breasts and my mouth."

"And because your eyes are dark brown and deep-set, he now thinks that deep-set brown eyes are the most beautiful."

"But surely he will get over this and take me for granted. I've seen this happen with some of my parents' friends. Once their passion is spent, they have nothing in common."

"This would not be the case with you and Beto. What you two feel for each other may be passion, but it is not madness because, as I pointed out earlier, it has a sound foundation."

After returning to the kitchen for the kettle and the box of chamomile, she said, "I hope you will not think I am being rude, but there are also other ways to assess Beto's feelings for you." She added a pinch of tea to Sofia's mug then filled it with hot water. "When you make love, does he proceed quickly to his own peak of pleasure?"

"Quite the opposite," Sofia said, leaning back against the cushions and sighing softly. "You must understand that I have no previous experience of men in this way, but Beto seems very inventive in finding ways to excite me, even discovering parts of my body that I hadn't known could produce pleasure, like the base of my throat or the backs of my knees. And when he is inside me, he controls himself until after he has brought me to my peak, at least once but often twice."

Maria Josefa leaned forward, gathering her hair in a knot, and said: "And what do you make of this?"

"I suppose this is to further his case for my agreeing to marry him."

"That might be so. But perhaps it is also because he takes joy in your joy—because he loves you. Now, wouldn't you rather have this fine, strong, albeit naïve man give you *this* gift than a bushel full of flowery words or a basket of pretty trinkets?"

Sofia let out a long sigh. "I suppose I have been a fool."

"Not a fool, exactly. Maybe blinded by your city notions of courtship. Though I must admit that few well-brought-up young women from the capital or even from Veracruz would have abandoned themselves quite so thoroughly as you have. Anyone with eyes could see that you are as much in love with Beto as he is with you."

"But you agree that the passion we now feel can't last."

"Oh, it is bound to fade. Otherwise, a couple would never get anything done, including raising children. But if you can hold in your heart and your memory what you are feeling right now, and if you can always speak up when you disagree, so that resentment doesn't form a barrier between you, you will be able to rekindle that spark—even after thirty years and five children, even when the gallant lover of your youth has begun to develop a paunch."

Smiling slyly, Maria Josefa patted Sofia's knee.

They spent the next few minutes quietly sipping tea. Sofia reflected on how fortunate she and Valeria were to have this warm, wise friend, who was like a second mother to them.

Suddenly, they heard the splash of hooves in the street outside, then three raps on the door.

"I wonder who that could be at this hour?" Maria Josefa asked, setting down her mug.

Standing on the doorstep was Beto. The rain had stopped, but water dripped from the front of his hat brim, and he was soaked through. Reaching around Maria Josefa, he drew Sofia to him.

"Thank God you decided to spend the night here." He clasped her to his chest. "I've never been so worried in my life. When I saw the storm building, I had images of you washed away in an arroyo or hit by a boulder on the way home. I couldn't just remain at the ranch and pace around, so I headed up here to Santa Fe, thinking that if you'd come to harm along the road, at least I could help you. I knew you'd come to see Father Antonio, so I stopped there first. He sent me here."

"You're drenched," Sofia said. "We have to get you out of these clothes and into something dry."

"First, I have to take care of my horse. She needs to have this wet saddle off her back and have me rub her down. And feed..."

"We have a stable behind the house," Maria Josefa said matter-of-factly. "It's small, but Carlos is away on maneuvers, so there should be room for your horse between mine and Sofia's. You'll find rags in a burlap sack hanging on the wall just inside the door and some old army saddle blankets, too worn for riding but fine for keeping that noble creature warm. Help yourself to the feed in the bin and to the fresh hay."

Maria Josefa looked Beto up and down appraisingly. "None of Carlos's things will fit you. While Sofia shows you to the stable, I'll find a muslin sheet for you to wrap yourself in. If you hang your clothes near the fire, they should be dry by morning."

Taking Beto by the hand, Sofia led him to the stable. His mare followed obediently. He set the horse in the one vacant stall, put two handfuls of oats in a feedbag, and removed the saddle and the sopping blanket. As he wiped down the mare's flanks, he turned toward Sofia. "Please, please do not frighten me like that again," he said softly.

He set his hat on a peg and came around to face her. Then he steered her toward the back of the stable and set her gently onto a stack of fresh hay bales, where he spread her full brunette hair out like a fan behind her head. Using his teeth, he pulled off his work gloves and began massaging between her thighs. He lifted her legs onto his shoulders so that her knees were next to his ears and entered her.

By his third stroke, she was moaning with pleasure. As he was finishing, she could feel that his cheeks were damp. Were they still wet from the rain, or were those tears of relief?

Then, as he tucked himself into his trousers and brought her eye to eye, he declared earnestly: "This isn't enough for me. I want you in my bed, not on a hay bale. I want to fall asleep with my arms around you and my hands cupping your breasts, with the smell of your hair and the sound of your breathing filling my senses. I want my first sensation every morning to be the touch of your skin. I want to make love to you as the light of dawn washes across your naked body. I want to hear the beautiful music you play on your piano, but mostly I want to hear your voice. I want to watch you nurse our children." Taking a breath, he kissed her deeply. "And I want you to promise to outlive me, so that the last thing I see in this world will be your loving face, and the last thing I feel will be the touch of your hand."

Sofia was almost too stunned to respond, but she

managed a simple yes.

"Yes what?"

"Yes, I love you. Yes, I will marry you. And yes, I am carrying your baby."

Beto embraced her and rocked her gently from side to side, with her head pressed to his chest. She could feel the beating of his heart.

"I love you," he said. "I have wanted you since that time on the caravan when you stood up to me about the lamb. Over the first days after we arrived at the ranch, I began to experience feelings that went well beyond lust. But I was afraid to admit them, even to myself."

"I understand. I felt much the same."

He kept his left arm around her waist as they walked to the front of the house and into the living room. Sofia could hear Maria Josefa upstairs in her bedroom. A muslin sheet lay draped across a bench in front of the dying fire. Removing his boots and clothes, Beto draped his shirt, pants, and socks along the bench and wrapped the sheet around himself like a Roman toga. He sank down onto a rustic wooden armchair, leaned his arms on his knees, and sighed.

"You must be exhausted, my love," Sofia said softly. "We should go to bed."

He glanced up at her and smiled wearily. "I like hearing you say both of those things, not 'exhausted,' but 'my love' and 'we should go to bed.' But probably I should fix myself a place down here."

"The spare room has a *cama matrimonial* that will fit us nicely," Sofia said.

"But wouldn't Maria Josefa object?"

Shrugging, Sofia smiled impishly. "Carlos might, for propriety's sake; but he's not here. As for Maria Josefa, given that I'm pregnant, the Pueblo half of her heart probably considers us married already."

"The Pueblo half of my heart does, too," Beto said and followed her upstairs.

CHAPTER NINETEEN

The road had dried during the night, so Sofia and Beto arrived back at Rancho de las Palomas before noon. He gave her a hand down and then unsaddled their horses, removed their bridles, and fetched them each one of the bruised apples from the stable's bin.

"Let's go tell my father," he said, opening the gate to the paddock so that their horses could graze on the fresh grass. "Perhaps I'm old-fashioned, but I would like to ask his blessing."

As they rounded the corner of the stable, one of the men working on the fence nearby called out: "Hey, Beto, you big stallion, I suspect the rumor my wife told me is true. You are going to be a father."

"He's been working hard enough at it," shouted one of the other ranch hands, pausing from hammering in a post. "Behind the stable, in the refectory, on that grassy bank below the mill pond."

"That grassy bank is indeed a nice spot," the first man

shouted back. "My wife likes it very much. In fact, three of our own were conceived there."

So much for discretion.

Sofia lifted the edge of her *rebozo* in what she hoped was a gesture of modesty but was, in fact, an attempt to conceal a laugh. Beto placed his arm protectively around her shoulder and changed his stride to a slight swagger.

"That filly of his is not bad-looking," the second man said. "Perhaps she will make up for his face, so the baby won't be too ugly."

Beto kept his arm around Sofia as they mounted the stairs to Don Emilio's library. She felt him nuzzling her hair, squeezing her shoulder.

"I am the world's happiest man," he said.

A second after Beto rapped on the door, Sofia heard Emilio call heartily, "Come in. Come in."

The *patrón* was seated at his desk, a quill in hand and a stack of papers in front of him.

"Father," Beto began, "Sofia and I intend to marry, and we hope that you will give us your blessing."

"It's about time." Setting his quill on a little silver tray beside his inkwell, Don Emilio rose to embrace them. "Your behavior was beginning to create a scandal. Two of the boys—I will not say which ones—have seen you making love—one behind the stable and one on that grassy bank below the mill pond. Of course, the boys were curious and asked their fathers afterwards about what they had seen. It is fine for children on a ranch to learn about the facts of life by watching the animals copulate, but not so good to have them do it by watching people do the same."

Sofia could feel herself blushing deeply. *My face must be scarlet.*

Don Emilio gave her a penetrating gaze and said in a mildly scolding tone, "Also, Consuela has reported to Inmaculada that you left class abruptly last Thursday to go outside and vomit. As a man I am mostly ignorant of these women's things, but I do know that such sickness early in the day in an otherwise healthy woman is one of the first signs that a baby is on its way."

Then he smiled broadly. "My first grandchild!" Then, softer, he said, "My Lucinda's grandchild...

"You must see to the banns immediately, my son, so that the marriage can take place next month. This will not be a fancy wedding. My wife would never stand for it. And besides, she and her widowed cousin are cooking up something elaborate—and I fear extravagant—for Alfonso and Valeria."

Sofia was relieved. She had been horrified at the prospect of a lavish celebration, for herself, although she was sure that Valeria would revel in one.

"Something simple and private for Beto and me, with only my sister and perhaps Maria Josefa and her husband as witnesses," she said. "By the way, yesterday I rode to Santa Fe to seek Father Antonio's advice about another matter. He begs your hospitality for tomorrow. He explained that he wanted to deal with Doña Inmaculada's potential charge of witchcraft against Marina. Also, he wanted to counsel Beto and me, together and separately. And he said that he would like the opportunity to beat you at chess."

"Aha! We will see who plays the better game of chess this time. But assuming that after he counsels you, he is satisfied that he can proceed with marrying you, he will be able to post the banns himself when he returns to Santa Fe."

Don Emilio strode back around his desk and sat down. "And now I have a wedding present for you, my son," he said unlocking his desk drawer. "I have decided to make you a gift of Rancho Valles Caldera."

Keeping his own clear gray eyes fixed on Beto's, he pulled out an official-looking document with elaborately scrolled borders and handed it to him. "You will notice that this deed bears a description of the property but neither my signature nor the date. While you two are in Santa Fe having your quiet little wedding in the side chapel at La Parroquia, I will be here at the *hacienda* availing myself of the services

of a notary. By the time you return, the ranch I inherited from
my mother will be yours."

Beto looked stunned.

"But what about my responsibilities here?" he asked.

Don Emilio sighed, the sunlight glinting from the silver
strands lacing his auburn curls. "Think about it. If you and
Sofia were to stay here at Las Palomas, the atmosphere
would become poisonous. As long as you have been single,
you have been able to avoid my wife, with the excuse that
you needed to oversee the tending of the animals and crops,
make sure that the fences and buildings were maintained, that
the mill and the forge were in working order, that the
acequias were free of brush. There is always so much to be
done on a ranch this size, and you have supervised it
admirably. I do not tell you often enough how much I
appreciate all you do."

Don Emilio rose and held his hand out for the deed. "But
now it is time for you to have your own ranch and your own
family. I am confident that you have found the right partner
for this life."

Pulling a white linen handkerchief from his sleeve, Don
Emilio wiped his brow and dabbed briefly at his eyes. "As
much as this gives me joy, it also pains my heart, knowing
that you will be a hard two days' ride away, not here where
we can talk about books or play chess, where I can look into
your eyes and see my own—or look at your glossy black hair
and your proud cheekbones and see your mother's."

As he slid the deed into the desk drawer and turned the
lock, the aging *patrón* took a bit longer than necessary. Sofia
suspected that he was concealing tears.

"Now to practical matters," he said. Apparently
regaining his composure, he looked directly at Beto. "You
visit Valles Caldera every month or so, and you tell me that
Jorge Martinez, the foreman, is doing a fine job."

Beto nodded.

"When you and your bride settle there, he can become
my foreman here, assuming he and his wife are willing. In

the meantime, you can move those new sheep of yours to Valles Caldera, so that they can become accustomed to the higher altitude before winter. As you know, the pasture is an old volcano, so the grass is exceptionally rich."

"But we bought that herd to improve our fleece production here," Beto said.

"And I've noticed that you have let that new ram loose with our regular ewes. I think he's done his job."

Ushering them toward the door, Don Emilio told Sofia sternly, "You must consult with Marina and do whatever she says. Eat and drink what she tells you to consume and avoid what she tells you to avoid. She is not a witch, but she is a wise midwife and healer." His voice softened. "She may not be able to prevent every problem, but she will help you and my grandchild to be strong and healthy."

Enveloping Beto in a hearty embrace, he said, "Bless you, my son, for being so persistent with this stubborn woman."

That night, as she and Valeria prepared for bed, Sofia announced her plans to her sister.

Valeria responded with shock. "I didn't even know that you *liked* each other." Her voice took on a mildly peevish tone. "Will you be wanting a double wedding? Alfonso hasn't proposed officially, but I think it's only a matter of days before he does."

"Don't worry, little sister," Sofia said. "Beto and I are expecting a baby, so our wedding will be small and quiet and will take place as soon as possible. We wouldn't dream of intruding on your special day."

"A baby? How can you be expecting a baby?"

"Sit down here beside me, and I will explain," Sofia said teasingly. "There may be some things about men and women that you don't yet know."

The following morning, Sofia left the teaching to Valeria and sought out Doña Inmaculada, who was seated at a small desk in an alcove off her bedroom, making a list of domestic supplies to be purchased in Santa Fe. Her head was covered with a simple kerchief, but she was wearing a long robe of iridescent green Chinese silk.

"I hope you'll excuse my interrupting," Sofia said. *La patrona* gave her a neutral look.

"Not if it is important."

Sofia explained that Father Antonio planned to arrive that afternoon, to hear her charges of witchcraft against Marina, to examine Marina himself, and to counsel her and Beto to help prepare them for marriage.

"Good," Doña Inmaculada said. "I believe fervently that we must stamp out witchcraft throughout New Spain, so I am pleased that Father is taking this matter seriously."

Sofia struggled to hold her tongue.

"As for you and Beto, your wedding is clearly overdue. We have had enough illegitimate children on this ranch. And I will add that your behavior this past month or more has been scandalous. In fact, if I hadn't recognized that you and Valeria have such different temperaments, your actions might have spoiled her own marital chances."

Although Sofia was confident that this wasn't the case, that Doña Inmaculada would overlook anything short of lewd public behavior on Valeria's own part before she would interfere with Alfonso's marrying a beautiful, well-bred, blond *peninsulara*, she bowed her head slightly and tried not to grind her teeth.

Turning back to her list, Doña Inmaculada said imperiously, "Tell Marina to be ready for Father Antonio to question her thoroughly, and see to it that that daughter of hers and the carpenter's boy are available, as well. I will have someone make up the room next to my husband's library. Father likes to stay there when he visits, so that he and my husband can play chess, and I suspect discuss heretical opinions, far into the night."

Sofia found Marina in the little room beside the weaving workshop, hanging a bunch of medicinal herbs from one of the low beams.

"Welcome, my dear *señora*." The elderly midwife's voice whistled a bit through her few remaining teeth. "We women of the *hacienda* have decided to address you this way out of respect for your condition, even though the wedding won't happen for a few weeks. I must say that everyone is happy for you, and especially for Beto. We all agree that he will make a devoted husband and father. As you may know, I delivered him myself. I have known him all his life."

She pointed a finger at Sofia's abdomen, which was as flat as ever. "I hope that Camila has told you what I said to do and what to avoid, and that you are following my instructions. Also, you must not make the mistake that too many women make and deny your man your embraces now that you are pregnant. This would make him jealous of the baby, and that would be bad for all three of you. You must let him know that you continue to welcome his amorous advances and that you are proud of him for making a baby with you."

"I am grateful for your wisdom and intend to be guided by your advice," Sofia said. "But I have some less pleasant news to bring you."

"And what is that?"

"As you may recall, when you treated Tomás's leg wound, Doña Inmaculada insisted that if the boy recovered fully, it would have to be due to witchcraft."

"That was superstitious rubbish," Marina said hotly.

"Of course it was. But Doña Inmaculada has a position of influence in this region, and she has called on Father Antonio to make a ruling in this matter. He has agreed to come here to question you and examine Tomás. He will be here this afternoon."

Tossing back her head, Marina glared at a point just

below the drying herbs. "I am ready for whatever he may ask."

"Good," Sofia said. "I will tell Tomás and his parents, and also Beto, because he was present for the accident and brought the boy to you for treatment."

As the gates swung open to admit Father Antonio, Sofia noticed for the first time that he rode his chestnut mare like a cavalry officer, rather than a provincial priest. Don Emilio, who was waiting just inside the gate, handed the reins to the stable boy, gave his friend a warm *abrazo,* and led him up the stairs toward the library. Sofia quickly alerted Marina, her daughter and assistant Elena, and Tomás and his parents. Beto was half a flight of stairs ahead of them. Despite the grave purpose of the gathering, Sofia couldn't help but feel a sharp yet sweet pang of desire as she admired the way his narrow hips joined his long legs.

Father Antonio stood to one side of the room, next to a tall bookcase packed with leather-bound volumes that looked to be at least a hundred years old. Doña Inmaculada sat opposite him in a carved wooden armchair. Everyone else stood around the perimeter.

"Doña Inmaculada," he said somberly, "I understand that you intend to bring charges of practicing witchcraft against the midwife Marina."

"You understand correctly, Father."

"Please describe for me, in your own words, the cause of your accusation," the priest said.

"Some weeks ago, the carpenter's boy here slashed himself badly while cutting brush. Apparently he slipped while holding his machete above his head. My husband's son Beto brought him to the refectory and called for Marina to treat him. Her daughter Elena accompanied her and set out and lit two beeswax candles, as though for some sort of occult ceremony. This woman also called for a basin of water, in which she and her daughter washed their hands with lye soap, muttering imprecations over the water. While she sewed up the wound, she chanted all the while in her own language. She continued to chant over the crushed herbs she used in dressing the wound and did not stop until she had finished wrapping it."

"And why do you consider this evidence of witchcraft?"

"I have seen such wounds before, where the flesh is cut so deeply that the bone shows through. The injured limb invariably is lost, which is why I was in favor of calling the garrison surgeon to perform an amputation before the wound festered and endangered the child's life."

Father Antonio turned to Tomás. "Please show me that leg."

Tomás rolled his pants leg to his knee and walked over to the priest, who bent down to examine the scar.

"This is indeed fine work," the priest said, rising. "I see no small cuts or patterns that could relate to Satan or to pagan gods. Can any of you, apart from Marina and Elena, enlighten me as to the purpose of the candles and the chanting?"

"Marina used one of the candles to sterilize the needle before stitching up the wound," Beto said. "Also, they provided light for this delicate task. She and her daughter were chanting over and over in Tiwa the Lord's Prayer and the Hail Mary and another prayer with which I was unfamiliar, but which seemed to call upon San Lucas and other saints devoted to healing."

"And what of the dressing?"

"She ordered the bandages boiled first," Beto said. "Then she wiped the area around the wound using one of the smaller boiled cloths soaked in brandy. She applied simple honey, plus those herbs, and wrapped the wound well."

Father Antonio then asked Marina to come forward and repeat the prayers that she had used. Despite her missing teeth, she chanted them in a clear voice.

"As Beto said, these are familiar Christian prayers, plus one to San Lucas the Physician and another that midwives throughout the Old World and the New have employed for hundreds of years," Father Antonio said.

"But I couldn't understand a word," Doña Inmaculada protested.

"That is because Marina chanted the prayers in Tiwa. God understands our prayers in any language. As your priest, and as hers, I am confident that Marina is no witch."

CHAPTER TWENTY

The premarital counseling with Father Antonio was straightforward. Speaking to her separately, he asked Sofia if her consent had been coerced in any way and if she was entering into the sacrament of marriage of her own free will. He asked her to confirm that she was free to marry and that she was certain that the child she was carrying was Beto's. He told her that if she wanted to back out of the marriage, now was the time to do so.

Whatever the priest went over with Beto, it took no more than ten minutes. For their joint counseling session, Father Antonio focused on each aspect of the marriage vows again. He concluded with a reminder that she and Beto had a responsibility to support their families and display caring and concern, even toward those they might not like. He looked pointedly at Sofia, as if reminding her that she needed to reflect on Alfonso's positive characteristics -- once she identified them.

The following Sunday, Sofia and Beto rode down to Pueblo San Miguel. Although she had met many of the residents during the overnight stop on the way north, Beto explained that his cousins, and especially his two aunts, would expect to be introduced to her as his bride and that they would undoubtedly make a big fuss about her pregnancy and give her all kinds of advice, which she should accept politely, even if she had no intention of following it.

As they rode into the *pueblo*, cheerful shouts greeted them. Even though their visit was unexpected, everyone within earshot seemed to join in the hospitable hubbub.

The chief embraced Beto as he swung down from his horse, then helped Sofia dismount.

"To what do we owe the honor of this visit?" he asked in near-perfect Spanish.

"I have come to introduce you to my bride and the mother of my first child."

Six young men rushed forward, clapping him on the back. Sofia suspected that some of what they shouted in Keres was probably obscene, given how heartily they laughed. The chief's wife stepped up and put an arm around Sofia's waist.

"The men are giving Beto a hard time, which is customary in such circumstances," she said. "They are praising your qualities, although in somewhat lewd terms. Among our people, this is considered the polite way for male friends and relatives to treat a man about to be married, especially if he has already fulfilled his duty of making the bride pregnant."

The chief's wife steered Sofia to a group of women who had been busily preparing the midday meal.

"My daughters and Beto's female relatives will have some questions for you. I will be happy to translate."

A woman who looked to be about sixty, with gray lacing through her long, dark single braid, called out something.

"Ahhh," the chief's wife said. "Beto's older auntie wants to know when the baby is due."

"Around Easter."

"In that case, it is too early for you to show," the chief's wife said. "But we will all pat your belly for good luck."

The women of the *pueblo* clustered around Sofia, chattering and smiling broadly. At least fifteen reached over to give her abdomen three pats, some of them mumbling as they did so.

"These are brief prayers to Mother Mary," the chief's wife said. "Or maybe to the Corn Goddess. Either way, they are wishing your baby a happy journey into this life."

Another older woman called out, holding up two fingers of her left hand.

"Beto's other auntie says it is fortunate our men have brought in two deer, so we will have roast venison for the midday meal. Venison is one of the things you should eat now. It will make your child a fast runner. Taking some honey in chamomile tea every day will make the little one sweet-tempered. And you must avoid wild boar. Eating that meat now would make your baby mean and cranky."

Doing her best to appear attentive, Sofia nodded.

A titter arose from the back of the group.

"That is one of Beto's girl cousins. You must forgive her. She is asking a question that you may not want to answer. She is always making jokes and other mischief."

"And what does she want to know?"

The chief's wife sighed. "She notices that Beto is a big man, with broad shoulders and long legs, and she wants to know if he is similarly big everywhere."

At first Sofia was uncertain what she was being asked. Then the meaning hit her, and she laughed merrily. "Tell her he is big enough to give me pleasure but not so large as to give me pain."

Once the chief's wife had translated Sofia's reply, and the women smiled and nodded their approval of it, she directed them toward the fire pit, where the succulent smell of roasting meat flavored the air.

Within a half hour, the men filed around the side of a

three-story building, Beto and the chief in the lead. They were sipping from mugs and singing some sort of chant. Beto strode over to Sofia, put his arm around her shoulder, and beamed happily.

"They all like you."

"They don't even know me."

"True, but they see that you make me happy, and they like me, so they like you."

The chief insisted that Sofia and Beto be served first and be given the choicest cuts of venison with blackberries and wild greens. They were seated at one of the trestle tables opposite the chief and his wife. Once the plates had been cleared, Beto stood, said something in Keres that Sofia assumed was by way of thanks for the warmth and hospitality, and held out his hand for Sofia to rise. Several of the younger men called out in disappointment. *Probably, they had hoped for an excuse to stay up late and drink more fermented corn.*

When the *hacienda* was in view, Beto turned his horse toward the mountains.

"There's a little stream back this way, where the horses can rest and you and I can enjoy some privacy," he said.

The sun had set by the time they rode into the stable yard at Rancho de las Palomas.

That evening, as Sofia was giving herself a sponge bath in preparation for bed, Valeria burst into their room and announced excitedly, "He proposed. Alfonso proposed. This evening after supper, he led me into the courtyard, knelt next to a rose bush, and asked me to marry him. Formally. Of course, he has asked me before, but not like this!" Valeria paused briefly for a breath. "The wedding will be the last Saturday in October. I hope you will stand beside me, even though you may have to wear one of those loose dresses that's only fitted under the bust. Doña Inmaculada and her widowed cousin will throw ever so grand a party for us after the ceremony."

Slipping on her short nightdress with its pattern of little purple birds, Sofia took her sister's hands and fixed her with a probing gaze.

"Are you absolutely sure you want to do this?" she asked. "Are you certain that you love him despite his flaws?"

"Oh, yes. I have loved Alfonso since the first moment I saw him, that day when you and I arrived at the ranch. He is *so* handsome and *so* polished. And he does adore me."

Those were indeed the only positive points Sofia had been able to come up with when she tried to follow Father Antonio's directive to find and focus on Alfonso's good qualities.

"And you are certain that you won't regret having given up all the fun and attention that would be yours if you remained single for a year or two?"

"It would be unfair to all those poor young men who would pursue me." Valeria sighed. "They wouldn't have a chance, because my heart would always be Alfonso's."

Sofia wasn't sure whether the sudden wave of nausea she felt was because of the baby or because of Valeria's bubbly expressions of devotion for a man who clearly didn't deserve her.

"See?" Valeria said as she plopped down on Sofia's bed and extended her left hand. "See the beautiful ring he gave me when I accepted?"

The ring was indeed lovely, a fine oval ruby flanked by two perfect pearls.

"I guess Beto didn't give you anything."

"Only his child."

CHAPTER TWENTY-ONE

Sofia and Beto married in the side chapel of La Parroquia at one in the afternoon on the day after the third posting of the banns. Having returned from maneuvers, Carlos donned his full-dress uniform and performed the fatherly duty of giving Sofia away. He and Maria Josefa served as official witnesses. As a minor, Valeria couldn't sign the documents, but she busied herself fussing with Sofia's hair and arranging her bright fiesta *rebozo* to drape just so over her ruffled white blouse and a white skirt just short enough to show off a few inches of her cutwork-trimmed petticoat. Beto wore a loose cotton shirt and deerskin trousers. His boots were polished. He beamed. Father Antonio made quick work of the ceremony, smiling throughout.

On their way out of town, they stopped at the Steiners' workshop. Just as Samuel Steiner was the best tailor in Santa Fe, his wife Rebecca was the top dressmaker. After warm congratulations to Beto, Señor Steiner went to fetch wine for a toast. Señora Steiner invited Valeria to sit next to her at the long trestle table, which was strewn with swatches of fabric, samples of trimmings and sketches of gowns.

"I suspect that you will want to go over the designs and materials with *la patrona*," she said with an understanding smile. "But let's pick out three or four that you really like, so that she won't be overwhelmed with choices."

After distributing goblets of hearty red wine and raising his own to the bridal couple's long and happy life together, Señor Steiner ushered Beto toward the back garden, saying jovially, "These matters can take quite a while and become numbingly tedious, at least for us men. Please, bring me up to date on the ranch. How is Don Emilio? He must be delighted that you are going to be a father."

Wondering how that news had traveled so fast, Sofia turned to the table, where Valeria held aloft a sketch of a regal-looking gown with a long train.

"What do you think, Sofia?" she asked.

The voluminous ensemble looked both ostentatious and unflattering.

Apparently noticing the expression on Sofia's face, Señora Steiner said tactfully, "You are so slender and beautiful, my dear. Why don't we consider some simple designs that will show off your natural charms? We can add some elegance by using a lovely lace and perhaps even some seed pearls."

Half an hour later, Valeria had selected three suitable designs and a dozen swatches of silk, tulle, and lace—nine for her wedding gown, three for her veil. She promised to return in a week with whichever options Inmaculada approved.

"That's when Señora Steiner will take my measurements," Valeria said excitedly as they mounted their horses. "Of course, Doña Inmaculada may also want something special for herself and for Consuela and Emilia, who'll be my attendants, along with you, naturally.

"Do you think you'll still be able to fit into your blue silk *robe à l'anglaise*?"

"In seven weeks? I think so," Sofia replied distractedly.

Could Valeria really be in love with Alfonso, and could he really be in love with her? When Alfonso told her and his father that he and Valeria fancied each other, that declaration had made a certain sense. Valeria went giddy over every handsome young man who crossed her path. And as Maria Josefa had pointed out, she turned the heads of men and boys of every age. Ever since childhood, her younger sister's beauty had prompted a mixture of envy and jealousy in Sofia—envy that Valeria had received this entirely unearned gift from birth and jealousy at the attention it drew.

And yet, Sofia now realized that such extraordinary beauty might be something of a burden. People praised her own musical talents. Sister Hortencia at the convent school in Veracruz even suggested that she might try composing a few piano pieces herself. In Sofia's estimation, Valeria possessed equal ability as an artist, but she seldom received more than passing praise for her paintings and sketches. No one said, "Your drawings of flowers and plants are so fine that they deserve to be published in a book of botanical prints," even though they were. Everyone was too blinded by Valeria's own beauty to see the beauty of her work.

Being noticed and appreciated only for what's on the surface must be lonely. Maybe Valeria and Alfonso recognize that loneliness in each other. Maybe they understand the isolation imposed by remarkable beauty and, building on this understanding, can bridge that gap.

Sofia herself was reasonably pleased with her own body, although she worried occasionally that age and childbearing might take their toll on her figure. Her face was another matter—not plain, but not pretty. As Maria Josefa had discerned, Beto seemed to find her overly deep-set eyes and her overly long nose endearing, just as she delighted in his prominent cheekbones and those long legs that gave him several inches of height over his already tall father and brother. Objectively, she and Beto were well matched in appearance, and that had allowed them to delve deeper into each other's minds and hearts—and to love what they found there.

And what would her sister and her fiancé discover if they explored similarly? *Alfonso would find a young woman with a nimble brain, a vivacious spirit, and a kind heart. And Valeria would find—what?* Here Sofia shuddered inwardly. Her sister would find a man who relished her beauty and her breeding and the esteem these would bring him when she became his wife. A man who adored her adoration of him. A man who was contemptuous toward those he considered beneath him. A man who could betray his family. And, yes, a man who was cruel to his horse.

Clearly, though, Valeria was deriving so much pleasure from Alfonso's courtship and their impending wedding that Sofia couldn't imagine what she could say to make her break off the engagement. Even if she were to disclose Alfonso's embezzlement from his family, which she couldn't do for fear of embarrassing Don Emilio, Valeria would probably explain it away as a past mistake, the sort of behavior that marriage to her would prevent in the future.

Sofia sighed. *I can't control my sister or even steer her away from potential grief and toward happiness. The only happiness I can influence is my own, and Beto's, and our children's.*

Riding beside this man who was now her husband, in the eyes of the Church and the Crown, as well as in her heart, Sofia let go of her protective anxiety about Valeria and replaced it with sisterly love. Her previous envy and jealousy dissolved. Valeria was of legal age to marry, and she had made her choice. *Perhaps Valeria feels as certain in her choice as I do in mine.*

Sofia felt a warm glow of contentment as she imagined the years stretching out before her and Beto, beginning with this night. Lilia, the stable master's wife, had whispered that she was transforming Beto's childhood room into a bridal bower.

"There won't be space for much besides the

matrimonial bed," she had said. "But that is all you should need."

As the three of them cantered south along the road, Sofia noticed dark clouds above the mountains to the east but thought little of them. It was late September, after all, past the time of regular afternoon thunderstorms.

But as they came to the wooden bridge over the arroyo just a few hundred yards from the *hacienda*, Beto gave a cry of alarm and pointed left. Water was backing up in the narrow draw. Brush and other debris had turned the bridge's crisscrossed support timbers into a dam, a dam that wouldn't hold much longer.

Although it hadn't rained at the ranch in weeks, clearly it had been raining in the mountains.

Raising his voice over the sound of the rushing torrent, Beto shouted, "Ride to the *hacienda* for help. If we don't clear this arroyo, the bridge will wash out within an hour. I'll need at least eight strong men. Tell them to bring their *machetes* and plenty of rope!"

Sofia watched as he flung his mare's reins over a squat juniper, scrambled the hundred feet down the steep slope, and began clearing the logjam with his hands. With Valeria by her side, she nudged her brown gelding into a full gallop.

Rounding the first bend, they almost collided with Alfonso, furiously spurring and whipping his white stallion.

Good. Somehow he's learned about the bridge and has come to help. How odd, though, that he didn't seem to notice Valeria.

Then Sofia heard him roar, "You half-breed son-of-a-whore! I'll see you dead before I see you own a square inch of Chavez land!"

Realizing that Don Emilio must have shown Alfonso the notarized deed to Rancho Valles Caldera, Sofia responded instinctively. Wheeling her own horse around, she gestured for Valeria to continue toward the *hacienda*, but with a shake of her blond curls, she joined Sofia in her dash back to the bridge.

As they crossed the now-trembling structure, Sofia looked to the right. The white stallion was halfway down the steep side of the arroyo, stumbling and sliding toward Beto, who stood bent over a snarl of debris blocking the rushing stream. The horse's eyes bulged. Rivulets of blood ran down his flanks. On his back sat Alfonso, his face twisted in fury, a pistol held high in his right hand. He was shouting. Although she couldn't make out the words, the tone was clear. It was murderous.

Sofia watched in horror as Beto turned toward the sound. From not ten yards away, Alfonso cocked the pistol, took aim, and fired. At the sharp sound, the stallion reared and let out a terrified neigh, his hooves pawing the air.

Everything seemed to slow as Beto cried out and fell back against the bridge timbers, and Alfonso tumbled off the stallion's back and onto the rocks. Valeria's scream echoed up and down the arroyo, almost drowning out the roar of the water.

"Get control of yourself!" Sofia shouted. "Ride to the *hacienda* fast! Send men to clear the bridge, and have them bring four long poles and some blankets. We'll need at least one stretcher, maybe two."

Valeria straightened her shoulders, turned the dappled gray filly toward the *hacienda,* and took off at a gallop.

Sofia slid down the bank, sending rocks and gravel ahead of her. To her relief, Beto was standing, his right hand cupping his left elbow, blood dripping from the flesh above and soaking the sleeve of his wedding shirt. He was wincing, but he didn't seem seriously injured.

"Don't worry," he said as she reached his side. "The ball went straight through the muscle. See? I can still move my left hand." He demonstrated, then added, amazement tinging his voice. "He was aiming for my heart. I never realized that he hated me quite that much."

As Sofia tore strips from her bottom petticoat, Beto cautioned: "A tourniquet could do more harm than good. I don't think he hit an artery, so a tight bandage should do the job for now, a tight bandage and a sling."

Fastening the sling around Beto's wounded arm, Sofia looked directly into his gray eyes, clouded somewhat with pain but still warm.

"I also never realized how much I love you," he said.

"Do you think you can ride?" Sofia asked.

"If we canter, but not if we trot or gallop. But first, I need to get back to clearing that brush pile. I still have one good arm."

"But, you're hurt!"

"Not as badly as Alfonso. Go see if he's still alive—and if there's anything you can do for him."

Sofia stopped briefly to rinse her bloody hands in the stream and wiped them on her skirt, leaving bright red streaks. Alfonso was lying on his back. His eyes were closed, and blood trickled from his ears; but his chest lifted and fell. His legs and arms twitched. He seemed to be mumbling.

Not eight feet away, the water swirled. It was rising.

Bending down toward him, Sofia heard him ask clearly, "Did I kill the bastard?"

"No."

He opened his eyes, eyes the same gray as Beto's but ablaze with loathing. As they focused, his face contorted with rage, and he flung his right hand toward something just beyond reach.

His gun!

Horrified, Sofia rose and kicked it into the brush.

"Stop moving," she said. Part of her wanted to seize a nearby rock and bash his head in, but her rational side won over as she recognized that Alfonso was no longer a threat to the man she loved.

Sofia glanced up at the edge of the arroyo. The white stallion stood there, stock still, his flanks and withers stained with blood.

Somehow, she knew it was urgent that Alfonso stay still and that she refrain from trying to haul him away from the rising water. Then she remembered. Mateo had mentioned describing a similar injury to his medical students in Veracruz. A man out riding with friends had been thrown from his horse, hitting his head on a rock as he landed on his back. Initially, the man had suffered only from a concussion and two cracked vertebrae high in his neck, but when his well-meaning companions lifted him out of the roadway, the damaged vertebrae had snapped, severing his spinal cord and stopping his heart.

"If you ever encounter an accident like that, keep the victim absolutely still and support his head, neck and back in a straight line before you allow anyone to move him," Mateo had told her.

Sofia knelt down next to Alfonso. Although he had tried to kill the man she loved beyond all else in the world, she felt a twinge of compassion. "Stay absolutely still," she said. "Valeria has gone for help."

Looking to her right, she noticed that the edge of the stream had receded somewhat and that the water was rushing straight down the arroyo, rather than swirling. She turned to see Beto using his good arm to haul a young aspen, perhaps seven feet tall, onto the rocky bank.

Sofia ran toward him. "Stop and sit down," she said. "You've cleared enough that the water has a narrow path under the bridge. The rest can wait until your men get here."

Beto nodded wearily. "What about Alfonso?"

"He's alive, and he can move his hands and feet. He's bleeding from both ears, but he was able to talk."

"What did he say?"

"He asked if he'd killed you."

Beto sank down onto a large flat rock and ran his right hand through his glossy black hair.

Suddenly, Valeria appeared above them, scrambling down the slope.

"Alfonso!"

Sofia hurried to join her sister beside her fallen fiancé, who now lay still except for his ragged breathing.

"Don't move him," Sofia said. "You could kill him if you do."

Kneeling beside Alfonso, Valeria stroked his forehead tenderly and caressed his auburn curls. Then she looked at her hands—and screamed. They were covered with his blood. She wiped them frantically on her skirt.

Everything was white and red. The white stallion with his red-streaked flanks. Beto's wedding shirt and sling. Sofia's own cutwork petticoat. Valeria's blouse and skirt. And somehow Valeria's innocent adoration of her handsome scoundrel. *And my wedding day. All of it stained with blood.*

Hoof beats clattered on the bridge. Several men shouted. Beto stood.

"Thank God you're here!" he yelled. "Tie up your horses, then get down here. Three of you get in the stream with your *machetes* and begin chopping up the larger branches. Two of you use ropes to haul the brush up the bank. And two of you take those poles and blankets and help get Alfonso onto a stretcher and out of here."

"Señor Beto," one of the younger ranch hands shouted from the top of the slope, "we heard what happened, that Señor Alfonso's horse tried to kill him. Do you want me to put that animal down for you?"

"That white stallion saved my life," Beto bellowed, clambering up the steep grade.

After patting the horse gently and speaking soothingly into his ear, he said, "Take him back to the *hacienda* and tell the stable master to treat his wounds."

"But, Señor Beto, surely this horse is ruined."

"He may be ruined as a riding horse, but he can still fuck. And he throws good foals. We'll give him a few days in the paddock to heal, then turn him loose in the pasture with the mares and let him enjoy himself."

Relieved that only one stretcher would be needed, Sofia explained to the two sturdy men who carried poles and blankets down to Alfonso why he should be moved as little as possible. Directing them to slide the longer blankets under him carefully and bundle the shorter ones up to support his head and neck, she had the men roll the long edges around the poles, lash them, then roll up two more blankets, one at Alfonso's head and one at his feet.

Valeria stood by looking helpless. Sofia realized that if she didn't give her sister something useful to do, Valeria would dissolve into hysterics.

"Don't take him straight up the slope," Sofia said. "You'll have to zigzag to keep him as level as possible. Valeria, find the gentlest way and lead them up."

By the time the men carrying Alfonso reached the top, the brush was cleared and the stream flowed smoothly, although it was still high.

As Beto had assured her, he sat the paint mare securely as they cantered the short distance to the *hacienda*. Marina and her daughter were waiting in the refectory. So were Don Emilio, Inmaculada, and their five younger children.

Inmaculada's face was a stone mask. "Where is my son?" she asked.

"The men are bringing him on foot," Sofia said evenly. "He has a serious injury to his head, and possibly his spine, so they couldn't risk carrying him on horseback."

Inmaculada nodded and pointed accusingly at Marina. "I will not allow that witch anywhere near my son."

Don Emilio grabbed his wife by the arm and spun her around. "You will allow this expert healer to give our son the benefit of her skills!"

Turning to Marina, he said, "While we wait for Alfonso, please tend to my son Beto. I understand he has a bullet wound."

"Of course, *patron*."

Beto drew in a quick breath as the midwife removed

Sofia's improvised bandage.

Nodding toward Sofia, Marina said approvingly, "This is good, that it stuck a little. It means that the blood is clotting well. Elena, go boil some muslin for bandages."

"You might as well use this," Sofia announced, stepping out of what remained of her bottom petticoat and handing it to Elena.

Marina held up a candle and examined Beto's left arm, front and back.

"I will need to take a few stitches—one here in front, two in back."

Just then, Valeria ran through the refectory door, the two ranch hands bearing Alfonso a couple of yards behind her.

She must have walked beside him, rather than riding. Good. She will have seen to it that the stretcher stayed level and that nothing jostled him. He was still breathing.

At the sight of her oldest son, Inmaculada let out an anguished wail. As the men gently lowered the stretcher to the refectory table to the left of the door, she spun on her husband furiously.

"If it hadn't been for your stupid idea of giving your bastard Rancho Valles Caldera, this never would have happened."

To Sofia's surprise, rather than shouting back in anger, Don Emilio reached out and drew his sobbing wife to his chest.

"No, my dear Inmaculada," he said almost tenderly. "If the gift of my mother's ranch hadn't set him off, something else would have."

For the next half hour, Marina focused her attention on Alfonso, mopping his brow, cutting open his shirt to help him breathe more easily, and using a blanket to cover his legs, which twitched occasionally. She and Elena prayed continuously—in Spanish. Valeria stood by his side, stroking his hand and murmuring softly. Alfonso never opened his eyes.

At nine o'clock that evening, Alfonso Chavez gave

three shuddering breaths and died.

As Marina looked up and made the sign of the cross, everyone in the room did the same. Don Emilio cradled Inmaculada in his embrace, rocking her gently. Juan gathered his siblings in his gangly fifteen-year-old arms and drew them toward his parents.

"You will need to learn some new responsibilities," Don Emilio told him. "But our discussion of that can wait a few days."

Valeria sobbed softly. Reaching for Sofia's hand, she whispered, "His last words were that he loved me."

"Should you go to your father?" Sofia asked Beto.

"No. Right now, my father needs to be with his wife and their children, not dealing with the conflict my presence would introduce. One of his sons tried to kill the other and died in the attempt. I think he is glad that I'm the one who survived, but he will still grieve for Alfonso."

Shaking his head slowly, Beto sighed. "Help me refasten this sling. Go comfort your sister. Let her direct the women who will wash Alfonso's body and pray over him tonight. Inmaculada is in no condition to do that. But don't let Valeria stay. She's too exhausted. Get Marina to give her something to make her sleep. Then take her to your room and sit with her and hold her. Don't say anything against Alfonso, not tonight. She saw what he was with her own eyes. Beyond that, let her hang onto her memories of her first love for a little longer, even if it was mostly an illusion."

Reaching out with his right arm, Beto drew Sofia to him.

"Our love is not an illusion. As soon as Valeria is sound asleep, join me in our room at the stable master's."

"Are you sure that's appropriate?"

"Alfonso attempted to deprive me of my life today. He will not deprive me of my wedding night."

An hour later, Valeria was snoring. She had become groggy so quickly that Sofia had to help her into her nightdress and use a damp cloth to wash Alfonso's blood from her face and hands.

Making her way to the little room at the back of the stable master's, Sofia found Beto naked except for his bandage and sling. He lay on his right side, his head propped in his right hand. The new bed did indeed consume most of the available space. The covers were folded back neatly. White and pink rose petals dusted the fine linen sheets. On a tiny table on what was apparently intended as Sofia's side of the bed was a plate of sugar cookies, creamy white with buttery brown edges.

"As you can see, despite this tragic afternoon, Lilia took care to make tonight memorable for us," Beto said as Sofia removed her bloodstained clothes and muddy boots. "Here in *El Norte*, these simple cookies are the traditional nuptial confection, not that heavy rum-soaked fruitcake that was served at Fernando's wedding. You are supposed to pick up the top one and take a bite, then pass it to me to finish. This allegedly ensures that we will have a sweet life together."

Sofia noticed that he winced as he took the cookie from her hand.

"Did Marina give you anything for the pain?"

Beto nodded toward the little table on his side of the bed, where an amber vial sat next to a cup of water.

"She did, but right now I don't want my senses dulled in any way. I'll have some later if I can't sleep."

Sofia stretched out with her back to him, aware of how nicely the perfume of the rose petals blended with the scent of wild sage.

"When Marina advised you about your pregnancy, did she say that you could allow me to do this?" Beto asked, nuzzling her playfully. "Or this? Or this?"

To spare his wounded arm, Sofia reached down between her legs and guided him inside her from behind.

"She told me that I should continue to welcome your amorous advances."

"Hmph," he said, obviously acting on the information.

"And she said that I should let you know that I am proud of you for making a baby with me."

"Marina is indeed a wise woman," he said and set about nibbling the back of Sofia's neck as she moaned with pleasure.

CHAPTER TWENTY-TWO

Sofia stretched as she awoke for the second time. She and Beto had made love again shortly before dawn. Then, as the morning wake-up bell tolled, he had clambered out of their wedding bed and dressed, leaving her to fall back into soothing sleep.

But now she recognized that she needed to check on Valeria. She hoped that her sister would still be unconscious, or at least that Camila would have come in to comfort her.

As Sofia dressed and made her way through the stable master's modest living quarters, she heard voices and the impatient pawing of hooves. Don Emilio was speaking to Juan, who was sitting astride his restless horse, holding a small burlap bag that jingled faintly.

"Go first to Father Antonio," the *patrón* was saying. "Explain what has happened and ask him to conduct a full funeral Mass for Alfonso in three days at La Parroquia. This is what your mother wants, and if it will give her more comfort than a simple burial service here, then it is what I want as well. Make it eleven o'clock, to give everyone a chance to get there. Afterwards, we will bring Alfonso back to the family graveyard at the ranch, so that he can rest with his ancestors. Apologize to Father for the short notice. Your mother insists on three days, because Mary and the Apostles kept their wake for three days between Christ's death and the Resurrection. You know how devout she is. But this is also practical, given that the afternoons are still warm. Waiting much longer would be, um, undignified."

"I understand, Father," Juan said somberly.

"Next, go to the coffin-maker's. Select a design that your mother will find suitable, something elegant but simple—a fine hardwood with brass handles but not a lot of other ornamentation, silk lining, gray, but if they don't have that, then white. Remind whoever will be doing the work that Alfonso was over six feet tall. It would be ghastly to have to break his legs to fit him into the coffin. And tell the coffin-maker you will be by with the wagon to pick it up day after tomorrow, in the morning.

"Finally, make a brief call on your mother's widowed cousin. She deserves to hear the news first-hand, rather than from the inevitable gossip. And she will want to prepare herself to receive the family and console your mother."

"Yes, Father."

As Don Emilio patted his son's long leg, Sofia wondered if the gangly boy might wind up as tall as Beto.

After watching Juan ride off, Don Emilio turned toward Sofia, who had just reached the stable gate.

"I would appreciate your advice on something, my dear daughter," he said.

Sofia brightened at the affectionate words. "Of course, Father."

"I am of two minds about Juan now that he will become the one to help me with the ranch's business affairs. Should I send him to university in Mexico City next year, or should I keep him here and educate him myself?"

Sofia thought for a moment before responding. "I think

he would have a better chance of developing into an authentic gentleman and an honorable businessman if you were to oversee his learning yourself, Father. Consider how well you did with Beto."

"True, but Juan is not as gifted intellectually as Beto."

"As his teacher, I have discovered him to be quite intelligent, especially when he finds the subject interesting. You might also consider exploring whether Hector Gutiérrez or one of Santa Fe's other successful merchants might take him on as an apprentice for a year or two."

"That is an excellent idea, my dear. That way, he could learn about business from more than one side."

Putting his right arm around her shoulders, Don Emilio gave her a fond hug.

"Your main challenge will be keeping Juan from joining the army," Sofia added. "He's fascinated by military history and tactics. He's always wanting to re-enact this or that battle."

"True enough," Don Emilio said, then changed the subject. "I will miss both your music and your wisdom when you and Beto are settled at Rancho Valles Caldera."

Pausing, he turned her to face him and took her hands gently in his.

"As you can imagine," he said, "I was up most of the night, doing my best to comfort my wife and children and also to receive comfort from them. And in the course of those hours, I came to recognize something. May I confide it to you?"

"Of course, Father."

"My fatal error lay not in giving my mother's ranch to Beto," he said softly. "It lay, and has always laid, in my loving Beto more than I loved Alfonso. From the moment Beto was born, both their lives were poisoned by Alfonso's jealousy."

"But you couldn't help loving Beto more."

Don Emilio squeezed her hands gently. "No, I couldn't."

Finding her old room empty, Sofia heard the repetitious intonations of the rosary issuing from the chapel. As she entered, she caught the overwhelming aroma of Alfonso's citrus and spice cologne and saw Valeria kneeling in the first pew, to the right of Inmaculada. To *la patrona*'s left sat her children Consuela, Diego, Emilia and Sebastian, all in black. Sebastian and Diego were squirming. In front of them, Alfonso lay in state on the altar, atop a white linen sheet. A gray silk cushion supported his head and set off his still-lustrous auburn curls. He was dressed in the suit he had worn to Fernando and Isabella's wedding—*perhaps, the suit he had planned to wear to his own.*

Valeria wore a black woolen *rebozo* over her head and shoulders, making her almost indistinguishable from the other women in the chapel. Only her slim build and erect posture gave her away. Sofia slipped into the pew, squeezed her sister's hand, and remained for ten Hail Marys and an Our Father. Then, raising her forefinger to her lips to caution silence, she took Valeria gently by the arm and led her outside.

"Shall we sit for a few minutes and talk?" Sofia asked.

Valeria nodded, and they proceeded through the refectory, Camila's room, and their own and out to the courtyard, where garnet-hued rose bushes still bloomed and scented the air.

"This is where Alfonso proposed to me," Valeria said.

"I'm sorry. I should have thought of that. Would you rather go somewhere else?"

"No. This is fine."

Valeria appeared to be done sobbing, at least for the present. Her blue eyes were clear, although the lids were still puffy.

"Doña Inmaculada told me that the funeral Mass will be in three days, at La Parroquia. Then they'll bring Alfonso back here for burial."

"Yes," Sofia said, patting her sister's hand. "I heard that from Don Emilio."

"We should unpack our black dresses. They're still at the bottoms of our trunks. I can't believe how ugly they are, and that high neck makes me feel like I'm strangling."

She gave Sofia a sidelong look. They both tittered and dissolved into hysterical giggles.

Wiping her eyes, Valeria asked, "I wonder what brought that on?"

"I think we needed the release."

"You know," Valeria said thoughtfully. "I think the children do, too. Is there some way we can get Inmaculada to let them get out of that chapel for a while?"

Sofia reflected for a moment.

"Why don't you tell her that I've offered to give a little concert of sacred music and that I would like Emilia to join me in the easy pieces? All the children can help by singing some of the familiar hymns. And we'll be in the refectory, so we can ask the cook and Jimena to prepare some simple pastries and fruit and cheese, and perhaps smoked sausage. No one has had a proper meal since yesterday."

"Maybe afterwards, Don Emilio could tell some stories about his family," Valeria said. "And Inmaculada could tell some about hers—assuming she's willing, that is."

Inmaculada approved the plan, although she elected to remain at prayer rather than joining in the hymns or recounting her family history. Valeria reported that she did, however, accept a small plate of bread, cheese, and grapes, "to keep up her strength."

The next two days passed uneventfully. Beto spent them supervising work around the ranch, even trying to pitch in until one of the ranch hands told him good-naturedly, "Go sit on your horse and tell us what you want done. With that wounded wing, you just get in the way."

Sofia visited the chapel for morning prayers and again in the early evening, and she urged Valeria to get Doña Inmaculada to leave her dead son's side at least twice a day to take meals with her surviving children. Don Emilio seldom emerged from his study. Sofia took to bringing him his meals there, then sitting quietly until he finished. On some occasions, he wanted to talk. On others, he didn't. Sofia thought she saw new strands of gray lacing his hair, but perhaps that was just the light. In the evenings, Beto and his father would play chess.

Lessons had been suspended until after the funeral, but Sofia made it a point to spend her mornings in the refectory. She would play the piano and work on lesson plans or simply read. The important thing was to be available to Alfonso's siblings in case they wanted to talk or simply have some adult attention that would be focused on them and not on their dead brother. The ranch hands' children busied themselves helping their parents with seasonal work, like bringing in the hay and harvesting apples, and such domestic projects as patching the roofs of their own houses.

Each afternoon after *siesta*, Emilia appeared at the refectory, asking to be taught a piano piece. The first day, she requested something sad. The second, she asked for something cheerful.

To Sofia's surprise, Consuela showed up the second morning, carrying a Bible and a book of devotions.

"I want to find some things that might give my mother comfort," she said. "Maybe something about Mary's life after Jesus was resurrected. And maybe a psalm or two. Mother's constant repetitions of the rosary and the Stations of the Cross are driving us all mad.

"Besides, Alfonso was not Jesus."

Giving her a hug, Sofia said, "What a thoughtful idea."

They spent the next two hours picking out appropriate pieces. Then Sofia coached her charge as she practiced reading them aloud.

Sofia also arranged to spend several hours a day with Valeria, taking her *siestas* in their old room and contriving to curry and brush her own horse at the same time her sister groomed hers. On the second morning, Sofia managed to persuade Valeria to go for a ride. The day was pleasantly mild. In the mountain draws to the east, the aspens had turned bright yellow.

Returning from a refreshing canter along the river, they found themselves at the mill pond. Yellow daisies, orange milkweed, and red lilies crowded the edge of the water. Small bright blue morning glories twined among them. To Sofia it looked as if nature were putting on a final spectacle of color.

"Could we stop here a minute?" Valeria asked. "The horses could use a drink, and I…well, I have something I'd like to tell you, where we can't be overheard."

They settled onto a flat rock while the dappled gray filly and the brown gelding slurped noisily.

"Everyone seems to accept that Alfonso was trying to kill Beto," Valeria said, "even Doña Inmaculada. I've heard her say that she wants his white stallion put down, but that's just because she craves revenge. If she can't blame a person for Alfonso's death, then she can blame that poor, abused animal."

Sofia was surprised that her sister had gained that much insight, including admitting that Alfonso had abused his horse.

"Beto wouldn't allow that, of course," Sofia said. "Neither would Don Emilio."

Valeria nodded. "I know that. I heard Don Emilio tell her that the stallion was valuable and that he wouldn't hear of his being harmed. He wasn't shouting. He's been very gentle with her since…but he was firm."

Now it was Sofia's turn to nod. She'd heard Beto use the same tone of voice, including to her and Valeria.

"What I really wanted you to know, my dear sister," Valeria said softly, "is that I recognized some time ago that Alfonso was not a good man. But you see, I thought that I could make him good."

Sofia smiled ruefully. "None of us has the power to make anyone else good—or for that matter, bad. The most we can do is to help bring out the good that is already there."

"Do you think he loved me?"

"I think he loved you as much as he could love anyone—besides himself."

With that, they remounted and trotted back to the stable.

When they arrived, Sofia noticed the white stallion in the paddock. His fresh wounds stood out in angry red gashes across his flanks and withers, but what shocked her more were the old scars, which formed nets of cord even whiter than his coat. Don Emilio's ten-year-old son Diego stood with his hand outstretched, offering the horse an apple. Crouched down beside the boy, Beto patted the stallion's neck, as if by way of demonstration.

As Beto rose and led his young half-brother back toward the stable, Sofia heard Diego ask, "Can I ride him some day?"

"Maybe yes, maybe no. As a result of being abused, some animals fear all humans. Others understand that only a single person was cruel to them. Eventually, they may come to trust others. Time will tell which category the white stallion falls into. Maybe if you keep being a friend to him—feeding him apples, patting and brushing him, speaking softly in his ear—in a few months he will let you on his back.

"But never, ever, approach him wearing spurs."

The two days moved so slowly that they seemed like a week. Sofia's morning sickness had subsided, and true to Maria Josefa's prediction, she felt better than ever. Her breasts had swelled noticeably, a development that seemed to delight Beto, who took to caressing them even more often than before.

After their wedding night, when Beto had taken six drops of the tincture of opium to help him sleep, the level in the amber bottle at his bedside remained constant. Sometimes he would roll his head and shoulders around, as if to relieve a crick in his neck caused by the weight of his arm in the sling, but he showed few other signs of discomfort.

Following Marina's directions, Sofia changed his bandage every morning, using a strip of boiled muslin lathered with honey and the midwife's healing herbal paste. Each day, the wounds on either side of Beto's arm got smaller.

He continued his daily practice of splashing himself with sage-infused water after shaving.

Rather than abating, as Sofia had feared it might during those somber days, Beto's ardor seemed to increase. Perhaps, she decided, he was experiencing something like soldiers felt when they survived a battle uninjured or with only minor wounds. She had heard that such men could become sexually voracious, so much so that brothel-keepers in nearby towns resorted to calling for reinforcements.

When she and Beto went to bed at night, Sofia would sit astride him to avoid any pressure on his wounded arm, which he removed from the sling when he undressed. After the morning bell woke them, they might be more playful and inventive in their lovemaking. What surprised Sofia was what happened several hours after they'd fallen asleep. They had taken to sleeping on their right sides, with Beto closer to the wall. He would rest his chin atop her head and encircle her with his long legs and arms, and she would feel so warm and secure that she would drift off immediately. Sometime around midnight or even later, she would float back into consciousness, buoyed by the sensations of his left hand stroking her breasts and belly and exploring gently between her thighs.

Although he would be hard, his regular breathing told her that he was asleep. By then, she would be reliably wet and would guide him inside her from behind. He would mumble as they both moved in their now-familiar rhythm. Sometimes her cry of pleasure would wake him. Sometimes it wouldn't.

On the second afternoon following Alfonso's death, the clatter of a wagon all but drowned out the Haydn sonata Sofia was playing. Rising, she strode to the refectory door and looked across the stable yard. Juan had pulled up in front of the chapel and had jumped into the wagon bed. He was untying the ropes securing a long rectangular object covered with a tarp. Don Emilio was hurrying down the stairs from his library.

"This must be Alfonso's coffin," he said. "Let me see it before you show it to your mother. I want to be the one to present it to her. That way, if she doesn't like it, she'll be angry at me, not at you. There is no way to predict her moods these days."

Resting her hand on her belly, where she thought she could detect the very slightest swell, Sofia experienced a stab of empathy. It was unlike anything she had felt toward Inmaculada before. *Children are supposed to outlive their parents, not the other way around. Of course, children frequently die of disease, but at least then there's warning, some time to prepare one's heart for the grief to come. Daughters die giving birth to grandchildren, but everyone knows that childbirth can be perilous. And during times of war, young men often die in battle, but at least parents know when they send them off that they might not return. But to have a son, a son so handsome, so clearly healthy and vital, die without warning at twenty-five years of age and just entering his prime? That pain is unimaginable.*

And then Sofia thought about Don Emilio. *What must he be feeling after having one son try to murder the other, only to die in the attempt?*

When Juan unwrapped the coffin, it gleamed in the late afternoon sun. It looked to be cherry wood, polished, and perhaps varnished. The handles were brass in a simple neoclassical design.

"This is good, Juan," Don Emilio said approvingly. "The work is fine quality, and the effect is dignified, not gaudy. Also, it appears to be long enough. I will go get your mother."

As Don Emilio walked toward the chapel door, Sofia

made her way back through the kitchen toward the room she shared with Valeria. She planned to read a while there in case Valeria wanted to talk when she returned from sketching wildflowers at the mill pond.

Passing through Camila's room, she encountered the young spinner combing and braiding her long black hair. A tan canvas traveling bag lay on her bed.

"I'm sorry that I haven't had a chance to tell you and Valeria how sorry I am about everything that has happened," Camila said, dropping her half-finished braid and embracing Sofia in a warm hug. "I wish I had been a better friend these past few days. And now I have to rush off to Santa Fe. Señora Gutiérrez, being Don Emilio's cousin, will want to offer the mourners a midday meal after the funeral Mass, so I must make sure she has heard the news and ask her if she'd like me to help serve."

The following morning, Sofia awoke well before dawn to the stamps and snorts of the two draft horses being led from the stable. Of course, she thought, if the funeral Mass was set for eleven o'clock, the wagon carrying Alfonso in his coffin would need to leave before daybreak. It would take more than twice as long for the wagon to get to La Parroquia as it would take the party on horseback. As she lay back down, Beto began nuzzling her neck and stroking her breasts.

After a mug of the thick *atole*, which she was beginning to like, Sofia bustled to her old room, where Valeria helped her into her high-necked black dress. The section across her bust barely buttoned. She hoped it wouldn't pop open in the course of the ride north.

"Do you think I can wear this on the outside?" Valeria asked, pointing to the gold rose pendant around her neck. "And this?" She held up her ruby and pearl engagement ring.

"Of course. Both would be appropriate, especially if they give you some comfort." Sofia paused. "But not the turquoise bracelet. It doesn't really go."

Sofia stepped back a couple of paces and gave her sister an appraising look. In the process, she noticed that Valeria had finished her portrait of Alfonso. It stood propped on the small rustic table next to her bed, a beeswax candle on either side.

"Let's put your hair down, not up in that severe bun," Sofia said. "It makes you look like—well, like a widow."

"But I am a widow... Well, almost."

"Almost, but not quite." Sofia undid the bun and brushed out her sister's honey blond hair. "And there is no reason to make yourself look forty."

Satisfied with the effect, she turned and rummaged through the layers at the bottom of her trunk.

"You should wear this *mantilla*," Sofia said, pulling out a large square of black lace fashioned in a pattern of roses and vines. "It's large enough that you can drape it over your face if you want, and the lace is open enough that your hair will show through. I'll wear this smaller, triangular one."

"Why should I care how I look, now that Alfonso is dead?" Valeria sighed.

"You know very well why you should," Sofia said as they went out to the stable yard, where Beto stood with their horses. His jacket and trousers were homespun black wool of a simple cut, not, Sofia noted, the elegant suit he had worn at Fernando and Isabella's wedding. Probably the britches would have been too tight for the long ride, she thought fondly. Somewhere Beto seemed to have found a dark gray piece of cloth from which to fashion a sling.

"Did you have something to eat, my love?" she asked.

"Some bread and cheese—and of course coffee. And I have more food in my saddlebag, in case we want something on the ride home."

"Señora Gutiérrez is preparing a meal for everyone after the Mass," Valeria said. "I imagine that it will be quite lavish, or as lavish as she can make it on a day's notice."

"I think everyone would be more comfortable if Sofia and I were to skip that."

Mounting up, the three rode north.

When they arrived at La Parroquia, four young men were loading the casket out of the wagon onto their shoulders. Across the plaza, Sofia spotted Maria Josefa, in a simple black frock, and Carlos, in his dress uniform. Valeria ran toward them, holding her mantilla bunched in her right hand.

"Oh, my dear Valerita," Maria Josefa cried, enveloping her in an embrace. "You must feel so sad."

Bustling up beside her sister, Sofia noticed that their wise friend hadn't said, "What a loss of a fine young man" or something similar.

"And Sofia, what a terrible thing to have happen on your wedding day."

Sofia could hear Beto's steps behind her. Even after almost three hours on the trail, he still smelled of wild sage.

Carlos clapped him on the right shoulder and pointed to the sling.

"From what I hear," Carlos said. "Alfonso tried to kill you, and his horse killed him instead. We shouldn't speak ill of the dead, but still…" Seeming to catch himself, he asked, "How is your arm?"

"It's just a flesh wound, and it's healing well." Beto wiggled his fingers.

"I had a wound like that once. If you can still work your hand, it should heal completely. See?"

Carlos made a fist with his left hand and jabbed the air.

"You're lucky it was your left arm, Beto. That way you can still use your sword, even now."

Sofia was sure she saw him wink in Beto's direction. "I mean your real sword," he said patting the scabbard at his side. "I'm sure your other sword works fine."

Just then, the gilded carriage belonging to Doña Inmaculada's widowed cousin pulled up in front of La Parroquia. Flowing from a huge rosette affixed to the roof, black crepe draped the windows. Don Emilio jumped out and extended his arm to help his wife and her cousin step down. Sofia noticed that it was Juan who descended next and gave his arm to his sisters. The family proceeded up the stairs and into the church.

"Go in now and sit beside Emilia, or whichever child is on the end of the pew farthest from the aisle," Maria Josefa prompted Valeria. "I have no doubt that you will cry, so keep your *mantilla* over your face during the service, but lift the corner and arrange it to show your face before you leave the church."

Here they were back in La Parroquia, Sofia reflected, the site just four days earlier of her simple but joyous wedding. The nave was almost full.

"Are all these people here to show their respects for Afonso?" she whispered to Beto as they settled into the pew.

"Most of them are here to show respect for our family," he whispered in reply. "Some, though, are Alfonso's friends—or maybe creditors."

Sofia wondered how many of the people present were counting their losses now that Alfonso was in no position to pay back his gambling debts.

"Who is that across the aisle?" she asked softly. The woman who caught her attention was wearing a black turban affixed with a black plume and a short black veil, through which Sofia could see almond-shaped eyes and full red lips.

Beto's reply was barely audible. "That's Madame Le Ferrier, the brothel-owner. Her girls are as renowned as her gaming tables are notorious."

In the loft behind them, the choir began "Dies Irae." Flanked by four acolytes singing the responses to the somber and soothing Gregorian chant, Father Antonio proceeded slowly toward the altar.

The Mass was dignified but not prolonged. Sofia realized that as a practical man, Father Antonio would be aware that Alfonso's remains needed to arrive back at the ranch before sunset if they were to be buried the same day.

After giving the final blessing, the priest closed the lid of the coffin and signaled to the six pallbearers. Juan took the left front. Diego, in the right middle, stretched up his arm to grasp the brass handle. At eight, Sebastian couldn't even reach the handle, but he marched solemnly behind Juan. The others rested the coffin on their shoulders.

Don Emilio, Doña Inmaculada, and their three daughters filed out next, with Father Antonio immediately behind them. Maria Josefa intercepted Valeria, enfolded her, and wiped her face gently. Sofia watched from her pew as her sister took a ragged breath, then nodded as Maria Josefa picked up the end of the *mantilla* and folded it back over Valeria's blond curls, revealing a face that looked lovely even in grief.

As Sofia exited the church on Beto's arm, she noticed Valeria standing to the side on the landing halfway down the stairs. Holding her left hand, Maria Josefa appeared to be whispering something in her ear. Sofia released Beto's arm and made her way to her sister's side. A tall young lieutenant with glossy dark brown curls approached. Bowing, he introduced himself and told Valeria that he was sorry for the loss of her fiancé. Once he had bowed again and departed, Maria Josefa said softly, "He is the son of a prosperous wool merchant in Albuquerque, currently unattached. I think you may have danced opposite him at the Gutiérrez wedding."

After another young man, this one in civilian clothes, offered similar condolences, Maria Josefa cautioned, "That one drinks a lot, and his father is having financial difficulties. You don't need his problems."

As the last of the mourners exited, Father Antonio closed the church doors. On the left was a piece of lettered parchment, nailed at four corners, announcing the banns for Beto and Sofia. Apparently, the priest had forgotten to take it down after the wedding.

Doña Inmaculada glanced up at the notice, then wheeled on Don Emilio. Even through her black veil, Sofia could see angry red blotches appear beneath the tears streaking her cheeks.

"I will stay here in Santa Fe for a while," Doña Inmaculada said clearly, "at the convent, where the nuns can help me pray for my son's soul and console me in my grief."

Giving Beto a spiteful look, she added, "I expect to be there a month."

"And what of *my* grief?" Don Emilio asked.

Descending the steps, Father Antonio clapped the *patrón* gently on the shoulder. "I will come visit you at the ranch. There are a couple of books I received recently I would like to discuss with you. Also, the last time we played chess, you beat me twice. You need to give me the opportunity to return the favor."

"We did not end on good terms, Alfonso and I," Don Emilio said sadly. "I feel like I caused my son's death."

"Of the Seven Deadly Sins, Envy is the worst. Your eldest son has always suffered from it and from its cousin Jealousy. It was not Adam's fault that Cain killed Abel, nor is it your fault that Alfonso attempted to kill Beto and died in the process."

Nodding, as if he understood but would like to explore the concept further with Father Antonio, Don Emilio turned to Beto and Sofia and sighed.

"Under the circumstances, I think it would be best if you moved to Valles Caldera as soon as possible, while Sofia can still travel safely and before my wife returns home," he said sadly. Sofia could see what her father-in-law would look like at eighty, and she suddenly understood the reason that Doña Inmaculada had been so specific about how long she planned to stay at the convent.

Sofia recognized that Valeria had shown herself to be a gifted and caring teacher, more than able to manage the ranch children's instruction on her own.

"We can leave directly from here, Father," Beto said. "The distance will be shorter that way. Camila and Lilia can pack our personal things, and one of the ranch hands can bring them up in the next few days. Maybe you would be willing to loan us a few books..."

"Of course, my son. I will send you a couple of crates, in both Spanish and Latin. And for Sofia, a few in French, although I must warn you that those will be a bit radical."

Beto and Sofia exchanged a look of mutual understanding. Leaving directly from Santa Fe would avoid the awkwardness of having Beto present at the graveside when the half-brother who tried to kill him was lowered into the ground.

Don Emilio added, "I will send the piano along in the wagon with your personal things. I plan to order another to be delivered by next spring's caravan. You know, your piano sits just below my study, my dear daughter. I have enjoyed hearing you play while I do paperwork or read in the afternoon. I also enjoy hearing how Emilia has been progressing. I would like her to continue with her lessons, but, alas, you won't be there."

"Surely, there must be nuns at the convent who teach music," Sofia said. "Perhaps one of them would be willing to give Emilia a lesson once every week or two. Valeria could accompany her to and from Santa Fe and work with her on reading music in between."

"What an excellent suggestion!"

And it will give Valeria an excuse to call on Señora Gutiérrez and other well-positioned ladies who might have presentable sons or nephews.

"Now, if she agrees, I will send Marina's daughter Elena to you," Don Emilio said. "She has a clubfoot, but she is a hard worker, and Marina seems to have trained her well in the healing arts. She can help you cook and keep house, and then when the baby comes..."

"But what about you?" Sofia asked. "You will miss the birth of your first grandchild."

"I am fortunate to be in good health," the *patron* said, drawing himself up to his full height and looking once again like a man in his early fifties. "In seven months, I should still be vigorous enough to make the ride to Valles Caldera to see my new grandchild, who will be one of the famous early babies of *El Norte*."

Smiling broadly, he embraced them both.

CPSIA information can be obtained
at www.ICGtesting.com
Printed in the USA
BVHW042325160621
609642BV00006B/1727

9 781633 635234